Secret Keepers

A Domestic Suspense Novel

Teddie Peacock

Speckled Hen Press

Book Cover by Andrew Thompson, Cincinnati, Ohio

First edition 2024

ISBN 979-8-218-36014-6 (Print)

Library of Congress Control Number:2024902744

The author is available for speaking engagements. Please contact via email: teddiep eacock@gmail.com

For my daughters Lauren and Sara who inspire and motivate me everyday.

For John, my constant!

Contents

— • —

EPIGRAPH

"The truth will NOT set you free. Truth will take everything, everybody you love, stomp on you, wipe her
feet on you and laugh on the way out."
    Mindy

PROLOGUE

Tessa 2010

I punch in the numbers quickly of a phone number I know by heart. The phone rings two, three, four times and just when I think the voice mail recording will start; someone connects the call. And then, there is total silence on the other end.

"Hey, it's me again" I sigh without meaning to.

"Look, you don't have to say anything, just listen and please don't hang up. Please!" I beg softly into the phone.

"I know, we don't agree about this. I know you need time to heal, think, scream, forget, I don't know exactly what you need right now. I wish I did" I say quietly. "But this thing is bigger than just you or me. Whatever it really is. It involves all of us. We have to tell, and then stick together. We can't carry this secret alone. It's too big and possibly dangerous. I'll help you but we have to- we just can't keep" I think I hear a click on the other end, and I am pleading with an empty, open phone line.

But then a small voice, so quiet I might have imagined it, breathes into the phone "No, I won't, I can't". And then a click, and I am left alone in silence cradling the biggest secret of my life. One that threatened to bring us all to ruin, and there's not anything I can do about it.

TESSA 2015

It's Independence Day weekend. Happy Birthday America and all of that. I should be happy, deliriously happy. My family and I celebrate with a nearly perfect weekend at our family weekend place, Storybook Cottage at Lake James - one of Alabama's up and coming *best* lake vacation areas. This sweet little place has been in my family for generations, long before Lake James and the surrounding area got trendy. Originally, our place was just a fishing shack; the place where my family has made so many happy memories throughout the years. With our daughters Afton and Reagan, extended family, friends, and neighbors; it is the perfect way to celebrate. Except, except that in reality, not so perfect a weekend- not even close.

None of our closest friends show up. Not one, even though we have been friends since college. Three fraternity brothers who were best friends, met three college girls who became best friends. The rest is straight from a sappy, feel-good Hallmark movie. We all married our college sweethearts, remained friends, and became godparents to our friends' children. We vacationed together almost every single year, until now. Now, this year, this time it was different, and nothing will ever be the same again.

Jackson and I have the biggest, most awful fight of eighteen years of marriage. Sure, we've fought before. Plenty, mostly over the usual suspects, kids, money, jobs, things every couple argues over, eventually. But this argument is different. It ended with Jackson leaving the lake house in the middle of our party and heading home, a two-and-a-half-hour drive with not much more than a terse "I'm going home, carry on without me" and a hand salute. He left without even a backward glance in my direction. He refused my calls and left my text messages unread for two days.

I want to believe that I don't know what caused his behavior or why all that sudden anger is so focused on me? But I know, I know what and I know why but what I don't know is how to fix it? So, I do the only thing I know to do. I pick up my phone, scroll through my favorites contact list and press the number.

It goes straight to voicemail. But I'm determined to reach out anyway, even if it is to an overly cheerful, self- assured voice brightly telling me that the owner of this phone number is busy, but please leave a message. So, I do as I am told.

"Hey Mindy, it's me, but you already know that" I say feeling *out of sorts*, struggling to find just the right thing to say to one of my oldest friends.

"We missed y'all so much! I sure hope Theo is taking good care of you. Those summer colds are the worst!" I carry on, trying to match Mindy's bright tone in her voice message.

"You know, I'm sure with being sick you've forgotten, please call me in a day or so, no rush just when you are feeling better and up to it" I say into the phone not even knowing if the message was still recording.

I am worried about Mindy. She and Theo have never missed a summer get-together. Not both of them, anyway. But Mindy has been distant this year- I rationalize that it's their infertility struggles; but something is nagging at me. It's not just that- something is eating away at her, and I can't quite figure it out. So, that makes me feel even more guilty about the *check in* call. I've been doing it **every** year since **that summer**. Jackson, Mindy and I do a *check in* every July 4th and talk about what happened. Well, (in all honesty), it's me who initiates the conversation.

We promised each other that summer- we wouldn't tell our secret then- but sometime in the future. Weeks, turned into months and then years. Mindy has insisted this heavy secret, stays between us. Just three days ago, Jackson not so elegantly told me "To give it a break and leave Mindy the hell alone". It's pretty clear where he stands on all of this!

So, here I sit, five years later with a secret that I don't even really truly know all the details. It grows heavier by the day. I have an angry husband, and close friends who have distanced themselves. I have a growing fear that hiding what happened that day is going to be the worst decision that I have ever made. Instead, to avoid causing issues within my marriage, lose my closest friends or deal with all the awful fallout that certainly will happen; I keep quiet- just like I was asked to. What other choice do I have?

TESSA (2022)

How is it July 4th already? Summers just seem to fly by now. Anymore, it feels like entire years are whizzing by. It's a new year, shiny and full of promise, then blink, and it's the middle of summer, catch a breath and it's Christmas time. Before you know it, you are ringing in another new year (again). Wash, rinse, repeat!

This year's summer celebration is happy, sad, but mostly happy. Mindy, Jackson and I carry on the annual tradition, with family, friends and neighbors. The years have been hard on our friendship- the Invincible Six. We are now three. Theo is gone, Kate and Kelly split and wandered off their separate ways leaving so much destruction behind them. All that's left are the three secret-keepers; bound together by loyalty and deception. We try our best to hold it all together for everyone, just like we always have.

Last night, I tried again to convince Mindy and Jackson to finally tell the secret. Mindy came down two days early to help me set up and spend some quiet time together catching up. We have both been so busy, she with her fabulously successful vacation real estate rentals and interior design business on the famous 30A beach strand and me with my editing job with a small but growing publishing house in Nashville; we rarely see each other anymore.

Forever, we've had a tradition of watching the sunset together. Sometimes together, and sometimes via text or video calling wherever we happened to be in the world. Even Kate, our midwestern bestie, joins in whenever she can. It is our chance to drink a toast to the good things of the day, wave off the bad and be amazed by the wonder of God's handiwork.

After we finished cleaning the cottage, shopping for the long list of food and putting up all of Mindy's collected decorations; we held our sunset toast. Kate, our savvy and highly notable Midwest investment banker, joins us virtually. After Kate and Kelly's divorce, Kate renewed our friendship even if somewhat sporadically. I have missed her so much!

Mindy raises a glass of top shelf bourbon, sniffs it, put it back down and raises her champagne flute filled with sparkling lemon water. Kate raises what appeared to be a Northwestern craft beer in the bottle and I salute with my half-filled glass of white wine.

"To us," we all say in unison.

Mindy flips the iPad camera around so Kate can see the pink, purple and golden clouds hanging low in the sky, painting the lake in iridescent colors. This view, this sunset, these friends who have seen me through so very much through the years; it sustains me.

"Okay superstar besties, it's another few hours of work for me" Kate says as she waves goodbye and signs off.

"Mindy," I start. She must be a mind-reader because she knows exactly what I'm going to say.

She interrupts me, by holding up her hand as if blocking my next words.

"No, Tessa, let's not" she frowns. "It has been a great day, let's not ruin it with gloom and doom".

"But Mindy, it's been almost thirteen years, don't you think it's time?" I gently ask her.

"Time? Time for what exactly, Tessa?" Her voice hardens and her body grows rigid. The loose stance and happy tone in her voice is gone.

"I think", I begin.

"That's your problem. You **think** too much," Mindy's face scrunches up with dislike written all over it. Her voice emphasizes the word *think* like it is a dirty word.

"Think, think, think. All these years, you think," Mindy's voice becoming more animated and louder.

"So, tell me Tessa, how has all your thinking, all these years changed anything? Anything? Not a damn thing!" Mindy looks at me expectedly as if she is really expecting an answer.

It throws me off a little, (honestly) it shocks me a bit. Mindy's body language is aggressive, and her tone is hard, her words hurtful. I look at her, not quite knowing what to say.

She continues, now on a roll. "To be so smart, with your nose always in a book, your *touchy feely* sixth sense crap, how can you ***possibly*** be so unaware?"

I breathe slowly in and out for a few seconds, unsure of what my response should be. This is escalating very quickly. What is the right thing to say or do? Although I do know what she is referencing, I'm not nearly that *unaware*, I ask just to be sure.

"Unaware? Unaware of what, Mindy? I'm not exactly sure what you are talking about?" I say in a soft, even voice trying to diffuse the situation a bit. Let her talk, let her tell me what has gotten her so fired up. It might not even have anything to do with me at all.

"Do I have to spell it out? Apparently, I do to the genius in the house. No. We. Do. Not. Need. To. Tell. Anybody. About. That. Day." She says each word very slowly for emphasis.

"In fact, never would be a great time. Okay? No more asking every July 4th! No more badgering me and Jackson to change our minds" she is now almost shouting at me.

"Mindy, the truth, what about the truth?" I am devastated having this conversation, this way.

"The truth? Forget the truth. The truth will NOT set you free. The truth will take everything, everybody you love, stomp on you, wipe her feet on you and then laugh on the way out" Mindy spits out.

I don't recognize this person in front of me. My friend, my confidante, godmother to my daughters has been replaced by a yelling, cynical, broken person. I collect myself and carefully consider my response.

"Mindy, haven't we carried the burden of this long enough?"

"Are you willing to lose it all? Your marriage? Your closest friends? Maybe even your professional reputation you've worked so hard for? Is the truth worth all of that?" Mindy asks, her voice finally softening as she is calming down some.

"I don't think it's as bad as that, and y'all say I'm the exaggerator" I laugh trying to bring some lightness into this serious moment.

"Telling the truth now, after all this time will change nothing about that day. But it can ruin absolutely everything for us. For **all** of us. Haven't I lost enough already, Tessa?" Mindy looks at me with deep sadness in her eyes.

"If you tell anyone, and I mean anyone, what happened then you will lose my friendship forever. You might just lose Jackson in the process too!" Mindy sounds so defeated in this admission.

Stunned, I struggle to answer. She is waiting for my reply. Then I answer with the only thing I can. "Okay" I sigh heavily. "I will not press you about the secret; I do not want to lose you or Jackson. And I will quit asking either one of you about it" I say almost whispering, and with a very heavy heart.

Mindy studies me for a long minute. After looking so deeply into my eyes that I think she could see into my soul, she breaks her gaze. Turning around, she walks quickly off the deck and into the house. I stand staring after her. Then I see the light come on in the upstairs guest bedroom, decorated in tropical colors she loves so much.

Jackson warned me before Mindy came, begged me in fact, not to bring this up during the visit. But as usual, being the inquisitive *truth seeker* that I've always been, I couldn't help myself. Talking to Jackson, would be worse. If he would even talk at all, it was to immediately shut me down. Over the years, Jackson and Mindy have developed very detached feelings about what happened. With each passing year, they seem to believe they are untouchable. Secrets couldn't hurt them -so they hid this one down deep and went on with their lives.

I struggled with this. I still struggle with this. Not a day goes by that I don't think about what we should've done. I think about what we still could do differently- today. Every time I've almost talked myself into telling what I know- I stop. I'm afraid. Just like Mindy said, I'm afraid of losing her, possibly Jackson and other important people in my life.

Now after all this time, is the truth worth all of that? I don't know. I truly don't know. . I have given my word to both Mindy and Jackson. So, I carry this burden a little longer.

— · —

TESSA

The breeze blows gently through the windows of our sunporch at Honeywood Farm (aka The Money Pit) on this late June day. In the summer, southern Tennessee can be as moody as a teenage girl. The rare coolish day with temperatures in the 70's and no thunderstorms is a welcome relief to the usually hot and humid weather. I take full advantage of these days since they are as rare as sighting white squirrels.

I have a writing office inside of this sprawling heap of boards and stones we call home. But most of the time, I prefer working out on the sunporch. I love looking out over the ten acres that against all common sense, made me fall in love with this place.

Originally part of a large cotton plantation, all that remains is the dilapidated, shabby, once majestic plantation house and ten acres. The other four hundred and ninety acres have been parceled off through the generations. All that is left of Honeywood Plantation is what we, the idealistic Carmichaels and the mortgage company now own.

Thankfully, the house and land sit just far enough outside of our small town, Fayetteville that it hasn't been gobbled up by commercial investors and developers. They want to put in acres of ugly strip malls and fast-food restaurants standing shoulder to shoulder, like soldiers in formation.

The other acreage, once attached to Honeywood is a collection of small farms, a boarding horse stable and even a bed & breakfast inn catering to tourists visiting the nearby Jack Daniels Distillery. It is quiet and peaceful out here. If you close your eyes, you can almost see what this place looked like in all its glory. Me, I always see scenes from *Gone With The Wind*. I am no Scarlett though, not even close!

I was a tough sell on this place, in the beginning. Jackson saw potential in being a gentleman farmer and living almost exactly halfway between his company headquarters in Huntsville, Alabama and my home office in Nashville. I saw work and money, lots of it to make this place livable.

When we bought this place, we could barely afford it. Correction, we couldn't afford it- not without my parents' help. But between Jackson's romanticized dream of the *country* life, my mother's uncanny ability to instinctively know a fantastic real estate deal and Mindy's otherworldly interior design talents for turning ordinary spaces into magazine worthy covers; I was outnumbered. My vote didn't even really count.

We bought Honeywood with the idea of restoring it and maybe opening an event venue. After the girls left for college, Jackson had a five-year plan to slow down. He planned not to be so involved in the daily operations of his company, ADT (Advanced Drone Technology) which specializes in search and rescue missions. Jackson, his business partner Martin Land, and their investor partners adopted drone technology very early, on the ground floor. The business was doing well. Jackson likes to be involved in daily activities. He spends a lot of time on the road, all over the Southeast and beyond, traveling with his teams. There are always emergencies, and someone, somewhere always needs rescuing. Not really complaining but he has been away from home and missed so much, for a very long time.

I keep my day job, because while the business was young, I had to. My editing job kept our household running and helped pay for two daughters' very expensive life experiences. I stay with my editing job now to pay for upkeep and upgrades on Jackson's dream life experiences that have yet to happen.

Mindy insists Honeywood could help pay for itself as a photo opportunity location. We've allowed photo shoots for magazines, commercials, and print materials. A movie company approached us wanting to use Honeywood as a film set. As exciting and profitable as that might have been, I turned it down. Even the thought of so many people traipsing through my home, changing things, and invading my privacy made me physically ill. Jackson was not happy with that decision.

Through the years, I have gotten to a first name basis with the various work crews that have shuffled in and out of Honeywood, shining her up to her Sunday best. With Jackson's many long-term absences, I've also made friends with Clancy Jones, my nearest country neighbor. Mr. Jones, a 75-year-old farmer, has lived all his life on family property in this valley.

He kindly checks in on me, dispensing little life lesson moments. He brings me produce, firewood and little gifts from his farm, he knows I will like. Mr. Jones is on my favorite contacts on my phone to remove unwanted animals from the pool, reset ancient electrical fuses and help me build a fire in the cantankerous fireplace when the electricity goes out in the winter.

He even tolerates my stubborn and possibly irrational dislike of our naturalized, stone pool, awful basement with root cellar and the carriage house. He does not even raise an eyebrow when I tell him those places *feel bad* and give off bad sensations, making me sick. He is lonely and maybe I am a little bit too, out in this beautiful yet isolated location. Clancy Jones is my one true friend here and that makes me both happy and just a little sad.

I jolt myself out of daydreaming and stare at the document on my computer screen. This novel section is giving me so much trouble. I've read and reread this section at least a half dozen times in the last two days. Nothing is clicking- no help, and no ideas. Sorry, new author- I've got nothing for you.

I'm so behind in editing these past months. I blame it on staffing at our small regional publishing house, and that's partly true. We are growing, and the workload is growing faster than what the owners wish to fund. But it's not just that. It's most likely me. I've grown bored, restless and distracted. I've been incredibly distracted.

My distraction though has little to do with my workload or increasing *meh-ness* over my current work situation. My distraction is a 6'1 man with black hair and gray accents. More precisely, it's a blue eyed ball of energy named Jackson. Jackson Carmichael, the center of my universe is causing my unsettledness and not in a good way. There is a growing distance between us. It's there, just below the surface. Empty nest syndrome? Maybe. Mid-life crisis? Something isn't right in Jackson's world and he's not sharing.

His trips back home are getting more infrequent. He jumps at every opportunity to go to all the work sites even though his work crews are entirely competent. He doesn't need to supervise them. He checks in with me briefly on arrival and departure and maybe one or two times in between.Our conversations are short, mostly about work, the girls, and the latest work on the Money Pit. We don't argue. We aren't tense, but there is a distance hovering in the background just pressing in. Sometimes, I feel just like the little Dutch boy at the dike in the Netherlands holding back the great sea by plugging the hole in the wall with just his finger. If I move, adjust, or change directions just a bit, it might all come crashing down. So, I do nothing and wait for whatever is coming.

I am still sitting at my screen, staring, starting and stopping. I've been doing this same routine for almost three hours now. If I can't be more productive, it is time for a break. Maybe a short walk with the dogs, and a light lunch will clear my mind. I have to make progress on this project and get it out of my inbox. There is a noise in the front hallway, the front door lock turning and unlocking. I wait expecting to hear someone call out "Mrs. Carmichael" one of the work crew guys or "Ms. Tessa" Clancy Jones' usual greeting. Instead, I hear footsteps clomping down the hallway. Our Irish setter Rudy raises his head, staring intently and starting the beginnings of a low growl. Our silly, pampered King Charles Cavalier, Daisy continues sleeping completely unaware on the sun dappled loveseat.

"Whoa boy," I whisper to Rudy. "Stay," I command him.

"Hello, can I help you?" I yell in the direction of the hallway. It's unusual for our work crew or even Mr. Jones to come in unannounced. Maybe Mindy or my mother has decided to surprise me with a visit. They both have keys. But Rudy knows them and wouldn't growl. Heck, he would already be running down the hallway expecting to be petted and fed treats.

"Hello" I shout again. This time I'm getting a little scared. I rarely lock the door during the day, but whoever this is has a key or knows the door security code. Just as I am looking around for something to use as a weapon and to command Rudy to attack; a face appears at my end of the hallway.

I see a familiar face; no wonder Rudy didn't make any more fuss. And here I was thinking he was a worthless guard dog. That face belongs to my husband Jackson who isn't supposed to be home yet from the latest work site.

"Jackson?" his face is blank almost as if in shock.

"Jackson" I repeat again hoping for some reaction. He goes straight to the small bar cart and pours himself a very liberal glass of bourbon. He gulps it down in one long drink. Placing the glass back on the tray, he rubs his temples as if trying to rub away a massive headache. He stands there quietly with his eyes closed saying nothing for what seems like a long time.

"What's wrong? Is it Afton, or Reagan, my parents? What the hell is wrong? You are scaring me!" The air is so still in this moment, but I feel a crushing, unseen something in this room. Something I don't want to hear or deal with. But it is here and cannot be undone.

Jackson looks at me, as if he is trying to formulate words that just won't come. Then he finally gets them out.

"Kelly is dead" he says before he breaks down in tears.

"What?" I ask, not expecting this.

"Did you say that Kelly, Kelly Ryan is dead?" which is completely stupid for me to say. What other Kelly does Jackson know? Who else would upset him this much?

"Kelly Bradley Ryan, one of my best and oldest friends, your best friend's former husband and godson's dad is dead" Jackson says this slowly in a tone reserved for people who need extra help understanding things.

I'm not stupid Jackson. Shocked, shocked just like he must've been when he first heard. I have so many questions. Right now, so many thoughts are running through my mind all jumbled. But with Jackson's current state, I know to wait and let him tell me what he wants me to know.

"Big Ed notified me early this morning- as soon as he heard. We are leaving in two hours; he thinks it's best to tell Kate and Jason in person. They are out at his farm" Jackson hurriedly tells me.

"Poppy and family got news first, then Big Ed. We need to get to Kate and Jason before it makes the news. Poppy's father was able to get the news story bumped until he gets word from us to go ahead" he continues, already turning to head out of the sunroom

"Jackson," my voice stops him. I go to him hugging him from behind. His body is knotted up with tension. He is stiff and unyielding in my embrace.

"I am so, so very sorry" I say, and I am, for so many things.

Jackson is packed and ready to go within fifteen minutes. Years of emergency response has prepared him for quick departures. He keeps several bags of seasonal clothes *at the ready* in his closet. With a quick kiss to my forehead and a promise to call when he has more information, he is out the door and headed to Huntsville to catch the flight on a private jet that Big Ed, Kelly's famous father, has arranged.

I pour myself a drink, and yes, it is very early in the day for me. I've poured too much Irish whiskey in the small glass. I try to down it just like Jackson, I cough and sputter, I feel sure I might throw up. There is an immediate burn down my throat and all the way to my stomach. I drink the second half of the glass much slower and try to process the fact that Kelly Bradley Ryan, the man with at least nine lives, is truly dead.

To say I'm shocked is a major understatement. Of all of us, Kelly Ryan always had the luck of the Irish and a well-connected, famous father. Hell, even though Kelly was always doing stupid things for as long as we had been friends, we all expected him to be the last man standing. One time, in college after a particularly long night of drinking and hanging out, we took a bet that Kelly would outlive us all. He was just that lucky!

All the questions that were jumbled in my mind, are now finally calming down and arranging themselves in some kind of order. I realize several things almost all at once.

Jackson knew about Kelly since early this morning and didn't tell me- why? He also knows how Kelly died. He didn't ask if I wanted to go to Indiana to be with Kate and Jason. He didn't even ask when I could come. My best friend, godson, and Big Ed could use support. Why doesn't he want me there?

Jackson did what Jackson always does, *takes charge* and then tells everyone else information on a *need-to-know* basis. He always shoulders all the responsibility, all the burdens and then tolerates very few questions, particularly when he is stressed.

Kelly's death, just like his life will be complicated. He is the only son of a very noteworthy, famous military general, Lt. General Edward Oscar Ryan, a living legend in his own right. Kelly's second wife Poppy Hawthorne is a model/social media influencer and daughter of gazillionaire Henry Hawthorne, media and satellite communications mogul. Still have no clue how Kelly landed her, other than he truly was a lucky guy. Kelly's death will be a media circus. The only reason this high-profile breaking story is not already everywhere is because a famous dad and a super-rich father-in-law have made some calls, called in some favors and maybe even exchanged some sacks of money to delay things. But that won't last long. I'm sure Hawthorne's personal public relations entourage is already *handling things*.

Kelly is dead! I feel so bad for Big Ed, and Kimberly, Kelly's younger sister who lives in California. I even feel sorry for Poppy, the beautiful, stereotypical, trophy second wife. She does seem to really love him-enough to stay with him and produce perfect twins Avery and Amos, who have their father's flaming red hair and Poppy's signature green eyes.

My mind is racing. Somewhere behind the shock and grief, a slow realization creeps up on me. Now that Kelly is gone, the secret does not have to stay hidden anymore. I know, I know, I promised Jackson and Mindy that I wouldn't do it. I wouldn't tell, but I'm not going to the grave carrying this horrible weight. We all deserve to know what happened that day.

— · —

MINDY

My phone buzzes, it is early. Too early! I open my eyes, stretch and try orienting myself to the surroundings. I'm not at home. Where am I? When my eyes adjust to the dim light and sleepy brain fog clears a bit, I realize I'm staying in one of our company's luxury beach rental houses. And my phone is still ringing.

"Okay, okay" I shout out to the ringing phone. I am not at my best before 8 am. Hell, who am I kidding as I squint at the time on my phone's home screen. Does that phone really say 6:30 am? Six-thirty a.m.? It better be the zombie apocalypse or immediate end of the world for someone to be calling me at this ungodly, early hour. Very early and very late phone calls are never good!

I wait and look a little cross-eyed at my phone screen. Where are my reading glasses? Why is eyesight one of the first things to go, after the late forties? I can see well enough to know there is a voice mail notification – the number is Jackson's. Why on God's green Earth is he calling me this early? He knows me very well and I do not function beyond basic breathing until after 8 am and at least two very strong cups of coffee. Whatever it is can wait until after at least one cup of coffee.

After the caffeine hits my bloodstream, I pick up my phone and listen to Jackson's message. His message keeps cutting in and out. He must be driving in some backwoods, no cell tower area in the middle of nowhere. Something about Kelly, Jason and going to Indiana. Why hasn't Tessa called or texted me yet?

I call him back. He answers on the third ring.

"Mindy" he answers gruffly.

"Jackson, why the early wakeup call?"

There is silence on the other end, has the call dropped? Is he still there? The phone is still connected but I'm not sure he hears anything.

"Mindy" he says again, louder this time.

"It's... I'm... Uh... Min"

He's starting to scare me. I straighten up and pay close attention. Jackson is never at a loss for words. He is usually calm, direct and to the point. He's exactly the guy you want to take charge in a natural disaster or zombie apocalypse.

"You mentioned Jason and Kelly in your message. What?" He cuts me off before I finish my sentence.

"It's Kelly. He's gone. He's dead" Jackson starts sobbing.

I'm not sure I've heard correctly. Dead? That's not possible. Kelly? He was supposed to outlive us all.

"Oh Jackson, what happened?" I'm still wondering why I am hearing this from him instead of Tessa or even Kate? Tessa is a morning person- maybe Kate doesn't know yet.

"Car accident in Virginia, taking the nanny to the airport. He was driving the Ferrari and wrapped it around a tree. They didn't survive".

I wait, still trying to process what he is saying.

"There's more, Mindy. Apparently, he was driving drunk, and his luggage was found on the scene" Jackson says.

"Wait, what?" I ask. This makes even less sense. Kelly is, **was** an ass. But for the last six or seven years had been a sober ass. Poppy, the supermodel was good for him. A suitcase though? Where was he going? And why was he driving? Along with Poppy the supermodel, came massive amounts of money and a Bentley with a chauffeur. Daddy Hawthorne insisted on it. Nothing adds up! Poor Poppy- Kelly Ryan is the bringer of chaos and destruction to everyone around him.

My phone drops and the call disconnects. I try calling Jackson again, but his phone goes straight to voicemail. Either he doesn't want to talk right now, or he's hit another area of bad cell service. I will wait for him to call back with more details. Immediately, out of habit, I call Tessa. But just before the call connects, I hang up. I don't trust myself to talk to her right now. Tessa is very perceptive and I need to get myself together before I talk to her or anyone else.

I have hated Kelly Ryan with a fury that knows no bounds for a very long time. I disliked him way back in college. But after that horrible summer day, I have imagined at least a dozen ways to end Kelly Ryan. But never in any of my imagined plans, would I have come up with this ending. God does have a wicked sense of humor.

I'm sorry for the people that care about Kelly. He always had a terrible impact on other people. He was a walking, talking, tornado that often blew in quickly from nowhere. Always catching people unaware and causing destruction to everything that lay in his path. But still people that I care about, love him and that is enough for me.

Listening to Jackson's message again, I piece together that he and Big Ed are headed to Indiana to notify Kate and their son, Jason. I don't know how Kate will take the news. That man put her through hell, every year they were together. She might laugh- I would! But Jason, that poor sweet, tortured boy, how he will react is anyone's guess.

The timing is terrible, but then when is a good time to die accidentally? Jason has just come out of a short hospital/rehab stint. He had a relapse. Kate and his grandfather have been trying so hard to get him to a good emotional place. Jason always does so much better at Big Ed's farm. Maybe, he will stay there this time.

I have a soft spot for Jason. I won't say it out loud, but he truly is my favorite godchild. I love Afton and Reagan; they are great girls. They are beautiful and so together. They also have a large and very loving family. You couldn't ask for better parents than Tessa and Jackson.

I connect with Jason because he is broken, too. Broken gravitates toward broken. Kate and Big Ed have tried their best for Jason, but there is something so incredibly chipped in him that he may never be whole again. Jason is the little bird who doesn't know how to fly. He's just more collateral damage in the self-absorbed world of Kelly Ryan.

Because Theo and I could never have children, I've focused on being the best possible aunt and godmother. I would've been a good mother. Instead, I pour myself into other people's children sacrificing for them just like a mother would. I believe Jason and I may be the only godmother/godson couple to go through rehab together. "Ha", not one of my finest life moments.

Right after Theo died, I found myself in a bad place, blaming everyone, and pushing everyone away. I started drinking heavily, so I didn't have to think anymore. I probably would've managed with grief therapy and AA but then there was the Jason problem.

Jason turned 18 and wasn't doing life well. He hated his mother, his dad and new perfect family, and mostly, himself. He had been dabbling in booze and drugs, on and off since he was fourteen. Kate and Big Ed sent him to rehab when he turned sixteen. It helped, for a bit. Then at eighteen, with adult freedom and a bad college semester, Jason found trouble- real trouble with misdemeanor charges. The judge was lenient and offered community service and rehab instead of jail time. Jason would've died in jail.

So, by the end of it, the only way Jason agreed to the plan was when Aunt Mindy decided to tag along to Healing Time Rehabilitative Services. Going to rehab with Jason gave him the *reset* he desperately needed. It likely saved my life; even though that last part I probably wouldn't admit to anyone.

Does Kelly's death really change anything? All the damage has already been done. Kelly Ryan possibly destroyed our lives forever and I'm to blame too. Because all these years, I've known. I've known Kelly was warped. The day I met him, I should've run away screaming and I didn't. I sat there smiling like the sweet, southern, stupid girl that I was - not wanting to hurt anyone's feelings or have an *awkward* moment.

Kelly Bradley Ryan was a predator and likely had been for most of his life. And I have protected him all these years, almost thirty years, because I am a coward. Tessa and Jackson only know part of the truth of what happened that terrible day. The rest, I have carried myself, my biggest burden and worst mistake ever. Will there finally be any peace when they put that miserable excuse for a human six feet under?

Jason

I'm lying on the bed, in my room at Grampa Ed's farm. The house is quiet, all except for the home health nurse Grampa hired to annoy the hell out of me every day. Thinking I'm asleep, Mom stands out in the hallway whispering to the nurse. I wish I was asleep instead of staring up at the ceiling wondering how this happened again.

I've been here under Mom's imposed house arrest for almost two weeks now. Before that, a week in the hospital and a week in a psychiatric transitional unit. My setback (freakout) as Mom and the medical staff calls it, happened last month. At the same time, I was all set to start a job with a regional Job Corps unit.

It really isn't as big a deal as all the grown-ups are saying. I got stressed about starting a new job- who doesn't? If Mom had just asked me instead of lecturing and talking, talking, talking about *finding myself,* she would've known. Known that I didn't want to go that far from home, known that I wasn't ready. Known that living with a bunch of people I don't even know- I don't want it. If she had really been paying attention- instead of always trying to find ways to *fix my broken shit*- I wouldn't have stolen some controlled substances and intentionally failed the Job Corps drug screen.

I just didn't plan on passing out in the middle of Orientation Day in front of a bunch of unknowns with their phones out videoing my stupid face plant and posting it all over the Internet. That will live on forever. I only meant to fail the drug screen, so I didn't have to go to whatever other backward ass, nowhere place they were going to send me.

If I could've just talked to Mom and have her really listen for once, to what I was saying- there would've been no relapse. I've been clean for a long time now; Aunt Mindy and Poppy convinced me with their own stories that I had enough problems without adding *wasted* to the pile. I know, even though I wouldn't tell Mom, what I did was stupid! But me doing smart things? I'm not even sure I know how to do that.

Getting the drugs was easy. Grampa Ed's medicine cabinet is like a pharmacy. Prescription drugs, not really my thing- so no clue on how much or what to take to fail a drug test. Anyway, I did it up right and here I am – on house lockdown and with Mom hovering over me All The Time.

Well, I won't be going to Job Corps now- at least I got that part right. Mom wants to know where I got the drugs. I lied and said from some kid at Orientation week. They will be looking for that imaginary guy for a while. I'm worried about Grampa, there's A LOT of pain meds in his bathroom. He travels a lot and is old as dirt. Something's wrong with him and I don't think he's told Mom. I'm sorry for worrying him like this. Sometimes I'm just a stupid idiot with an empty head. I don't mean to hurt other people, not even myself. For once, I want to wake up and be happy. Is that too much to ask?

I love Mom but I really, really wish she would just shut up and go away for a while. She hovers, she babies, she worries and then I feel like shit for making her feel this way. But damn, if she doesn't treat me like one of Grandma Ella's old antique dishes downstairs. Sometimes, she's afraid to be around me- afraid I might break. But what she doesn't know, as smart as she is, is that I am already broken. I may never be put back together again

Mindy

Chase Fontaine, my work assistant, is not only one of the most handsome men I know, but he is also highly efficient. He saves me, more times than he will ever know. I don't pay that man nearly enough, even though I try to be a good boss. I secretly hope he never gets discovered by a Hollywood agent and moves to LA to live his big dream. That would crush me and break my heart neatly in half.

Chase travels with me to our luxury rental properties. He helps scope out potential properties and he is one hell of a home stager. He has no school training but does have a great eye and inherently good taste you just can't teach in classrooms. The fact that he is breathlessly handsome, and oozes Southern charm is a check in the plus column too. If HGTV signed him tomorrow, he would become instantly famous and make them at least a gazillion dollars. Women naturally hang on every word he says and want to spend massive amounts of money, usually without much encouragement on his part. He is my secret weapon, my guardian angel, my *ride or die* workmate and a totally hot specimen of a man all rolled up in a perfect package.

Thank God, we respect each other, and he understands that any kind of romantic entanglement would ruin our chemistry. Because if this man left me, I might literally die that day. Chase is so important to me and our company that losing him would be like losing part of myself.

Chase immediately steps up to stand in the gap with the latest adopted family situations. Between Jason's meltdown and Kelly's death (still processing this) my family needs me. I know that I can leave town and Chase has it all under control. He is such a blessing.

I haven't been up to Indiana to see Jason yet. Kate hasn't wanted me to, not just yet. I've respected that. It's her call- and she knows best. But now with all this mess with Kelly; I'm going to the farm, invited or not.

Chase drives me to the Destin airport. Always busy, it is particularly busy right now just before the 4th of July holiday. Probably not the best time to travel, but hey I will work with what I've been given. I hate flying and avoid it like the plague. I especially hate flying solo but sometimes, I just can't avoid it. The old me would pop a valium and have a drink or two to calm the nerves; the new me, the recovering alcoholic knows better.

I sit in the airport waiting area, trying to get ahead of all the upcoming tasks I'm dumping on Chase. I check both my phone and text messages. Work, work, work, junk (delete). I see two phone messages from Tessa, but no voicemail. She and I have been playing phone tag over the last week. Talking about our dead former friend via text or phone messages just doesn't feel right. Tessa has been a little distant recently. I think, trying to rationalize to myself, we've both been busy with work projects. It is that, but Tessa and Jackson aren't on solid ground right now. When Tessa's world gets out of balance, she retreats and withdraws. I'll call her once I've seen Kate and Jason and update her.

There is a text from Jackson- "call me" short and to the point, that's Jackson especially in a crisis. I press his number, "Hey Jackson" I say quietly into the phone.

"Mindy, are you on the way yet?"

"Yes, sitting here waiting for the flight to board. How is everyone?" I ask knowing this is a silly question. They are likely just like you'd expect, sad, angry, maybe even relieved (in Kate's case). I feel awkward talking to Jackson right now. Something in our relationship has shifted. It seems too personal and a little too uncomfortable. I don't like it!

"Well," he pauses with a deep sigh, "not good, about what you would expect".

"And Jason? How did he react?" I'm most worried about him.

"He didn't take it well. He laughed hysterically like a mad man. Then he started yelling and we had to restrain him so he wouldn't hurt himself. The nurse gave him something to calm him down and help him sleep. That killed Kate! She's gone into her room, and I haven't seen her since" he says clearly worried.

I'm not surprised either by Jason's outburst (real or theatrical) nor Kate's stoic reaction. It's how they handled things, especially messy, emotional things. I need to get there quickly to help calm the situation with Jason. What an ever-loving mess and of course, Kelly Ryan is right at the center of it.

"When is Tessa coming in?" I ask.

Jackson pauses on the other end for a beat longer than necessary.

"Tessa isn't coming right away until we make arrangements. She's busy with work. With the dogs, and construction work, arrangements have to be made" he says.

This troubles me. Tessa never misses showing up for her friends. She's always been the one that holds us all together. She helped Kate and Jason through their difficult years with Kelly. She was the first one there and the last one to leave with Theo's sudden death. No, Tessa is a giver, something is definitely not right.

"Mindy, I need... We need you here, hurry" Jackson says so softly, I barely hear him over the airport noise.

"Jackson, they're calling my flight. I'll let you know as soon as I land. Bye" I hurry off the phone.

And there it was, the growing feeling of uncomfortableness with Jackson. So many things not right with this interaction. I would have plenty of time to dig in and try to figure it out on my flight to Indianapolis. Delta flight 2575 was not boarding just yet, but the conversation with Jackson was getting awkward and that on top of everything else already on my plate. I just can't handle it all right now.

I treated myself and got a first-class ticket on an expensive direct flight. It's still an hour drive out to Ed's farm from Indianapolis; Ed's farm manager will be picking me up. Jackson doesn't want to leave the family alone. Leaning back in my seat in the first-class section, I begin relaxing a little. A few glasses of chilled sparkling water and a classical music playlist will have to do.

Only God knows what mess I'm walking into on the other end. I need every ounce of peace and calm to handle things without losing my mind. Besides, I'm still trying to convince myself that Kelly is dead, that we are now all beyond him hurting us and I've made the right decision.

Jason

I've imagined Bio Dad dying and being erased from this earth in about a thousand different ways. I've never talked about it to anybody, because that's probably a one-way ticket straight to a mental ward somewhere. Besides, it's not like I would ever have the guts to do anything to make that happen. I would probably screw it up - just like I've screwed everything else up in my life. Then I would end up in prison. I can't go there. Or maybe get sent to Happy Daze crazy hospital for life, and that useless waste of air would still be alive, walking this planet and ruining everything and everybody.

It's still hard to believe he's dead. I've read the online obituary so many times I can quote it now by heart. Read all the comments too- so many people leaving messages about what a great guy he was. Did they have him confused with someone else?

Grampa Ed was away on business travel when he got the news. He showed back up at the farm with Uncle Jackson. That was different, they don't usually travel together. Their work is completely different. I guess it was probably hard for them to tell Mom and me. Especially since I was just coming off an *episode*. I had to act upset when I heard the news, because I couldn't hurt Grampa's feelings. I think I overdid it a bit. What they thought was grief, is really happiness. But since I couldn't possibly be happy about what happened, they filled in the blanks. All but Uncle Jackson, he kept looking at me really intently. Pretty sure that he wasn't totally buying my act.

Grampa though, was so torn up he could barely speak. I was worried he might fall over with a massive heart attack. I guess it's true what they say about parents outliving children and how tough that really is. Even losing crappy children must hurt bad based on Grampa Ed's reaction.

I don't really get Mom's reaction. She should be so happy- she is finally rid of that guy for good. Sad, was not what I was really expecting from her. She has hated him for so long! Even when she finally quit talking about him and acted like he didn't exist; she was still so mad at him. Even though she thought she had me fooled; she didn't.

With his serious face on, Uncle Jackson tells us that Kelly had a car accident driving the nanny from their mansion in Virginia to the airport. Grampa Ed was so upset, he had to leave the room at this point. I'm glad he did cause he didn't need to witness the freak out that I was about to unleash.

I didn't trust myself not to bust out laughing, do a happy dance or about hundred fist pumps in the air at this happy news. I was so freaking happy, but I had to conceal it. So, I did the next best thing. I had a total meltdown. There was some Academy award winning acting going on. I'd seen some crazy guy lose his shit in the psych ward when I was there for observation. I just did the same stuff. I needed to get Mom out of the room before she started her *forgiveness* speech. My freakout was impressive enough to get Nurse Ratchet back in the room with some good drugs. Yep, I'm calling it a success!

When I wake up, Aunt Mindy is sitting in the room with me. How long have I slept? Aunt Mindy tells me, I've been out almost 12 hours. Now that was some good drugs.

"So, Jase, how are you doing?" Aunt Mindy takes a long, knowing look at me.

"Yeah, you know this whole thing has put me behind on my Ironman marathon training schedule. But back at it, soon" I deadpan giving Mindy my most innocent smile. This smart-ass going back and forth was our thing.

"You sure? Ironman huh? What's this- your third or fourth race now?" Mindy is playing along with me, both of us avoiding talking about the real thing.

"Nope, it's my first, been training for months. Out here at Grampa's to run the trails. Mom needs to let me out of solitary soon or I won't be ready for the race".

Mindy nods her head and breaks into a wide smile, "My godson the superhero, so when were you going to tell me – or were you planning on keeping it a secret" Mindy asks, the smile slowly dissolving on her face.

"I was gonna surprise you Aunt Min, you know me Mr. Spontaneous" I smile again hoping to charm her.

"Jason, stop!" her voice has an edge to it I don't recognize.

"Can we just talk about what happened without all the clowning around? Why didn't you tell me, or tell your mom what was what going on?" she says with a sad look.

"You know there's no talking to Mom. She never really hears what I'm telling her" I say.

"Or what you don't" she finishes my sentence for me. Aunt Mindy knows me, she gets me like nobody else on this sorry planet could.

"But Jase, you can always talk to me about anything. You know that right? I'm not saying there might not be a bit of judgment, but I will listen, and I will help you. Always!" Aunt Mindy looks at me with her eyes watering. *Man, I hope we aren't gonna cry. I feel crying coming on and I'm not cool with it*".

"I Couldn't Do It" I finally say.

Aunt Mindy looks at me, quietly waiting for more.

"You couldn't do what Jase? Who was trying to make you do something?" Aunt Mindy asks somehow knowing that whatever *it* was, is not my idea.

"All of it, Job Corps, going to work at Grampa's friend's dude ranch. All Of It. But after the college screw up, Mom and Grampa kept pushing and pushing wanting me to do something. Anything other than laying around all day feeling sorry for being the pathetic loser that I am" I finally admit.

She stares at me for a long minute, probably trying to sort out what to say to such a loser.

"Jase," she says, sitting on my bed and grabbing both of my hands.

"You are Enough. It's okay to not be everything or sometimes, anything that someone else wants you to be. You, and only you, get to decide who and what you want to be. And don't you forget that". I wonder right now if she's really talking about me or herself.

"We can get so lost and cause ourselves so much pain, trying to live up to the hype. *Feel the feels,* Sweetie and then decide what is good for you, what makes you happy and what is true to the incredibly awesome person you are meant to be" she says, fixing a bright smile on her face.

If this was anyone else, Mom, my therapist, Poppy, any self-help expert or literally anybody else- I would probably puke in protest over such basic bull shit! But this is Aunt Min, who has always played straight with me. She's been right down in the gutter with me. Yep, she knows what it's like to be so far down that's its just too much effort to claw your way back. I'm just too tired to challenge her on this and I'm trying to stall because I know what's coming next.

"Please, please, please let's not do this now. Nope, don't want to talk about Bio Dad, now or ever. But I know Aunt Mindy and here it comes".

"Let's talk about your dad Jase, you can't keep it bottled up inside forever" she gives me a determined look.

"You mean Sperm Donor?"

"Your dad Jason, Kelly Ryan, you know the guy that's listed on your birth certificate" she rolls her eyes at me.

I try not to laugh. That's just like something I would do. Maybe that's why Aunt Mindy and me are close. I do not want to talk about this, I do not!

"Aunt Mindy, it's okay- I'm okay. Can we not talk about this right now? I'm hungry. Do you think you could get me something to eat?" I ask trying to get her off this topic, at least for now and I am hungry. I don't exactly remember the last time I ate.

"Are you up for my famous Slamma Jamma sandwich? If I can find everything in the kitchen?"

I smirk without really meaning to. Aunt Mindy is a lot of things, but she can't cook worth a damn. We figured that out a long time ago, when she used to burn up everything, she tried to cook for me. One time we got so desperate to eat after burning a meal, Aunt Mindy started pulling out everything out of the frig and then the Slamma Jamma was born. Peanut butter, honey, and dill pickles on toasted white bread. As disgusting as it sounds, it's pretty awesome. Then we made it a game to put together sandwiches that sounded awful and tasted delicious. Aunt Mindy is always fun that way.

A few minutes later, I hear footsteps outside of my door. Aunt Mindy pushes the door open carrying a food tray. I quickly close my eyes pretending to be asleep. I'm good at this- pretending. Especially when I'm avoiding stuff I just don't want to think about. She puts the tray at the foot of my bed on top of Grampa's old army trunk. Leaning in close to see if I'm asleep, she ruffles my hair just like she's done since

I was a little boy with crazy curls. She probably knows I'm faking. I hear her soft footsteps and the click of my door closing shut.

I open my eyes and stare at the ceiling. I will eat, and then stay up here inside this room until they won't let me anymore. Poppy, the two perfect littles and Moneybags Daddy with the security team will be here tomorrow. Afton, Reagan and families aren't coming in for the hurried up memorial service. I don't blame them- I don't want to be here either. Afton and Reagan were like my sisters when we were little. At least up until I turned crazy. I spent some of every summer at Aunt Tessa's lake house. But then, hey you know how people are, they don't want to be around sick or crazy people- they think both are contagious.

I get cards from the girls on my birthday and Christmas. I especially hate the Christmas cards where Afton and her model perfect family are wearing color-coordinated lame ass holiday outfits and their big fake-ass smiles. Reagan's cards aren't much better; it's some great adventure shot of her and Jonas in some crazy awesome place living their best lives. I know they mean well, trying to keep in touch with their scribbled "miss you" and smiley faces on the cards. But damn, those cards depress the living hell out of me and remind me what a world class loser their *almost brother* really is.

Aunt Tessa isn't here yet. I expected her already. I overheard Uncle Jackson tell Aunt Mindy that she couldn't leave right away but she would be here as soon as she could. Sounded like a lot of excuses to me. And it really didn't sound much like Aunt Tessa. What is going on with her? All my life, Aunt Tessa is the first to show up in any crisis with a stack of books relevant to the situation and dozens of her world-famous chocolate chip cookies. She claims the cookies are a secret family recipe handed down generations in the Donovan family. That's a total lie, she ripped off Hillary Clinton's famous recipe. But Aunt Tessa is cool, so her secret is safe with me.

I think she's stalling if she can, it's going to be a shit show around here. It will be loud, awkward and memorial services are just ridiculous anyway. But I think it's more than that with Aunt Tessa. She is an empath and everybody here being all in the *feels* is gonna get to her bad. She's always downplayed her abilities which I have always thought were super freaking cool. But Uncle Jackson doesn't really believe in it, always says she's overly dramatic from reading too many books. Sometimes, I would like to punch him right in the nose. He is so unaware of the people around him. Mom and Aunt Mindy believe her and joke about her *witchy ways*.

When I was a kid, hanging out with Afton, Reagan and Uncle Theo's small nation of nephews and nieces, Aunt Tessa would always know when we were up to something or lying or both. She isn't a mind reader but somehow, she always knew. She always knows.

The first summer that I lost it, went a little crazy and did some time in rehab; everyone came to see me, eventually. Aunt Tessa was missing in action for a while. When she finally did get around to visiting, I knew it was hard for her. She always thought her ability was connected to places and not people. She was so wrong! Everything I was feeling crossed Aunt Tessa's face. She felt everything I felt and all the feelings in that place. It was so hard to watch her be in so much pain. Since that day, when I am low, I try not to be around her. It hurts her too much.

When the memorial service day rolls around with Grampa Ed, Poppy and the minis, Jackson and whoever else is here; Tessa will be feeling all their feelings. It's hard enough to feel your own crap; dealing with everybody else's must be absolute torture! Maybe, I can flip out enough just to get me and Aunt Tessa out of the freak show service. At least, I can do that for her.

I am tired, so insanely tired! I can't go downstairs and deal with Mom's long face and side eye looks at me making sure I'm holding my shit together. Grampa Ed can barely keep it together; it makes me so sad looking at him. He loved Dad, like really, really loved him. Even though Kelly didn't deserve a father like him. If I could just sleep. Where is that nurse with her bad breath and awesome drug stash? I stare up at the ceiling. I can't go to sleep. I have to stay awake. If I don't stay awake, I will dream of redheaded, red-faced, blue eyed monsters chasing me. I will dream about him.

TESSA

I spend two days planning so I can get to Kelly's memorial service in Indiana. It will be a private service, only family and close friends. There was some maneuvering by both General Ryan and Henry Hawthorne to (1) contain the story as much as possible and (2) get Kelly's body released, cremated and quickly buried. Having friends in high places, calling in favors and who knows what else, can get things done in the Beltway when you are on a tight time schedule.

I question the speed of this but the journalist in me knows that the quicker and quieter Kelly goes away; the faster any possible scandal might too. By himself, Kelly is not particularly noteworthy but being associated with three high profile people makes his death news on a slow news day. It doesn't take a genius to get a copy of the police incident report and realize this event is problematic. Murder and mayhem, gloom and doom, someone else's misfortunes creates website clicks, newspaper sales and higher ratings during news shows.

Kelly's death has potential to be scandalous, if the right person knows how to read a police incident report and dig a little around the edges of the story. What can be verified is, and what can't be is sometimes embellished, all in the name of creating a story that people can't get enough of.

The circumstances surrounding Kelly's death trouble me. My mind has been working overtime, putting the known facts together like a puzzle. There are some missing pieces, some gaps that I hope possibly someone at the farm can fill in. But this is not the appropriate time to play investigative reporter. Our friend, our daughters' godfather and the son of a man that I greatly admire is dead. There will be a right time and place to get answers to the persistent questions that will not leave my mind.

The drive from Tennessee to Indiana is long. Freeway miles stretch endlessly, mile after mile of concrete expressway interrupted by occasional town exits. I'm prepared with my 90's playlists, podcasts and a full queue of audiobooks that I may never get to. Jackson encouraged me to fly. I hate to fly! I have horrible flying anxiety. Being locked in an oversize tin can held hostage by 200+ passengers' feelings and the residual energy left behind in the plane, no thank you! Even with Big Ed's offer of a seat on a private jet, I decide to drive. Jackson doesn't really understand the flying anxiety but then again there are a lot of things he doesn't seem to understand, these days.

Without a big editing task and short deadline closing in on me, I have time to think and breathe a bit. This long road trip is exactly the excuse I've needed to think about all the little things that have been bothering me. Jackson, Mindy, Kelly's death, Jason's emotional well-being; they all crowd my mind threatening to cause my brain to explode.

I've had two short conversations with Mindy since the news of Kelly's death. She's at the farm now, taking care of Jason and Kate. There is a reservedness in our talks. I don't know if it's the shock of Kelly's death finally seeping in or something else. Mindy seems distant and intentionally careful with her words. This is very unlike her- but I know when I see her, we can work through whatever is bothering her.

Jackson however, I'm unsure how to deal with him. Kelly's death is hitting him extremely hard. Expected, after all it is one of his closest friends. Or if I'm being honest- was one of his closest friends until that summer that changed it all. Jackson tried to remain friends with Kelly through the years. I'm racking my brain trying to figure out what's going on with him? Is it work, he's tired of me, he's sick? I've asked these questions many times in the past eighteen months or so. He's *off-* we're disconnected and a little wobbly and he definitely won't discuss any of this with me right now. It's very confusing and hurtful.

Jason is going to take some time to heal and maybe recover from everything. He's fragile. I worry that even as much as he says he hates his father, Kelly's death may be the one thing that truly sends him over the edge. Big Ed and Mindy are calming influences on him. They will help Kate get Jason through the rough patches. I try, I love Jason as much as Afton and Reagan. But when Jason is *out of sorts,* I can't be around him much. Even though my empath perceptions usually are dampened around people; I still pick up strong emotions. Jason is full of those. Anger, rage, hate, rejection, abandonment, hurt, fear, hopelessness; these are just a few of the emotions he projects often all at the same time. When he is like this; it hits me like a great impenetrable wall that threatens to suffocate me. At times, I've been physically ill around him- the worst was when I passed out. Mindy and Jason let me off the hook during these times. I support them at a distance doing all that I can for them while avoiding them. It's unfair and I feel like such a bad person, but they understand and love me anyway.

The miles tick by, bored with my audiobook, my mind keeps coming back to the details of Kelly's death. There seem to be big gaps in the story- those might be filled in by Jackson, when I see him. I try to sort out the knowns and unknowns hoping there may be something significant that answers my unanswered questions. I talk out loud to myself, hoping to find the missing links.

"1. Kelly Ryan is dead. 2. Car accident 3. He was driving 4. Under the influence of alcohol 5. The 22-year-old nanny was with him. 6. Kelly had luggage discovered on the scene." I list off all the facts I know, so far.

"Things I don't know. 1. Why was Kelly driving? His family has around the clock driving service 2. Kelly was drinking? He is an AA graduate and had been sober for at least six years 3. Why was he driving the nanny? Where was she going? 4. Had Kelly planned to travel somewhere?" I ask myself.

It is this second list that greatly bothers me. For every question I have, there are two or three more questions right behind them. Something isn't quite right with all of this, and I intend to find out one way or another.

When I finally pull in at Big Ed's farm, after clearing the security teams stationed at the entrance, it is late afternoon. I dread what I might find here and wish I could've somehow made some believable excuse not to come.

Poppy, the twins Avery and Amos, and Henry (along with a security team) are settled in a swanky hotel in downtown Indianapolis. They will be here tomorrow for the graveside service, back to Indianapolis to catch the family jet and travel to a remote beach getaway for a while. They will stay gone until they are no longer newsworthy. Ah, the woes of the rich and famous.

Mindy, Jackson and I are staying at the farmhouse with Ed, Kate and Jason. It is large and has been remodeled through the years. What started as a small one-story white clapboard farmhouse on a few acres has grown into a very spacious six-bedroom farmhouse on 200 acres.

Big Ed's Meadowview Farm is rural and remote enough to offer privacy but still close enough to civilization to suit its 21st century guests. Being in the middle of Amish country, with neighbors who mind their own business is a plus.

I see Jackson sitting with Big Ed on the wide front porch. They are deep in conversation. These two have always had an easy relationship. Jackson looks up to General Ryan with awe and admiration. In return, Ed has taken Jackson in, treating him like a second son.

Ed looks up, waves and gets to his feet. Jackson is a little slower in response. I put on my brightest smile and walk up the steps right into Big Ed's waiting arms. He's gotten frailer since I last saw him.

"Big Ed, how are you doing? I got here as quickly as I could" I say, staying in this sweet man's hug.

"I'm... we, we will all be fine," his voice falters a little.

"Yes, we will. But I am so very, very sorry. I will be here for you. Just anything, anything you need. Please just ask" I reassure him and it's true. I love this man dearly, despite his son.

He looks at me with intense sadness in his eyes. "I know, honey" he says, choking on his words. It is almost too much for one of the strongest men I've ever met.

Jackson stands off to the side. He has his hands shoved deep in his pockets, standing awkwardly and a little unsure of what to say, if anything. I glance over at him waiting, waiting for him to make the first move to welcome his wife, to welcome me. He just stands there for a minute.

"Jackson, I missed you" I say wrapping him in a hug. And I had, even if things did feel so weird between us right now.

"Me too, Tessa," he replies, his body feels tense. It has been a very stressful week. I'm being silly.

I tilt my head back so I can look into his face. There it is again, that quick flash of emotion followed by a neutral blank face, showing little emotion. His face changed so quickly, had I imagined it? With all the emotions that Jackson must be feeling right now; I feel nothing. There is a blankness radiating off him that doesn't match the situation. But then again, I had never been very good at *reading* Jackson. I purposely avoided doing that, giving him some privacy with his thoughts and feelings.

"What can I do to help?" I ask them, stepping toward the massive double front doors. "I'm here now, put me to work." I'm sure there are things still to be taken care of and I need to be busy and not so alone with my thoughts.

Inside the former parlor, now a modern den, Kate and Mindy sit with their heads huddled close together. My heart is filled with joy at the sight of them even though there is so much sadness here. I can feel it in the house, radiating from every room. It's stifling. I take a couple of deep breaths and try pushing away the feelings. What I don't feel though is anger and rage, which is a good sign. I hope. I don't feel Jason's usual crazy mix of emotions swirling around and for that, I am thankful.

"How is he?" I ask Kate, noticing the tiredness in her eyes, and the dark circles ringing them. Of the three of us, Kate was always blessed with the most beautifully radiant skin that always looked like she had been airbrushed. Today, she looked faded and tired.

"Jason or Ed?" she asks.

"Both, I'm sorry, long drive and my brain is a little addled" I explain.

"Ed is holding up as best he can. Jason is quiet and somewhat calm, for now. Mindy has a lot to do with that. He's been asking about you" she says, glancing at the upstairs stairway.

"Should I go up and say hello? I can sit with him a bit."

"I think he's asleep, or at least he seemed to be when I took his supper up earlier" Mindy says.

We sit for a few minutes, uncomfortable in the silence, each deeply lost in our own thoughts. Jackson comes through the front door lugging my suitcase and complaining about the weight of it. "Tessa, are you planning on moving here? This thing weighs a ton," he says ,trying to lift it rather than rolling it across the floor.

"Well, I didn't really know how long I would be staying," I say, trying especially hard to keep the irritation I was feeling out of my voice.

Jackson ignores me, barely looking in my direction. Talking to no one in particular, "I 'll take this up to our bedroom. I'm sure you've way overpacked as usual. But you can never have too many clothes for a funeral, right?" he laughs a little at his own joke, and hauls my not so overly packed luggage up the stairs and down the long hallway to one of the guest bedrooms

An awkwardness settles on the room. Jackson's subtle dismissal and comments don't go unnoticed by Kate or Mindy. I shrug, smile, roll my eyes "Men" I say, as if that explains it all. Jackson wasn't unkind to me, but there is a new tone in his voice and the comments he makes that haven't been there before. Not exactly fault-finding but almost *put downs* disguised as jokes. It is embarrassing and I'm not exactly sure how to respond.

The realization suddenly hits me as I stand there, watching him walk up the stairs; we are sharing a bedroom. It's been a while since we have slept in the same bed, months maybe. A quick calculation in my head tells me its been at least six months since we've slept in the same bed. How did that happen? It was a gradual thing, so gradual that I didn't even really notice that it is another problem, in the bigger Jackson and Tessa Problem.

We eat a delicious vegetable frittata and homemade bread, prepared by Celia Thomas, Big Ed's longtime housekeeper. We are all tired, it's been a long day. With the memorial service set for tomorrow, everyone decides to turn in early and try to get some sleep before we say goodbye to Kelly.

Jason hasn't come down from his bedroom. I take a tray up to him. His back is turned to me, and he seems to be asleep. His breathing is even and shallow, it feels peaceful here, at least for the moment. I sit on his bed.

"Hey Sweetie, I'm sorry you're asleep but I know it's been a big ordeal and you need your rest", I say gently to him lightly rubbing his back.

"We are here, all of us, here for you. We will get through tomorrow and what lies on the other side of that, together okay? If you need me to stay with you, I will. You will eventually be alright. Maybe not soon, but I promise one day- you will be so much better than you are right now".

I get up to leave. Jason's hand reaches out for mine. He is crying softly. What this sweet young man has been through breaks my heart. The worst part- we don't even really know the hurt that he carries within him. Jason has never talked to any of us, not even Mindy, about the real reason why he hates his dad so much. Whatever it is, has ripped him to shreds. We can only hope that Kelly's burial will finally bring Jason some peace.

Suddenly feeling nervous, I walk down the hallway and open our bedroom door. I didn't expect to see Jackson propped up in bed, reading an engineering industry magazine. It puts me off balance a little. Hell, who am I kidding? This whole crazy situation has me on edge. I stand looking at my husband of so many years, like I'm seeing him for the first time. He is still very attractive, very fit, looks younger than a man almost in his 50's. I know every feature of his as well as I know my own. Yet, looking at Jackson right now, it's almost like looking at someone I don't know.

When he doesn't look up, I take my things into the bathroom and start my bedtime routine. Pajamas on, teeth brushed, face washed and moisturized; I come back into the bedroom and slip into the bed beside Jackson. It feels strange, even though I have been sleeping beside this man for more than 25 years. Have we really come to this? He is sleeping lightly with the magazine on his chest. I lean over to turn off the lamp, kiss him goodnight and put the magazine away. He stirs lightly.

"Jackson," I say quietly. "Are you awake?"

His breathing tells me that he is, even though he is slow in answering.

"Jackson?"

This time he turns and faces me, even though I can't see his expression very well in the darkened room highlighted only by the glow of nightlights.

"Are you okay" I ask in a small voice? What I really want to ask, and cannot, is "are we okay?"

"Yes", he answers. I wait for him to say more, and he says nothing.

Taking his hand in mine, I ask him again, "Are we really going to be, okay? Is it finally over with Kelly?".

"Yes, Tessa, I believe it is" he answers me in a quiet, defeated tone that is not really like Jackson. In that moment, I feel sad, incredibly sad about that summer, sad for Kelly's senseless death and the impact on those who loved him most. But mostly, sad for myself. In that quiet moment in the dark, holding Jackson's hand, I have a startling realization. My husband no longer loves me.

The day dawns bright and early on this already warm July day. I know because I'm sitting on the front porch, sipping strong coffee and watching the sun make its dramatic appearance in a quiet sky. I slept little last night, overly tired and overwrought emotionally which led to a very restless sleep. When I finally slept, I dreamed over and over about another 4th of July, that summer long ago- the one that made us secret-keepers. After I startle myself awake for at the least the fourth time of this same nightmare, I would fall asleep again only to dream of Kelly's death and burial. It too seemed like a nightmare on repeat. Only, Kelly's death and memorial service are all too real.

I hear some noises in the house, I expect it is Big Ed and Jackson. They are both early risers, old habits die hard. I hope to avoid Jackson this morning. It is going to be a long and emotionally draining day for all of us. Whatever weirdness last night was, I really can't deal with it right now. Maybe I even imagined Jackson's feelings? After today, Jackson and I need to sit down and have a long talk. It feels like our marriage depends on it.

Before long, Celia is here and, in the kitchen, laying out brunch and prepping today's funeral food. I feel bad for her. It's a holiday. Surely there must be somewhere else, anywhere else she would rather be than here. Celia has worked for Big Ed a long time. Once Kelly left for college and Kimberly left for California as quickly as she could; Celia has kept Big Ed in food and cleanliness.

Kimberly won't be back for today's service. I'm not surprised. In fact, I would be surprised if she showed up- shocked even! Kimberly and her dad are close and have stayed that way through the years. But after Kelly left for college and Kimberly graduated from high school, she left Indiana, moving thousands of miles away. I've always thought she wanted to get as far away from Kelly as possible. But that might just be the *overactive* imagination that Jackson believes I have. Kimberly begged to go to college on the West Coast. Big Ed agreed, only after they compromised, and Kimberly consented to living with her mother's first cousin. Ed had stayed in touch with Connie and trusted her to take care of his little girl.

I try to remember the last time I saw Kimberly? Was it Kelly's wedding? No, I think it was Jason's baptism or maybe one of his early birthday parties. It's been a long, long time and she's made a good life for herself out in California. If I could be any other place in the world except here, I would be!

Poppy and the twins are here, along with her dad and the celebrity force security team. The mourning group is small. Afton and Reagan asked to come, and I told them "no". If I'm being honest, I've run interference on any contact with Kelly for a very long time. Today would be no exception. Same with my parents who wanted to come and support the family. The fewer people here, hopefully fewer possible problems or a chance for rogue media types to crash the memorial service.

There is a large law enforcement detail placed at the perimeters of Meadowview Farm. Our own ADT is monitoring any possible unauthorized drones in the farm's air space. It sounds like *overkill* but with a high-profile wife, father and father-in-law; it will take many moving parts to keep the press away and have a private ceremony. It doesn't help any that the Beltway news outlets aren't moving past this tragedy as quickly as they should. There have been no more public statements by the family beyond the initial one. This has not satisfied the news media and they have continued looking for juicy tidbits, anything to keep the story going.

Kate, Jackson, Mindy and I have even been briefed by a public relations team hastily put together by Ed, Henry and Poppy's people. We've taken down personal social media accounts, removed our phone numbers from business websites, and directed our work associates not to give out our personal information. We've also been hypervigilant about answering our phones and our front doors. Honestly, it's been a real pain in the ass!

Kelly is a relative nobody outside of his family connections. Even that **should** only make him newsworthy possibly one day. But with the circumstances surrounding his death and rumors circulating about the nanny's family pursuing wrongful death ligation- it has been one awful mess. But then that's Kelly Bradley Ryan, he was never one to fly under the radar or lead a boring, ordinary life. So, I guess it's ironically fitting that on this Independence Day with the hurried up, hushed memorial service that we all just hope not to become collateral damage in Kelly's life-long train wreck.

Jason drew a line in the sand and vetoed attending the graveside ceremony and burial in the small family cemetery. That's no surprise really, it's his expected response. Kate doesn't push him on this, and I think we all are glad. General Ryan and Poppy will have enough dealing with their own raw emotions without Jason's unpredictable behavior.

The home health nurse is here. After Jason's *incident* labeled a suicide attempt by his mental health team; he isn't allowed to be alone for lengthy periods. Especially, not on a day like today. I volunteer to go up and sit with him a bit. His *show out* this morning likely wore him down. I don't plan on going out to the service, unless necessary. Too many feelings, and regrets are connected to this event. I'm not sure that I am strong enough to withstand it.

Sitting in Jason's room in the corner club chair, I open a dry biography on famous World War II general Douglas MacArthur that I found downstairs in Big Ed's library. Between the boringness of the book, the hum of the ceiling fan, and Jason's rhythmic breathing; my mind begins to wander. I try to piece together exactly when Jason started having so many emotional issues. It has been a part of him for long, it's hard to pinpoint a certain age, behavior or event that triggered his emotional fragileness.

My mind keeps drawing a blank, but just on the edges of my thoughts, I keep coming back to the summer of the fire. But Jason was so young then, maybe six or seven? That day was traumatic for everyone. Watching the boathouse burn at Storybook Cottage on Independence Day, just as dusk was settling in, will be forever etched in my life memories as one of the worst days ever.

Thankfully, no one was killed or very seriously injured. Even though the boathouse was a total loss, and the party a complete bust afterward - it was all okay. But no, no it really wasn't okay. Not even close. Something happened that day- that changed all of us. Kelly was at the heart of it and Jackson and Mindy are protecting him. There are a lot of unanswered questions about that day. I've tried through the years to get them to tell the truth about what really happened and how Kelly was involved. Jackson gets angry and Mindy threatens ending our friendship. I can't lose either of them, so I stay quiet and wait, wait until the truth finally makes its way out in the world.

Shortly after the fire- the Invincible Six began having problems, real problems. The loss of the boathouse was painful to work through; but it wasn't the most painful thing to come out of that whole mess. The Ryan family was the first, slowly withdrawing from our inner circle. Unreturned phone calls, cancelled plans, missing events without any explanation, there was a growing distance between us conveniently explained away by forgetfulness and busyness.

Then, Mindy and Theo began a quiet retreat. At the time, I explained it away with the infertility issues they were having. It was stressful and with each miscarriage and false pregnancy Mindy became much more introverted and more unlike herself with each one. It wasn't that I didn't see Mindy- I visited her often during this four-year period. There were just no more Invincible Six family get togethers. The inner circle slowly fell apart and drifted away.

Right after the fire summer, Jason began having awful nightmares, refusing to eat, sudden crying outbursts, wetting the bed, becoming very moody, temperamental, and extremely unhappy. The change in him, almost overnight, worried his mother and infuriated his father. Kate would spend the next year and a half taking him to doctors trying to figure out what was happening to him. Because of his young age and failure to find anything physically wrong with him, the mental health team decided it was a *phase* exaggerated of course, but one he should outgrow in time.

I glance at my watch, yes, I wear one. It is a gold Cartier that belonged to my grandmother, Esme Donovan. It's worth a lot of money- a shocking amount of money. Enough that we have to insure it separately and Jackson never wants me to wear it out in cities unless we are dining with his wealthy potential investors. It is one of the few luxuries that my grandmother allowed herself. I always remember her wearing the watch and I feel close to her when I wear it.

I need to get the day nurse back upstairs so I can get out to the graveside service. Although, I've been *excused* from attending the burial - I know that Jackson will latch on to this. Maybe not today, but some day soon it will be added to the arsenal of the *Things Tessa Didn't*

Do list. I really have to convince myself to go. The last time I was out at the family chapel and cemetery it didn't go very well.

Jason is settled, as much as possible with the nurse and I head back downstairs. I hear noises in the kitchen thinking it is Celia preparing the post-service meal for the few mourners. I walk into the kitchen expecting to see Celia, working away on the feast Big Ed has requested. Instead, I run smack into someone else that I wasn't expecting.

"Finn?" I know I must have the most surprised look on my face. I almost smacked heads with my first cousin, Finnigan Michael Donovan. Finn has always been more like my brother, instead of a cousin. But *"what the heck was he doing here? I didn't invite him."*

"What are you... why are you here?" I ask him.

He places a hand on his heart in a gesture of being wounded. He fakes a shocked expression on his face.

"Contessa Tanner Carmichael, your manners have NOT improved, since I saw you last" he squeaks in a falsetto voice.

"No, really. I didn't know you were coming. Why didn't you tell me?"

"Jackson invited me, I thought he told you."

"Nope, but welcome. Are you planning to head out to the graveside?" I ask him, realizing that I needed to get a move on if I didn't want to be late.

"No, I don't want to intrude on family time," he says even though ironically, he is intruding on family time. "Jackson asked me to come out, he needed to talk to me about something before he heads back out on the road. I thought I could meet him here, help if y'all needed me" he answers looking a little sheepishly at his feet to avoid looking at me.

Something is up with him; I've known Finn all his life. Know him better than I know myself sometimes. He's not looking at me because he doesn't want me to sense anything going on. *"Well played-Finnigan- well played".*

"I'm going out to the chapel then; we'll catch up later when I get back" I give him a big hug. I've missed him so much. Between taking over my mother's share of the family real estate law practice and partnering with Claire Beth Donovan Tanner on all her post-retirement, side hustle real estate deals, he was a busy, busy, man.

As I'm heading out the kitchen door, I turn back and ask him" Hey, would you like to go up and sit with Jason for a bit? He's having a good day (mostly) I'm sure he would love to see you" I tell him.

"Give him a break from Nurse Ratchet" I stage whisper and wink at him.

Finn and Jason have always gotten along well. They have a kind of *cool, fun* uncle relationship. Jason is comfortable with Finn. Finn is easy to like, and he's always gone out of his way to spend time with Jason and foster a relationship with him. Not being married or having children of his own, maybe he enjoys spending time with Jason or is just compensating for Jason's lack of a decent father.

"Sure, and if he acts out. I will get Nurse Ratchet on him" Finn laughs.

"Yes", I yell as I'm hurrying out the front door.

The chapel and family cemetery are not close to the farmhouse. They are in the middle of the property. Originally a community gathering place, the little chapel in the meadow is old, probably dating back to the early 1800's if the grave markers in the small adjacent burial site are any indication. Maybe while I'm here, I will have the opportunity to spend a little time in the cemetery learning the names and bits of history resting there. Cemeteries are usually peaceful places for me to sit quietly with my thoughts.

Driving out to the chapel, I feel distant echoes of negative emotions lingering in the landscape spread out before me. It is a beautiful breathtaking property with a clear, open blue sky that seems endless and huge white puffy clouds that are hanging lazily. The hardwood trees hugging the tree lines along fence rows will provide a spectacular show in the fall. The fields are lush and green holding square after square of late summer corn stalks. The sunflower and wildflower fields are my favorites. It is the most perfect photo opportunity if only I had time to stop.

Underneath the beauty, I feel the pain of Settlers' difficult travels, disease, sickness, starvation, Indian attacks and massacres. I feel the essence of migrating buffalo herds and wild horses. Joy, happiness, pain and sorrow mingle together in a disjointed melody. I feel war, families fighting against each other. Hardships, successes, failures, hope all permeate this land, what went before fills my senses, almost making me dizzy.

After parking, I struggle to regain inner balance and control of my senses before slipping in the graveside ranks. The priest is doing his bit, talking about Kelly's virtues and reassuring the very small group of mourners of his next destination. I quickly scan the group gathered in a semi-circle around the Ryan plot, which is the largest and most prominent in the small graveyard. General Ryan, with his flaming red hair, piercing blue eyes, lean, fit frame wearing his finest military dress uniform is struggling to maintain composure. Jackson stands beside him, incredibly handsome in his slim cut, precisely tailored black suit, white shirt and tie. Mindy is to his right wearing a perfect mourning jacket and slim black skirt with just the right amount of accessorizing. Her long blonde, wavy hair is pulled away from her face with a chic black headband. Her pale blue eyes are hidden behind huge Hollywood style black sunglasses.

Kate is a little harder to read. Sadness seeps from her mingled with what surely must be regret and maybe even relief, if she could be honest. In this minute, Kate looks defeated, not peaceful like I had hoped she would. With her tall willowy frame and short blonde hair, she has more than a passing resemblance to Princess Diana. Throughout the years, she has cultivated an excellent fashion sense in classic style. In the early years, she was mistaken multiple times for a Di double. Today is no different with her black and white sleeveless sheath and a Kentucky Derby style black hat that would put all the Derby ladies to shame.

Mr. Hawthorne, Poppy, and the twins stand off to the left side of the general. Hawthorne's attire, a custom designer suit that normal people have never heard of reeks of casual elegance- the kind that 99.5% of the population can never achieve in their wildest dreams. Poppy who is even more breathtakingly beautiful in grief with her black suit dress, gloves, sky high pumps, is so beautiful and broken in this moment. It hurts to look at her. The couture black hat sitting on top of her shiny shoulder length, thick caramel colored hair and ridiculously large sunglasses just add to the impression. She looks as though she has come straight from a Vogue shoot. I expect to turn around and see a fashion photographer. The twins, Avery and Amos, looking like little replicas of the grownups glance around dazed and confused. Perhaps, they are waiting for Kelly to show up and explain to them what is going on.

I opted to wear light gray. Not that I am particularly a rebel, but I refuse to wear black unless there is no avoiding it. The color has such a negative impact on me, that I swear I can feel some of my energy draining from my body whenever I wear it. That and I look completely dreadful in this color. So yes, there is a little narcissistic something going on here. Besides, standing next to my beautiful and striking companions, with my mud colored brown hair, small light brown eyes, and chunky body, I look just like a mouse in comparison.

The mood is somber, the priest serious, General Ryan seems to be holding on simply by his determination to do so. Jackson and Mindy are distressed. Henry Hawthorne is quiet and respectful – neutral- there are no strong negative emotions emitting from him. Poor Poppy has so many emotions swirling around her, it is amazing that she is not deliriously dizzy. Neil Frazier, the longtime farm manager, Celia, Ed's housekeeper and cook, and Lollie, the stable manager, look on at a small distance from the family. Each seems caught up in their own thoughts, likely imagining Kelly as a younger boy and not the man he became.

I stand across from the family, just a little back from the group, not wanting to be disruptive. They sense my presence. Standing here gives me the unintended opportunity to see their facial expressions, take in body language and absorb some of their emotions without feeling overwhelmed. I see a glance pass between Jackson and Mindy. I don't quite know what it is. A knowing glance, shared pain, possibly. I wait for Jackson to look up at me. I *will* Jackson to look up at me. He does not. Instead, he looks intently at the hole by Ms. Ella's grave that will hold Kelly's cremated remains. He does not look up; he does not share a moment with me. It is odd, I file it away for later when there is space in my brain for only my own thoughts and feelings.

The ancient priest finally finishes up with his remarks, the whole *ashes to ashes, dust to dust* stuff. In all the millennia of the Catholic church and humankind's long standing burial traditions, you would think we could come up with some better material. Why isn't there maybe just something a little more original and inspirational? Any moment I expect to hear the chorus of Kansas' hit song "*Dust Blowing in the Wind*". Damn, that song will be in my head all day long now. But wouldn't it have been pretty cool if the priest had started singing it? I mentally slap myself back into appropriateness and the present moment. This was the trouble with an overactive imagination, it peeked out at some of the most inopportune times.

It's not that I'm not mourning Kelly- I am. In a weird way, I guess, but I am. But between energy echoes of the farmland , others' emotions and Jason's sonic boom emotional projections; I can't allow myself to feel too much right now. Because letting down the walls, taking it all in and feeling all that surrounds this day is too much. I will lose myself and I Can Not Do That

I wait just on the outside of the group, feeling more like a viewer than participant in Kelly's memorial. It's not necessarily intentional, more to shield myself from a tsunami of emotions. Jackson will likely perceive my actions as closed off and distant. He doesn't really believe in the whole empath thing and at times, he reacts cynically and even a little harshly. It's hard to get him to understand that whether it is a physical or emotional reaction or is just all in my mind; it's real to me.

Jackson holds Big Ed by the elbow and guides him to the edge of the burial plot, they both toss white roses into the hole. In this moment, Edward Ryan looks so frail and fragile. He is just a shell of the man who led soldiers in the jungles of Vietnam. Or the man who with his charismatic smile and sharp sense of humor, quickly rose through the ranks and retired as an Army lieutenant general. This is not the same man who wrote best selling military books, appeared as a subject matter expert on many news shows and had connections with enough important people that he has a standing invitation to the White House, no matter who was the sitting president. But today, he is a broken old man staring down into his son's final resting place and coming face to face with his own mortality.

Poppy, Hawthorne and the littles trail after Big Ed tossing handfuls of dirt and white roses on Kelly's funeral urn. I was a little surprised that neither Poppy nor Kelly's father decided to keep his remains, but Ed insisted that Kelly be buried by his mother Ella. Honestly, I don't blame Poppy for not putting up a fight over Ed's request. After all, who would really want to have a constant reminder of your husband's possible infidelity taunting you every day?

As Ed's farm staff walks by to pay their final respects to Kelly, Mindy stands motionless at the edge of the plot. She seems rooted to the spot where she is standing. She glances down at Kelly's remains and then sideways at the others who have started making their way back to their vehicles. She doesn't really know what to do. I walk around to her and grasp her elbow, speaking softly to her.

"Mindy, sweetie are you okay?" I ask.

It's as though she hasn't heard me, she is looking so intently at Kelly's remains.

"Mindy" I say again.

It takes her a few seconds to come back into the *now*. I don't know what this day is really like for her. That day long ago, that summer, somehow changed her. She has the scars from the fire to prove it. But it's the internal scars she carries that worry me most. There are things about that day, something to do with Kelly that deeply affected Mindy. She's held it inside of her, all these years, refusing to talk about it. Jackson has supported her in that decision all along. Maybe he knows, they seem close, closer now than ever. I hoped that with Kelly's sudden death, she would find some peace. But maybe there is none to be had.

By now, the others have left, heading back to the farm for the funeral meal. Mindy continues staring down into the open hole, in a trance-like state. I'm unsure what to do. She is not herself, and I am feeling dizzy with all the residual emotions lingering here. I reach out my hand placing it on her arm. I flinch. She is hot to the touch and her body has a vibrating sensation.

"You are burning up; we need to get you back to the farm. The day nurse can check you out. How do you feel?" I ask.

At first, I think she has the flu or some other virus she's picked up from traveling and all the stress of this trip. Then, suddenly I recognize these feelings. It is anger and rage. The intensity of these emotions is overwhelming. They almost bring me to my knees. I've only sensed this one other time. Jackson felt just like this, the night the boathouse burned down at the cottage.

Then Mindy says something so quietly that I have to strain to hear her. "I hope you are enjoying Hell, Kelly Bradley Ryan, because it's much too good for you" she says in a tone that is so quiet, so matter of fact, that it is truly scary.

The moment is broken by the sound of a light wind stirring through the branches in a huge, ancient oak tree by the small chapel. The motion and sound snaps Mindy out of her mood. She leans heavily against me like she is almost too weak to walk to my SUV. I wonder if we'll make it on the short walk to the Pathfinder. She is weak and I am dizzy with the onslaught of all of her emotions. We walk slowly, leaning heavily on each other looking like two drunk ladies after a girls' night out on the town.

Somehow, we both get in and I take a sip of barely cool water from my travel Hydro-flask tumbler. The water feels good, it clears my mind a little and chases some of the dizziness away. I offer the water to Mindy. She takes it, swigs a long drink, staring straight ahead. I don't know what to say to my best friend. What is going through her mind? What is the source of all that rage? It's the secret that she has kept buried for years. She knows, by my physical reaction, that I know some of what she is experiencing right now.

We drive slowly back to the farm in silence. I wait for Mindy to speak- she does not. She continues staring ahead, lost in thought and unwilling to share. Some of her anger has dissipated. I can breathe now; the dizziness is gone and the air around her feels a little lighter. Not red, black and electro-charged like a lightning storm. This sounds crazy but sometimes, strong emotions present themselves as colors.

I park behind all the other vehicles, leave the SUV running with the air conditioning on. It is unforgivingly hot this 4th of July holiday. I tell Mindy to stay, I'll be right back. The mourners are gathered in the large kitchen and dining room picking at plates of food. Jackson glances up at me. I can see the question on his face. I ignore him and find Finn.

"I need your help" I whisper to Finn.

"It's Mindy, she's either very sick or having some kind of break-down. Please help me get her in the house without a fuss" I beg him.

"Okay" he says,putting his plate and glass on a table and following me nonchalantly outside.

Mindy is exactly where I left her, in the same position still staring into nothingness. Finn opens her door and leans inside.

"Hey, Min, you aren't looking so good, right now. How about I give you a little help getting in the house?" He flashes her that boyish smile and puts on the charm that most women find irresistible. He is a hard one to say no to and he knows it.

Mindy looks at him and nods her head gently "yes" as if the effort is hurting her. She extends her hand, Finn takes it and helps her out, walking her slowly to the front porch. This scares me, I've never seen Mindy like this. Not after the miscarriages, not even after Theo's death. This quiet, almost catatonic version of Mindy terrifies me. There is something terribly wrong with her.

Finn gets Mindy up the porch and to the front door with me following close behind. I open the front door and we slip quietly past the front of the house toward the large staircase. Thankfully, no one is in the hallway, and we make our way up the stairs undetected. It is a miracle too, because Mindy is walking like a 90-year-old woman who is afraid of stairs. I find the day nurse in Jason's room. Out in the hallway away from Jason's door, I ask her to check on Mindy, explaining my concern. She hurries down to Mindy's bedroom where Finn has gotten Mindy to lie down and is sitting with her.

I slip back into Jason's room. He is a smart guy and will know something is going on. I decide it's better to tell him something. He is sitting at his desk, dressed for the day, watching some action movie on his laptop screen. He hears me come in and pauses the movie. Spinning around in his chair, he looks intently at me. And my heart is shattered. With Kelly's piercing blue eyes and fair skin and Kate's wavy blonde hair, this young man that I have loved fiercely, all his life, is beautifully perfect. And yet so damaged.

He is peaceful in this moment, this is the rare Jason sighting, that is so unusual and yet so beautiful. He looks normal, almost happy, he looks like the grown-up version of the five-year-old boy that forever stamped himself on my heart. I'm quiet, taking in this moment, filing it away, knowing that I will treasure it forever.

He breaks the silence first. "So, who passed out?" he asks with a sly grin on his face.

"Is Mom okay?" he asks.

"Yes, Kate is fine. Big Ed is unsteady today. That's to be expected", I tell him.

"Hard day for Grampa Ed" he says.

"Hard day for everyone Jase".

I see the concern in Jason's face. I can't read his emotions, nothing strong is bubbling beneath the surface. He loves his grandfather so much and would be devastated if something happened to him. Through the years, Ed Ryan has more than made up for Kelly's parental shortcomings. He's close to Kate, treating her as his daughter all these years. I worry about Jason and what will happen to him when his grandfather is gone.

"Actually, it's Aunt Mindy. I think maybe she has a little heat exhaustion or is possibly coming down with the flu or something. I asked the nurse to check on her. I'm sure she will be fine", I tell him, in a reassuring voice that was meant as much for me, as for him.

"What do you think about maybe coming downstairs for a bit? Avery and Amos have been asking about you. I think it would do Big Ed a world of good to see you up and about", I say encouragingly.

Jason considers this. I am hopeful he will go downstairs for at least a little bit and be around other people. Staying cooped up most of the time in this small bedroom with nothing but Netflix movies and memories to keep him company can't be good. Downstairs, everyone loves him and wants to spend time with him. Well, everyone except maybe Henry Hawthorne and he seems to only love himself.

I leave Jason to check on Mindy. I hear a door close softly and footsteps in the direction of Jason's room. I smile to myself and hope he will enjoy some time downstairs.

Mindy's door is closed, I knock softly and go in. Mindy is asleep, in her funeral clothes, laying on top of the bed with a lightweight cotton blanket covering her. The nurse is not in the room, but I'm surprised to see Jackson sitting in a chair in the corner.

"Jack," I say, the surprise clearly in my voice.

"Where's the nurse? What are you doing in here?"

He uncrosses his legs and stands up to stretch. "I came upstairs to check on Jason. I heard voices coming from this room. Finn and the nurse were talking. I walked down to see what was going on", he says. This is Jackson, always the *take charge* guy in any situation.

"So, what did the nurse say? Mindy didn't look well at the graveside" I tell him not asking him why he was sitting with her instead of coming to get someone else.

"Maybe coming down with the flu, more likely heat exhaustion. Possibly just a stress reaction" Jackson tells me, with his usual sparse language. He does not believe in using extra words when only a few will do.

"Well, what do we need to do? Did she leave instructions on what we needed to look for?"

"Tessa, you know flu, heat exhaustion and stress symptoms," he says.

"Mindy wanted to take something to help her sleep. She had some Valium, the nurse approved. She took some medicine and drifted off to sleep."

"But that still doesn't explain what you are doing just sitting here. She doesn't need you to watch her sleep" I say, a little more sharply than I mean.

"Tessa, I was worried okay. Is that a crime?" he asks. I can tell he is agitated because he rakes his hand through his hair. I've seen this gesture many times. It is you're *trying my patience* reflex.

"Okay" I say not wanting to provoke anything. This has been a stressful week for all of us.

"Why does everything have to be such a deal with you anymore? You are constantly reading into everything" his voice rises a bit. He is getting animated.

No, No, No, I silently tell him. Let's not do this here, not today. I give him a look that is something between frustration and disappointment. I turn to walk away. But something stops me, and I turn around to face him.

"Jackson, something happened between Mindy and Kelly. I believe it has to do with the fire" I tell him- knowing this is not the time or place. But it is now or never.

He glares at me and comes around the bed. He clasps my elbow and leads me out of the bedroom and in the hallway, shutting Mindy's door firmly behind him. He angrily whispers, "Jesus, Mary and Joseph, woman, can you not **EVER** drop anything? Yes, they were in a fire together, they got burned trying to put it out. We lost the boathouse because of it" he explains as if he is talking to a small child or someone incapable of advanced thought. His face is angry, and his eyes are flashing.

"You keep trying to make something of nothing. It was an unfortunate accident and that is all. Let it go" he says, his face close to mine.

"Jack, you didn't see her at the burial plot. She was shaking, shaking with rage. So angry that her body was reacting physically. I felt it. It was so strong, I felt ill" I tell him trying to convince him yet again that something happened that day.

"Tessa, you and your empath crap! If you felt anything, if that is even a thing, you probably felt the effects of heat stroke. Not some *touchy feely* woo woo psychic crazy stuff".

I have a sharp intake of breath. I always knew Jackson questioned the whole empath thing, that's why I've always been so careful around him. Mostly, we have joked about it through the years, or I didn't mention any occurrences. But the accusatory tone in his voice is new. Another *new* Jackson behavior that is a recent thing. I breathe deeply and take a moment before I respond.

"Jackson, Mindy is very angry and closed off about that day. That's not like her! If there's nothing more to what happened that day, then why did you beat up one of your very best friends?" I ask him and instantly wish I could take it back.

There is a tic around his eye, and then his facial expression smooths. He laughs, a fake laugh but still a laugh to lighten the moment and deflect my questioning. "Tessa, my overly dramatic girl with an overactive imagination" he says trying to be humorous. "I always said you should quit wasting away your time at that small time publishing house and write your novel" he says evenly, looking directly into my eyes.

"Maybe you should direct all that pent up drama and write a mystery. Make it a murder mystery, then you get to spin the story however you want. You are good at making stories out of nothing" he smiles a charming smile at me that doesn't quite reach his eyes.

I stand there for a moment or two, shocked. Shocked into silence, which doesn't happen very often. I decide to say nothing. There's nothing that I can say in this moment that is helpful or will help diffuse the tenseness of the conversation. He looks expectantly at me, waiting for a reply which he is sure will come. When it doesn't, he turns away and heads down the hallway and downstairs without a backward glance.

Leaning up against the wall outside of Mindy's room, I feel weak, and tired. No, exhausted, emotionally and physically worn out from today. Even in death, Kelly is somehow able to shake us to the core. Mindy is angry, Jackson is very tense and distant, Kate seems lost, and I am truly, completely puzzled by it all. But two things I know, the look on Jackson's face when he was watching Mindy sleep and Jackson's deflection about the fire. Two people that I've loved for so very long are keeping secrets from me. I will know what they are, even if it threatens to destroy us.

I head back downstairs, feeling a massive headache coming on. Maybe some Tylenol washed down with a little alcohol, will head it off. Only a little alcohol, I'm very much a lightweight. Hopefully, Mindy does not have some kind of contagious virus. That would be awful for everyone to come down with something especially on top of everything else this week. The twins and Big Ed, particularly need to stay away from viruses. I'm worried about Big Ed; Kelly's death is taking a toll on him. But it feels like something more than that. He seems frailer than when I saw him last summer. Something feels out of balance. But maybe, it's just dealing with the death of a child, that would throw anyone off balance.

I hear noise and music downstairs. I smile. As I come into the kitchen, I see Jason and the twins playing a cutthroat game of *Go Fish*. Someone is cheating by the sound of the twins' protests and giggles. Avery and Amos love Jason. He seems to love them back. I will forever be appreciative of Poppy including him in their family, even as awkward as it must have been. Poppy seems to really care about Jason, and I respect her even more, for that.

Kate is standing at the sink, smiling and watching Jason play with the kids. Poppy is sitting on a kitchen stool, looking effortlessly beautiful and carefully studying a fruit platter. In my mind, this scene is perfect. It feels like a commercial on tv. The mood is relaxed. As I leave the kitchen, I hear Poppy and Kate discussing the fall/winter couture fashion designs. There is an easiness in their relationship. They have seen the best and worst in Kelly and now share a kinship. Poppy has always been so kind to Jason, inclusive and able to reach him when he withdraws into his shell. She understands the struggles of addiction having wrestled with some of her own. In another universe, she and Kate would probably be good friends. Maybe, they still will be.

I hear the men talking quietly and intently in the den. The conversation is about business and technology of some sort. I hear ice cubes clinking in glasses, I expect Big Ed has broken out some of his finest Irish whiskey in memory of Kelly. As I pass through the wide hallway, to head back upstairs, Jackson looks up and holds my gaze. I nod my head up and down, it's an old thing between us. Even though we probably are not okay, maybe will not ever be okay again. In this moment, I have forgiven him.

Opening Mindy's door, I find her propped up in bed, with all the pillows looking just like the queen she always is. Her color is better, her hair is brushed and she is scrolling on her phone. I place the tray of food on the bed beside her.

"I thought you might be hungry, so I brought you a sampling of the food downstairs. It's all so good. Celia really outdid herself."

Mindy looks up from her phone, sets it on the nightstand and looks at the food tray. She picks it up and sets it carefully on her lap. I stand at the foot of the bed not quite knowing what to say or do.

"Are you feeling any better now?" I ask her.

"Yes, much better, thank you. I guess the heat and all of it was just too much," she says, not looking up at me.

The silence between us lengthens. I start again. "Come on, Mindy. It's me, you can talk to me about anything."

"There's nothing to talk about. It was hot as Hell's front porch out there and I just got a little weak. Don't make this into something big, Tessa," she says, finally looking up at me. Her face is calm and composed. She seems *almost* back to her usual self.

"I felt it, Mindy. Felt all the feelings you were feeling. That wasn't heat exhaustion. You weren't okay," I tell her, silently pleading with her to finally tell me what is wrong.

"You felt that? Of course, you did. Sometimes, I forget."

"It wasn't a little something, it was overwhelming, intense. Mindy, what is it?"

She takes a moment carefully considering her words before answering, "That jackass- Kelly, he can still piss me off, even in death" she says with a little smile on her face.

"Yep, it was a special talent of Kelly's. Finding trouble, weaseling out of it, and pissing off his friends along the way," I say, my tone matching hers.

"But why were you so angry with him today, today of all days?" I gently ask.

"He was a miserable, poor excuse of a human. He was toxic, Tessa. You know this. He burned down everything and everybody around him" she says. For emphasis, she waves her arms in the air. Her right arm is scarred from the burns of the fire that she and Kelly tried to put out at the boathouse.

My attention is drawn to her scars, they aren't so bad now. There are multiple long, white lines criss crossing down her forearm. Several expensive plastic surgeries have corrected most of the damage. Immediately, my mind goes to that night and the gaps in the story that remain. It isn't the fire, but something connected to the fire that troubles me. Kelly and Mindy lied about that night, Jackson too. I want to ask her, beg her even, to finally reveal whatever secret she's been carrying for so many years. The secret that we hid from Theo, Kate and everyone else. The weight of this is heavy, but the ironic thing is that I don't even know who, what, or even the why of this secret. But I do know there is one.

"Please tell me, Mindy. Whatever it is, tell me. Kelly can't hurt us anymore. It's over" I plead with her.

"Don't, you, see?" she asks me in a detached voice. "It's never over, Kelly ruined us. All of us and we may never be whole again. Any of us" she has that same glazed look in her eyes, the one that scared me earlier.

"Mindy, we can get through it together just please..."

"No," she interrupts me. "No, I can't."

I start to say something else, and she holds up her hand to stop me. This isn't productive, and we are both emotionally exhausted. It can wait, after all these years, today it can wait.

"I think Poppy and the kids are getting ready to leave and catch a flight back to Virginia. Will you come down later, only if you feel up to it?"

"Yes," she answers and picks up her phone again. That is my signal this conversation is over.

I go to the door, open it and step out in the hallway.

"Hey, Tessa" Mindy calls out quietly.

I peek around the door and look at her.

"Thank you, for everything."

Downstairs, Poppy and the twins are saying their goodbyes. I'm happy to catch them before they leave. Hugging sweet little Avery with her angelic face and bouncy curls and Amos with his mischievous grin and flaming red hair is like seeing the best parts of Kelly. I will miss them. Even when grieving, Poppy is charming. She offers a girls' weekend for Kate, Mindy and me in D.C. when things settle down. I return the offer with a stay in Tennessee, at Honeywood, for her and the twins. Maybe Afton and the grandkids can come too. I really hope Poppy will come visit soon. Home gets so lonely now.

The guys, including Jason, are on the porch planning to ride out to the stables and take a look at Big Ed's latest horse breeding efforts. Finn is a huge Kentucky Derby fan and racehorse breeding fascinates him. They head out to the stables. It is probably good distracting Big Ed, and besides men are not very good at sitting with their feelings. Being outside, doing something physical and focusing on something else is the best thing for all of them as they grieve Kelly.

The house is finally quiet and feels *clean*. Just like a regular house and not full of intense emotions bouncing off the walls in every direction. It has settled back into itself for the time being. I feel the calm, steadying, lasting echoes of Ella Ryan floating back into place. I never knew her; she died when Kelly was ten. I sometimes feel the echo of her presence in the house. She was a lovely, kind, determined woman that I am sorry I didn't get to know.

Kate is sitting outside on the terrace by the pool. It is a beautiful space. The calm blue expanse of the pool is contrasted with the jungle like colors of the many plants and trees that line the terrace and pool areas. You almost feel that you are in a swanky Caribbean resort rather than stuck in the middle of Indiana cornfields. It is extravagant but tasteful, exactly the sort of thing that Ella would love.

"Room for one more?" I ask Kate. Which is ridiculous since the terrace is huge and empty, but I don't want to invade her privacy if she wants to be alone.

"Of course," Kate says as she sits nursing a large glass of red wine. It is likely an expensive brand of Cabernet Sauvignon, her favorite.

"Kate, I feel like I've not been paying you enough attention through all of this. Are you okay? Is there anything I can do for you?"

She turns and looks at me with sadness etched in her face. For a split second, I could swear I was sitting across from an older Princess Di. The resemblance is sometimes startling.

"Tessa, always the worrier. Always the giver. My sweet friend, I am fine. As fine as I am ever going to be," she tells me.

"It seems like Jason has handled this pretty well. It's been a day."

She looks down into her wineglass before answering. "You know, I was worried, really worried. How he would handle this on top of the setback he just had. But he seems to be handling it okay, so far" she says, not saying the very thing we both are thinking.

So far, but Jason is fragile, and has a lot of pent-up anger directed toward his father and who knows when that might come bubbling up to the surface? Hopefully, Kelly's death will finally give Jason the opportunity to have some closure and peace in his life.

"How are you holding up? This must be difficult for you." I ask her, leaning over and putting an arm around her shoulder. Kate is not naturally a hugger, but I sense she needs some reassurance right now.

She replies in a quiet voice, "All these years, especially during the hard years with Kelly" she struggles to maintain her composure, "sometimes I wanted him to just go away, and other times after the bad arguments, I wished him dead".

"I'm ashamed of that, I know it's not healthy thinking. But there were times when I felt the only way I could be free, truly free of Kelly was if he was dead," she hangs her head and begins crying.

I wait a beat or two before I answer her. Kate and Kelly's marriage turned volatile towards the end. There were lies, rumors of infidelity on Kelly's part, bad arguments, and verbal abuse directed at Kate. Mindy and I suspected possible physical abuse, but we didn't see any signs and Kate wasn't talking. It finally got so bad, that Big Ed intervened and convinced Kate to divorce his son, for the best of everyone.

"Kate, that's understandable, it was a horrible marriage towards the end" I try consoling her.

"I prayed and prayed to be released from the hell that Jason and I were living in. Do you know how many times, even early on, I considered leaving him? But every single time, he would smooth talk me into staying and make a lot of empty promises, he never kept. And I stayed time after time, thinking it might get better. I was foolish enough to believe that it was best for Jason, that he needed his father, even if his father hated me," she says, sobbing now.

She doesn't have to say a thing, I feel the pain, years of pain bubbling up inside of her. It is so overwhelming; I almost can't bear it.

"And you want to know the crazy thing? Even during these last years, when I pretended that Kelly was dead to me; as soon as I heard the news, I wondered if I somehow caused this? How messed up is that?"

"Even his death is somehow my fault" she laughs a sarcastic laugh.

"No, no, no, Kate" I grab her into a hug and hold her until she calms down.

"After today, we can move forward and really put Kelly to rest. We will survive, put ourselves back together and go forward. One day in the future, this day will be okay."

I tell Kate this as much for myself as for her. Out there, where none of us can yet see, we might be beyond Kelly's long reach. Kelly's death didn't end the hurt and pain he subjected us to, with his reckless ways and inability to take responsibility for anything. I don't realize it yet, but burying Kelly didn't bury the past. I'm not sure we buried the secret with him. Bad things have a way of smacking you in the face, when you are the most vulnerable and least expect them.

Mindy

I'm tired of sitting up here in this room alone. But I'm hiding, not wanting to face anyone just yet. Taking a page straight out of Jason's playbook. It is awkward and I don't exactly know how to laugh and make my earlier behavior light, easy and more *Mindy like.*

Tessa knows, I let my guard down temporarily. So caught up in hating Kelly, I didn't turn it off quickly enough to fool her. When I saw her knees buckle at the graveside, I knew she was getting the full force of my anger, and rage. I've lived with both horrible emotions for years, since that summer. She only has some idea, what it feels like to be me.

I normally hide it pretty well. Underneath the southern girl charm, and my God given looks, I'm grossly underestimated. No one would ever guess at the raging, cold blooded, revenge seeker I could be, if forced into the situation. I'm sassy, mostly sweet, charming, loyal and have impeccable taste. My sometimes foul mouth, is a detraction, for sure. But otherwise, I am a fine, upstanding, citizen who just happens to be wildly successful in the vacation rental market.

But Tessa saw a glimpse of the other Mindy, the one I try to keep buried. She is too dangerous and must be tightly controlled. I am mostly successful at that. But today in a weak moment staring down at what remained of Kelly Ryan, she almost slipped out. The other me, has spent years imagining ways to kill Kelly Ryan. But the stupid jackass went and killed himself. Honestly, I'm more than slightly disappointed in that.

The house sounds quiet, Poppy and her family are gone. I like Poppy but what she ever saw in Kelly Ryan is beyond me. She has everything and I mean EVERYTHING going on for her. Looks, wealth, career, connections, impeccable taste; it must have been some type of *savior* complex. As much as I don't really want to admit it though, she did try to help Kelly. It seemed to work for a while, and maybe he was even trying to be a better person. That was, until he wrapped himself around a tree, driving drunk with an extremely young nanny in the car. It doesn't take a genius to figure out that it wasn't just an innocent ride to the airport. Poppy and the kids were out of town, visiting friends. Kelly just coincidentally *falls off the wagon,* decides to take an impromptu trip and drive the nanny to the airport when she hadn't cleared any vacation days with her employer? All that and the luggage found on the scene, screams something going on with the nanny.

Out of respect for Big Ed and Poppy, none of us mention anything about this. It was squashed in the police report, not reported by the news outlets and "hey" if you don't talk about it, it didn't happen. Right? Except it did. Even after Poppy rescuing him, Kelly could not stay away from other women. He had a sickness that we just didn't recognize and when we finally did. It was too late!

I make my way downstairs, grab a chilled bottle of seltzer water and some wine glasses. I see Kate and Tessa outside on the terrace. While I won't toast Kelly, it is time to reinstate our sunset toast. Kate and Tessa are talking quietly, Tessa is hugging Kate. They don't hear me walk up until I make some noise placing the tray on the table behind them.

"Well, it sure doesn't seem like much of a party, but I guess we must carry on" I announce bringing the glasses and seltzer water to the lounge chairs. It is my best attempt at lightening the mood and distracting Tessa from any probing questions. Once the reporter, always the reporter seeking out the "who", "what", "why", "where" and "how". Young Tessa hoped and dreamed of becoming an award-winning, human-interest reporter. She would've been amazing. She was amazing, until Life Happened. And then it became another one of our smashed dreams.

Kate looks up at me with watery eyes and a small smile that takes great effort. Honestly, it's all I can do to not shake her until her teeth rattle. If there is anyone who should be dancing in the street, that Kelly Ryan is dead, it is Kate Maynard- first wife. Her life was ruined the day she laid eyes on him. He was the first biggest mistake she ever made, and the second was not leaving him behind after a second date.

"Are you feeling better, now?" Kate asks.

"Much, you know this crazy heat, stress, just all of it" I wave my hand, like I'm just waving it all away. *Keep it light, friendly,* I tell myself, fixing a smile on my face. Why do women always feel like we need to smile, even if it's the very last thing we want to do?

"I thought we could do our sunset toast tonight. It's been a minute, we're all together. It's been a terrible week," I say looking at my best friends, then pouring drinks and handing each of them a glass. "It's seltzer water, you girls can move on to something stronger later" I wink.

The sun is beginning to dip low in the sky. It's almost sunset. We sit close together, watching the sun disappear and lift the glasses in our traditional salute "To Us", we all say. I hold my breath, hoping, hoping, hoping Kate won't suggest a toast to that former horrible husband of hers. Thankfully, she doesn't. We sit for a few minutes, watching the sky turn beautiful shades of pink, and purple. Each of us, lost in ourselves over recent events.

I sit expecting Tessa to say something poetic. She is, after all our well-read philosopher with an appropriate quote or little story for almost every occasion. I guess it's from reading so many books all her life. But it is not Tessa that breaks the silence, it's Kate.

"I loved him," she says in a quiet, pathetic voice. "I know, I know, it's crazy," she says, wringing her hands and looking up at us.

"Even after all, everything that happened. I Loved Him. There is a small part of me that will always love him" she says with a defeated look on her face. I cannot believe what I am hearing right now. Are you serious?

"Kate, that's normal. You built a life together; you had a child together..." Tessa is consoling her.

"Bullshit" I say in a loud voice before I can stop myself. Kate and Tessa, look at me, startled by my outburst. " Bull Shit", I say even firmer this time. I try to keep my voice down, but it is hard. Big Ed, Jackson, Finn and Jason are in the house. I don't want to make a scene. *Control, Mindy, Girl, get ahold of yourself right now* I tell myself and take a couple of deep breaths, trying to calm down and think before shooting off my mouth.

Kate and Tessa look at me wide-eyed, waiting for something. The outburst is uncharacteristic of me. I'm usually the *cheerful* one, Kate is midwestern *pragmatic* and Tessa is usually *reserved*. They wait for my follow-on because I certainly owe them one.

"You loved the ideal Kelly, The funny guy, the life of the party. You loved the guy you thought he could become one day. So did Poppy. We all loved the "fun" Kelly"I say, knowing that I should just shut up here. But I keep going.

"The other Kelly, the bad guy- the one we should've stopped. We," I say pointing at myself, Kate and Tessa. "We knew, all three of us knew, as soon as we met him, we knew."

Kate and Tessa stare at me, not really wanting to hear what might be next. But just like looking at a bad highway accident; they couldn't tear their eyes away. I feel myself getting worked up, and I take a breath and hold it a few seconds. *Do I finish this?* I asked myself.

"Look, I'm not trying to disrespect Big Ed or his love for his son. I love Big Ed, he's been kind to me, I think of him as the father I never had. Kelly was so lucky to have him. He didn't deserve Big Ed. You all have such great families. Well, all but Jackson, his family sucks" I say, and Tessa smirks a little. That's an understatement. "Only I won the bad life lottery and lost my parents early and got stuck with that God awful woman who was my aunt by blood only" I shudder thinking about my Aunt Tisha who made my life a living hell growing up.

Kate fidgets nervously and Tessa looks like she trying to find the right thing to say to interrupt my rant. I've dug the hole this deep, I may as well finish the job. "I knew the day; the very day I met Kelly Ryan I should've turned around and walked away. So did you Tessa and by God, whether you are willing to admit it or not, so did you Kate. You knew inside that there was something a little *off* about him. But just like me, you probably shrugged it off and thought you were being silly, and it was just your imagination playing tricks on you".

"Mindy, why are you doing this today? We've all been through the wringer with this. We are all trying to process and deal with our feelings. Is this really the best time for this kind of conversation?" Tessa ask me, with a very worried look on her face.

"Forget feelings!" I hiss.

Kate turns pale and her eyes look so big that at any second, they might pop out of her head.

"Have you been drinking Mindy? That's the only explanation I can come up with for your crazy talk right now," Kate tells me, the usually unflappable Kate is very upset with me.

"You know I haven't. Maybe a bottle or two of vodka would make this awful week more bearable. I knew I shouldn't have come here," I say worrying now that I have just done the wrong thing. But there was no backing out now.

"Tessa," I say, directing my attention to her. She is quiet, I can tell she is struggling with the emotions I am projecting. I try to rein in all the fire, I am currently feeling flowing throughout all my body. It is hard. She doesn't need to feel this too. But I cannot stop!

"How many years, after that summer, the fire summer have you asked me to tell the truth?" I ask her, my eyes boring into hers.

"Thirteen, today" she squeaks.

"Tell the truth about what? I don't understand," Kate is truly puzzled.

In this split second, I decide to tell her the truth. To tell Tessa the truth because all these years she's only known part of it. There is no going back now, Damn Kelly Ryan!

"Mindy, are you sure, do you think this is the right time or place? Could we talk about it later? Maybe when we are all in a better frame of mind?" Tessa asks me, she knows that something bad is about to be revealed. She senses it, she knows the truth, it's right on the edge of her mind and yet she just hasn't quite put it all together.

"No!" I exclaim, making Kate jump a little. "You have been hounding me for thirteen years. Thirteen years Tessa, every year asking me on the fire anniversary to tell the *truth*. You couldn't take a hint, you had to keep digging and digging and asking because you just couldn't leave it alone," I am getting emotional now. Oh, this is going to hurt, but it has to be done.

"Mindy, you don't have to do this right now" Tessa says, trying to diffuse the situation.

"I'm sorry, but I do. You only know part of what happened on the fire night. We did so wrong by not telling the rest," I look at Tessa and she is so unsure of what is coming next.

"That night, Kelly, it was" I start trying to decide how to start. After all this time, I didn't know how to tell what needed to be told.

"Shut Up!" Kate says whimpering.

I continue. "Yes, Kelly and I put out the fire in the boathouse. You know that I have the scars to prove it. But something bad happened before then" I say, hugging myself.

"Shut Up!" Kate says a little louder this time.

"Shut up, shut up, shut up" she pleads with me.

This secret that I have kept is going to wreck us. There might not be any *us* after this. But I can't seem to stop myself. I am starting to shake a little thinking about that night, my voice is hitching a little.

"Please stop," Kate says, holding her hands over her ears.

Tessa watches me, her body rigid and her breathing shallow. She has a look of resignation on her face for whatever is coming.

I say simply, "Kelly physically hurt me that night. He took advantage of the situation and he; I couldn't stop him. His best friend's wife, he..." I can't bring myself to say it.

"No, no, no" Kate is almost hysterical now.

Tessa looks at me, puzzled not quite putting the pieces together. I don't want to say the next part.

"Stop it, you are lying! I can't listen to any more of this. How dare you, Mindy!" Kate leaps up from her chair, crying. She runs across the terrace and lets herself into the house.

Tessa is still looking at me, not comprehending what I'm saying. Well, at this point, I'm unsure if I have the courage to tell all of it. So, I just tell the next part.

"Kelly was drunk, almost out of his mind. He was angry. I happened to wander into his path. We did start the fire accidently. Kelly hurt his best friend's wife and godmother to his son. He hurt me, Tessa. The rage in his face was terrifying. Jackson suspected something and then he covered it up. All these years, he did it to protect his friend.

Tessa stares at me for a moment with her mouth open trying to process what I've told her. "No, Mindy you and Kelly fell coming out of the boathouse trying to get help with the fire" she says looking at me for verification.

"That's what Jackson decided we would say. I got hurt in the boathouse. Kelly got hurt when Jackson tried to beat him within an inch of his life for starting the fire and hurting me," I gently tell her.

"Mindy, no that does not make any sense. Why would Jackson lie?" she seems unable to connect any dots.

I struggle with how much to tell her. I've opened Pandora's box but telling her everything will devastate her. So, I do the next best thing. I take in a deep breath and plunge in.

"Tessa," I say, taking both of her hands into mine. I would do just about anything to avoid this right now. Especially right now with everyone in the house, but she has to know.

"Sweetie, Jackson and I had..." I begin, choosing my words very carefully.

"An affair?" she interrupts me, her face crumpling.

"Mindy, how could you? You and Jackson are having an affair?" her voice is shaky, and she is staring at me unbelieving.

What do I do? Do I let her believe this? Do I tell her the truth about the fire summer and Kelly? Either option will destroy us. There will be no more Mindy and Tessa. There will be no more any of us.

"No," I snap at her "you silly goose."

"So, you are denying it?" Her voice begins to rise dangerously, and she jerks her hands away from mine.

The last thing we need is a messy scene in front of everyone, especially in front of Jackson. *Think fast, Mindy, you need to fix this.* I feel myself getting angry. If I don't get control of myself right now- I'm going to mess this up permanently. What was I thinking?

"No," I say softly. "You know me better than that. You are my sister, Theo was the love of my life, there is no one else for me" I tell her soothingly. Her body softens a little, I think that she believes me. She is simply caught up in the emotion of the moment.

"Mindy, Jackson is..." she breaks down in tears and struggles to continue. "Jackson doesn't love me anymore. He may be involved with someone else" she says, wiping away tears.

I look at her, now more troubled than ever. How can I tell her about Jackson? So, I don't.

"Look at me, right now" I say in my bossiest tone. "I honestly don't know what is going on with Jackson. I don't! You need to pull yourself together right now and listen to me and listen well" I feel bad about the tone I'm taking with her, but it is necessary.

"Quit feeling sorry for yourself, get your head out of books and alternative realities and pay attention, **close** attention to what is going on around you. Quit running from the world, when it gets to be too much" I hate these words as soon as they come flying out of my mouth. It's too late now. In this moment, Tessa will not forgive me, I hope that someday she will.

She flinches from me, like I've hit her. Her body goes stiff, and I see anger slowly creeping in her face. "I thought you were my friend, Mindy. All these years you and Kate have been the sisters I've never had. I've always been there for you. Pregnancy struggles, Theo's death, the alcohol issue, Kate's awful marriage? All Of It. Now," she is getting angrier. "Now,that I need someone and feel like my life is blowing up, where is everybody? Huh, where are the friends that I have fully supported for almost thirty years?"

"You're all so caught up in yourselves, there's no room or time to be around for me."

"Tessa, I'm telling you this with much love and concern. Be careful around Jackson" I tell her, biting my tongue to prevent myself from making this any worse.

"What does that even mean?" she asks with her eyes blazing.

"Sweet friend, Jackson is your kryptonite and if you aren't careful, extremely careful he's also gonna be your Apocalypse", I get up and start walking off the terrace away from this scene. I have to leave before I do irreparable damage. Later, I will tell her as much as I can, but not today, not on this god-awful day. I walk toward the gatehouse to clear my head. I hear a door close and footsteps on the terrace. I hope it's not Jackson. But I do not trust myself to turn around and look.

"Tessa, there you are. There's something I need to talk about with you" Finn tells her with much affection in his voice.

"No, not right now" she tells him sharply. "Maybe later".

"But Tessa, I will be leaving tomorrow and ..." Finn seems insistent.

"I said no" she almost yells at him. Even though I can't see his face I know Finn must be shocked.

I've stopped walking and I am standing around the corner, just out of sight of anyone on the terrace. I hear the French doors close once and then close again. I step back around so I can get a better view of the terrace. Tessa and Finn have gone into the house. The terrace is empty, a window is cracked open upstairs. I think I see a curtain flutter, but I don't really feel a breeze blowing. It's probably just my tired mind. This has been one of the most emotionally exhausting days in my life and I've had more than my fair share of those.

JASON

Anymore, being around people is wearing me out. Mom begs me to come downstairs more and *interact*. I'm so tired, I feel like I've run a long-distance marathon. I'm just out of practice with the whole *peopling* thing. Today, wasn't bad though. Grampa Ed needed to know I was okay. I could be **okay enough** long enough not to worry him. He has enough shit to deal with, without me adding to the pile.

It's hot in my bedroom, so I open the window a little. Sometimes, it gets stuck and will only open about halfway. It faces out over the pool. Sometimes, I look out this window and imagine I am in a sexy, tropical place with a hot girl by my side. Maybe even Chloe, nah – she's dead.

I'm staring out the window, wishing I was anywhere else but here right now. Mom, Aunt Tessa and Mindy are sitting by the pool. They are probably waiting for sunset to do their dumb toast thing that they do. They toast the sunset and start talking. I sit up on my desk, listening hard to hear what they're saying. Usually, I wouldn't give a damn; but today has been weird, so it's an easy way to read the room.

Mom is crying, which still makes no damn sense. Aunt Mindy's voice is louder and easier to hear. She is pissed. Mom is doing that thing with her hands; Aunt Mindy is talking loud now, and Aunt Tessa looks scared. "What the hell is going on?"

I hear a little only because Aunt Mindy's voice is getting louder. You can tell by the body language; something big is going down. I'm not proud of this, but I race downstairs fast in stealth mode and sneak into the butler's pantry. Uncle Jackson is on a call in the kitchen, Grampa Ed and Finn are glued to the Cincinnati Reds game in the den with the French doors closed. Nobody sees me. I open the pantry room window as quietly as I can. This one doesn't stick like the upstairs window. Now I can hear everything they are saying. The three of them are so into what they are talking about; they have no idea I'm listening.

And BOOM, there it is. I finally find out that I'm not crazy! This would've been an important share about a million years ago. Mom and Grampa Ed could've saved a lot of Benjamins on therapy, holistic doctors and a stint in rehab (more than one- but who's counting)? Bio Dad, Kelly Psycho Ryan hurt Aunt Mindy the fire summer and I saw it.

I Am Not Crazy! All those dreams I've had for so long of Bio Dad being a monster is true! Except it's worse than my dreams. In my dreams, Kelly was a big scary monster with snarling teeth who ate kids if he caught them. In real life, he hit women, assaulting his best friend's wife. And my mom too, even though she tried to hid it from me for years. Maybe they weren't the only ones- maybe, he didn't just stop at hitting them.

The truly messed up thing, at the lake house is I saw Bio Dad hurting Aunt Mindy. All those scary dreams that Mom, Grampa Ed and too many stupid therapists told me was my imagination. It was real, it happened!

No, those dreams didn't come from my imagination or feelings of rejection that the *little me* didn't know how to express. They came straight from the dark place in my mind. It came from little kid eyes that saw my hero doing things to his aunt, that my six-year-old self couldn't understand. I never told anybody about that night either. Little Jason didn't have the words- at least the head doctors were right about that.

Right after that weekend at the lake, things got heavy in the Ryan house, fast! Mom and Bio Dad went into full war mode. I went into retreat mode. I started having terrible headaches and was afraid of the dark. Started wetting the bed and had a sick stomach all the time. I remember hiding a lot, mainly from Kelly. I didn't want him to hurt me too.

One year, I missed so many days of school that I was one day away from having to repeat a grade. My mom found a child therapist recommended by my private school counselor. That lady was nice, like a grandma. She was the first of many head doctors that I saw. Kelly thought I was just going through a brat stage and acting out. The more problems I had; the tougher he got on me. Of course, I just got worse. It was like being on a crazy merry go round that kept going faster and faster and I couldn't get off.

Elementary and middle school boys being the little asses that most of them are, smelled blood in the water and attacked. Yep, soon I was crazy Jason. One of the moms was friends with the school counselor who ran her mouth that the grandson of already famous General Ryan was headed for Crazy Town.

So, coddling, worried mother, hard ass, screwed up father, famous grandfather, bullying classmates, too many therapists, much recreational drugs and alcohol later, and "Damn" if it really wasn't me after all! Couldn't I have found this out about two rehab vacations ago? If I had known it was all him- I could've calmed the hell down. Maybe I would have been a little more normal, whatever that looks like. Maybe I wouldn't have worried every second of every day since that fire summer that I was losing my freaking mind, tiny pieces at a time.

I'm so insanely angry right now. The crazy thing is I don't even know who to be furious with? Mom, Grampa Ed, maybe everyone else too? They all knew, they had to know something was wrong with him. All this time and no one said a thing. Kelly Ryan screwed up everything and everybody around him. If he was not already dead, I'd be headed to Virginia right now to take care of that little problem.

Mom is losing it. I don't think she can listen to Aunt Mindy any-more. I need to bounce upstairs before they catch me listening. I don't know what I'm gonna do with all I've just heard. Process it, I guess, like the head docs say. But today definitely isn't the day to confront them. All I know for sure, is Kelly Psycho Ryan has finally left the room and it's about thirteen years too late.

Mindy

After the truth bomb, I've just dropped, I hang out by the gatehouse for a bit. Mostly, trying to calm myself down and also avoiding the two people I love more than anything in this world.

I knew I shouldn't have come here. My mind is not in a good place and just blurting out the truth today was not the right thing to do. But right or wrong, it's done now and I will just have to deal with the fallout. I should feel relieved. But I don't because it's not done. I told the *varnished* version of what happened that day. The real truth, I'm not sure we can handle that without breaking into a million little pieces.

Sharing this is one of the hardest things I've ever done. It's right up there with becoming an orphan at age ten and finding myself a widow in my 40's after Theo's sudden death. This secret is as heavy as my four miscarriages and decision not to go through with in-vitro fertility treatments, when I had the chance.

Tessa and her yearly check-ins on the 4th of July. Her continual pleading to tell the truth, I guess it finally got to me. Or maybe it's wondering if this terrible secret might finally consume me? I've paid for not telling the truth about Kelly and that day in so many ways. We all have. I guess that's what really keeps me up at night. If I had just told the truth about Kelly, maybe all our lives would've turned out differently.

Not long after the fire, Tessa started asking questions about what happened that night. It was chaotic, scary and stressful. The less I wanted to talk about it, the more that she did. She didn't quite believe what Kelly, Jackson and I were telling her. Who could blame her? Our stories didn't line up, but we brushed that aside, blaming Kelly's stellar drunkenness and chaos surrounding the fire. If she hadn't talked to the babysitter Caroline, a few months after the fire she would've let it go. Theo and Kate accepted the stories we told without hesitation. But not Tessa, her reporter instincts told her there was more, much more, than we were telling. She was right, so very right.

Well, you know what they say about hindsight and all. I say it is a bitch! It's so very easy, after the fact, looking back on situations and seeing how you could've/should've acted differently. At the time, I wanted to forget, just forget what happened. Sometimes, I even fooled myself into believing that I made it all up and nothing really happened. Other than the fire of course. I didn't make that up. It was real and I have the scars to prove it.

Maybe Tessa was right. Maybe, we should've confronted Kelly, and held him accountable for what he did. He started the fire and tried to weasel out of it, blaming me. But what he did, what he really did, was so much worse than a fire that the insurance company eventually ruled an accident.

So much deception, and so many lies piled up, so much damage and destruction for all of us and for what? Protecting ourselves? Our relationships? Kelly? Tessa was convinced not telling the truth would end up hurting everyone. She didn't even know all that happened, but inside, she knew. We shouldn't have let Kelly get away with what he did.

At the time, I convinced myself what I thought happened and what really did were two entirely different things. Jackson, always the leader, stepped in and *handled* things. He dealt with the chaos, the aftermath and created the stories that we would tell. Only, he didn't count on Tessa having that *little* bit of doubt. He was arrogant enough to believe Tessa would completely accept whatever he said. He underestimated her! That was his first mistake. Underestimating me, is his second. Kelly lit the match that torched our world. Jackson watched it burn and walked away.

TESSA

Somehow, I make my way upstairs to the bedroom. I hear Jackson talking on his phone with one of the ADT teams. Big Ed is sleeping in front of the tv, with a baseball game playing in the background. It's been a very long and trying day for him. Thankfully, I don't run into Finn downstairs. I feel bad for yelling at him. I haven't done that since we were young. It's been a day!

I consider stopping in to check on Jason. But I can't right now. Any more emotional outbursts and I might just collapse. One thing I know for sure is I cannot stay here another minute. My mind is overwhelmed with what just happened. It's going so fast, I feel dizzy. But if even half of what Mindy said is true, I can not be around my husband Jackson Carmichael right now, much less share a bed with him.

Pulling out my suitcase and yanking down my clothes from the closet, I start repacking my things as quickly as I can. I don't really have a plan in mind, but I know I cannot be here. It's probably too late to drive much past Indianapolis tonight, especially in my current frame of mind. Maybe, I can follow Finn back, he was planning to stay there and fly out tomorrow. I have no idea about Jackson's plan, nor do I care.

I text Finn:

Me: Sorry about earlier. Forgive me?

> Finn: Sure! Long day. Headed back to Indy. Early flight tmrw.

> Finn: R U ok? Still need to talk very soon.

> Me: Ik, soon, ok?

I'll stay in the gatehouse tonight since it will be empty. I doubt I will be getting much if any sleep. I absolutely refuse to be in the same room with Jackson, if I don't have to. He will wonder what's going on. I have to come up with something quick.

I feel terrible about leaving without saying goodbye to Ed or Jason, but I can't see Mindy or Kate right now. Honestly, I can't deal with any of them right now. Feel like I'm drowning, being pulled down by something heavy and I can't get any air.

I drag my stuff downstairs and peek in the kitchen. Jackson is still on the phone, sounds like he is trying to manage some worksite problem. He hates working remotely. Seems like he will be busy for a while. I try to get his attention, he waves me off, points to his phone and turns his back to me. Alright then, I tried.

The gatehouse is unlocked. I walk in and pull the door closed behind me, locking it. It is a very nice space, cozy and spacious at the same time. Big Ed had it renovated quite a few years ago to accommodate overflow guests. There is a small master bedroom downstairs and a full, finished loft area upstairs, with a sitting area, full bathroom and bedroom with bunk beds. It would make a fabulous vacation rental place. But General Ryan would never allow that.

I call Jackson to make my excuses for staying in the gatehouse and leaving early. His phone rings and goes straight to voicemail. He must still be managing work issues. I leave a message.

"Hey, I didn't want to disturb you, your call seemed important. I'm going to stay in the gatehouse tonight. Too much today, I have a terrible migraine. I'm heading home tomorrow, Annie called. My meeting with the owners has been pushed up to the day after tomorrow. Can you believe that? So, anyway duty calls. I'm going to bed soon. Let me know your travel plans. Okay, bye," I talk quickly so the message won't get cut off. I realize after I hang up, I didn't tell him I loved him. I forgot, or maybe subconsciously I didn't want to say it, I don't know. It is another sign that our marriage may be in deep trouble.

I lied about my work meeting. My senior managing editor Annie Price did not call or text me. There **is** an upcoming meeting with the owners of my publishing house. However, it's not been scheduled yet. Usually, we do those remotely on Zoom. Jackson has no idea what my work schedule is anymore, and I don't know his, unless I specifically ask him. I need an alibi to be in Nashville for a few days. There is something I must do.

Today was full of shocking revelations. It was too much, just as it always has been with anything related to Kelly Ryan. As my mind has cleared a little in the last hour, and emotions have drifted away, I know these things:

1. My husband Jackson is involved in something, he very much shouldn't be. I don't know what, but it might be our undoing.

2. Mindy's confession hurt! But it was only a half-truth, at best. She's still hiding something. There's still so many unanswered questions about that day. Now that Kelly is gone, I intend to uncover the truth, all of it.

If that is not shocking enough, I got the most important and terribly unsettling news of the day. While Kate, Mindy and I were having that awful fight on the terrace; I had the most vivid, strongest impression I've ever had. The thought came to me so clearly, I was sure

God spoke down from Heaven. It jolted me a little and I still can't believe that Mindy and Kate didn't hear it too.

Kelly Bradley Ryan's death was not a stupid, reckless accident. He was murdered! With all the lies we've told ourselves and each other and the secrets that have corrupted our friendships since the fire summer; I can't trust anyone with this. Because it is very possible that someone who was at Kelly's graveside today is his murderer. This idea chills me to my very soul!

Who can I now trust? My best friends? Kelly's wife? My own husband? No, this is my secret that I will have to carry alone (for now). I'm going to Nashville to see the one person, I trust, probably the only person who can help me get to the bottom of this. Kelly was a troubled person who damaged our lives in so many ways. Still, he did not deserve to be murdered.

The drive from Meadowview Farm to Nashville is uneventful. I set my phone to meeting mode. Along the long and boring highway miles, I miss calls from Afton, Reagan and Finn. I check, no missed calls from Jackson, Mindy or Kate. After the awful scene with Kate and Mindy, I am okay with the silence between us. Jackson obviously doesn't care enough to bother checking in with me. It is not very unusual behavior, not anymore.

Normally, I would fill long drive times with work calls, or check in with family, Mindy or Kate, catching up for a few minutes. Sometimes, I listen to audiobooks, it seems this is the only time I can catch up on recreational books. Today, I'm embracing the *quiet*. After the past few days and Mindy's stunning revelation; I need some time to rewind and try to make sense of everything.

When did life unravel? Was it a slow, gradual process, with changes so subtle you don't notice them until it's too late? Was it a single incident, like the fire? That damn fire, I have believed for years that single event led to our undoing. I am the only one who thinks so though. Has Kelly's death sent us over the edge? Holding that secret for so long is bad. I felt it then, and I know it now.

We weren't always this way though, fractured and fragile. There was a time and space when the Invincible Six were truly well, invincible, or so we thought.

Tessa 1994

"*Why, why, why*" I wonder to myself as I'm sitting here at Auburn's Ralph Brown Draughon Library, or the RBD. I'm waiting on a new tutoring student to show up. I'm really starting to regret picking up these extra tutoring shifts. As a double English literature/print journalism major, I need to be catching up my homework and writing my own papers instead of tutoring bad writers. I have about a million things to do myself and helping dummies who can't spell or write coherent sentences is not very high up on my priority list.

Yet here I am, impatiently waiting for students to show up. I don't need money for being a student tutor. Thankfully, my parents and generous grandmother Esme Donovan have taken care of college expenses for me. If I make grades and stay out of trouble, I have all the money for college that I will need. This includes graduate school, law or medical school, if I choose to follow in my parent's footsteps.

I'm not even getting paid to tutor. These tedious and time-wasting hours count as participation hours for my sorority. Which was also not my idea, by the way. My mother insisted! Because she is paying a lot of my college expenses- I play along. So instead of reading and writing for my own classes or editing my latest feature article for the *Plainsman*; this overworked, stressed-out Delta Gamma girl is sitting here, furious that the dummies are late.

In the past, I would reserve a study room for these sessions. After a while I quit, when too many people stood me up. I spend so much time in the library and I feel comfortable here. I have an unofficially reserved space where I meet students. It is out of the main traffic areas and far away from the stacks area which is the notorious *make out* area. I learned that little lesson very early on.

I'm always tired at these sessions, and usually more than a little cranky. Why do people want to meet at 9 pm or later to get help with their crappy papers? I'm more of a morning person and am not friendly past 10 pm. If I'm pulling a late night, it's for myself and my grades. Not interested in losing sleep because of someone else who is a poor time manager and a super crappy writer.

I pack up my bag, thinking I've been stood up again. It would just be so much easier to make a bigger effort to go to the sorority events. I would get more sleep that way. Two people walk in my direction, both wearing Greek sweatshirts. The girl is small with long blond hair, pale blue eyes and a perfect face. I know her sort of, she's Mindy Thomas, a very popular Chi Omega girl. *"Great,"* I think to myself. The guy, who I don't recognize, belongs to Sigma Phi Epsilon. I wonder which one needs tutoring.

"Hi," the girl says.

"I'm Mindy Thomas, and this" she says gesturing to her friend "is my friend, Jackson Carmichael. You're Tessa? Tessa Turner?"

I slyly check out her friend Jackson, hoping hard he is the one that needs tutoring. Over 6' tall, with short black hair, sky blue eyes and a very attractive body, as far as I can tell. I would give up extra sleep for him.

"Yes," I point at the chairs across the table from me. "You're late, if I'm going to tutor you, you need to be on-time or let me know you will be late, okay?".

"So, which one of you needs extra help? Let me guess, English Lit Appreciation Survey class, right?" I ask, already knowing the answer. Auburn requires all students to take this class. It is considered a *make-or-break* class for people considering majoring in English or Writing. It is a *break* class for all others who hate reading and writing about (mostly) old dead white guys in a language that does not even closely resemble modern day English. If you get one of the hardcore professors, it is that much worse. Students routinely fail this class and sometimes wait until senior year to retake it- if they had a bad first experience.

Mindy and Jackson look at each other and laugh. I'm still waiting to hear his voice, wondering if it is as attractive as the rest of him?

"That would be me," he says, and his voice most definitely is attractive.

This surprises me a little, I was sure the pretty, popular Chi O would need help. This guy sitting across from me, looks smart, like he could certainly handle mildly challenging writing assignments.

"What's your major?" I blurt out.

"Mechanical Engineering" he looks amused at my question.

"Hmm" I say, "and you?" I ask, looking at Ms. Perfect.

"Communications? Video Journalism?" I answer for her.

"Actually, I'm planning to major in Interior Design, I'll have my own company one day" she is so confident, it makes me sick.

Jackson smirks. I don't know why I'm dissin Mindy. Well actually, I do. I'm tired, I don't want to do these late tutoring sessions. I don't even really want to be a DG. And she's just so pretty, perfect and of course, with the finest guy.

"You?" he asks.

"Double major, English lit/print journalism. Dean's list, feature writer for *The Plainsman*, DG girl who does not have any time for any crap, okay" I can't help myself. Probably not the best introduction ever.

"Well," Mindy starts in a sweet voice. "We both need to pass this class, no issues with us. Just please, please, please help us", she pours on the charm.

I'm unimpressed! That might work on Smart Guy, but not on me. Lord, I'm tired.

"This is a slot for one tutoring student. Okay, here's the deal. I'll tutor both of you at the same time. You will sign for double hours, so I get credit. No, you don't need to pay me, cause I'm not writing your papers. And, If I don't like you, or you don't show up and do what you are supposed to, I will drop you. Is that understood? There are much easier ways to get participation credit" I sound like a bitch, but at 10 pm, with my own work still ahead of me, I just don't care!

"Agreed," Mindy smiles wide, holding her hand across the table to me.

I sigh, shaking her hand. "And next time, you and your boyfriend there, need to be on time. No more meet times after 7 pm. I wait 10 minutes and then I walk", I say getting my bag and standing up to leave.

Jackson is now laughing. He's looking at me, puzzled. Well, I guess, I'm entertaining at least.

"Oh no, you got it all wrong," Mindy says, shaking her head.

"He's not my boyfriend, just a friend. He's my boyfriend, Theo Greer's best friend. They are both Sig Eps".

"I don't care," I say, turning around and walking away. She is still talking, and I keep walking.

Tessa (Before)

Mindy and I didn't immediately become good friends. At first, I really didn't like her very much. She was everything I was not. Pretty, popular, charming, always had the most friends and potential hot guy boyfriends hanging around. Even my stupid, younger cousin Finn is completely out of his mind over her. My mom, Claire Donovan, former semi-famous defense attorney, is *thrilled* to have a Chi O daughter, even if it's not me. Yep, Mindy has really inserted herself into my life. But she still can't write.

She and Jackson showed up for every tutoring session last fall. Jackson isn't a bad writer, but he is an engineering major. He is a great technical *to the point* writer. He does not understand writing about red wagons, glistening raindrops and white chickens that make absolutely no sense. He hated poetry with a passion. He didn't understand it, care about it and certainly did not want to waste any time writing about it. But once I convinced him that critical analysis is a technical form of writing and he could criticize the selections- he got it.

Mindy, bless her heart, is an awful writer. She has no idea that correct spelling exists. She's not simple-minded, she just doesn't have time to be bothered with writing. Why should she? She literally charms the pants off anyone she meets. Maybe that's why she tried so hard to be my friend in the beginning. I didn't think she was *all that*. I guess she saw me as a challenge to overcome.

Anyway, after the semester and tutoring sessions ended, somehow, we became a foursome. Mindy, Theo, Jackson and I were inseparable. But then we became a fivesome and that was not particularly cool, not at all. Theo and Jackson took in a stray red-headed boy, Kelly Ryan. He is an ROTC transfer student from Purdue, Indiana. I guess the guys took pity on him during pledge week. After Kelly became a Sig Ep, they have not been able to shake him since. I don't much like Kelly, I tolerate him. Mindy seems to like him even less and she tries to like everyone.

Kelly is weird, not necessarily in a strange way, but weird just the same. He makes my anti-social, introverted, self-look like Homecoming Queen candidate. He tries too hard to be funny, and is a very stereotypical drunk Irishman, most of the time. If Kelly is around, there's bound to be a drunken episode of some sort and at least one angry girl in the mix. He's way more trouble than he is worth. But Theo and Jackson have adopted him, likely because no one else would.

It's more than him just being an irritating pompous ass though, plenty of those here on campus. Sometimes, when he thinks no one is looking, he gives off a *bad* vibe. It's hard to explain really, just a little something that makes me really uncomfortable. I try hard never to be alone with him and discourage other girls too. At any event, he always gravitates toward young girls that don't know him. He has the tendency to stand too close, and place his hands wrongly, accidentally. He says inappropriate things and then completely laughs it off. He asks out unavailable girls, all the time. Available girls are just a game to him, just something to pass the time.

He's never tried anything with Mindy or me. I think knowing his best friends would punch his teeth out, prevents him from even trying. It doesn't stop him though from saying inappropriate things, just to make us uncomfortable and get a reaction. He's creepy at times, and what's worse, he knows he's doing it and he completely does not care.

I'm shocked he has a steady girlfriend back home. I wonder though how *steady* they would be if she knew he was two timing her all over campus. She probably won't find out though, cause his military friends and his Greek friends protect him-even though they know it's wrong. I guess secrets can't hurt you, if no one tells you. Well, his girlfriend won't be a secret much longer. Her name is Kate, and she is coming to the Spring Fling Sig Ep formal. Mindy and I are dying to meet her and see who puts up with someone like Kelly?

Spring Fling formal and Spring Break week at Florida beaches are a big deal for the Sig Eps. The only one from our friend group going on the Spring Break trip is Kelly. Jackson would give anything to go but can't afford it. He is a scholarship student, barely scraping by to make enough money in the summers for school expenses and helping out his mom and sister. I offered him a small loan; it wasn't a big deal. I have money that my grandmother put in a trust fund for school. My parents wouldn't mind, they really like Jackson. But he got offended and said "no".

Theo promised his family he would spend his week off, back home helping with their commercial landscape company. Spring is a very busy time for them. Mindy really wanted to go on the trip but didn't have any extra money. She is also a scholarship student. She is an orphan, and her awful aunt sold her parents' business and spent Mindy's inheritance money on herself. She gets a special scholarship for school and her other expenses are mostly covered by a college fund her hometown Clearview created when her aunt's scandal came to light. She supplements her clothes budget by freelancing some weekend decorating jobs and creating store display windows at local stores. I also offered to loan her money to go on the trip. But, without Theo going along, she was out of luck.

Instead, Mindy and I planned a long, quiet, fun week at Storybook cottage, my grandmother's lake house, in my hometown on Lake James. I love spending time there; it's been a part of my life as long as I can remember. The day I turn 25, it becomes mine. My grandmother left it for me, and I can't wait to spend many more happy summers there. Spending the week at Storybook suits me just fine. I have a ton of classwork to do, why do professors always assign papers or projects over the one break you get? It's sadistic! Mindy also needs to buckle down and put some serious work into her design portfolio. So, it all works out okay, even though it looks like Kelly will be the only one, having a great time at the beach. So surprised- Not! Kelly always seems to have a way of getting exactly what he wants.

Well, tomorrow will be all about having fun at the formal and seeing how Kelly acts when his girlfriend is around. That should be very interesting. Then it's eight beautiful days at the lake hanging out with my best friend and trying to put this long, long semester behind me.

MINDY (BEFORE)

Thank God, this semester is almost finally over. With Spring Fling formal and eight days of spring break rest to look forward to, I might actually make it to May. I'm disappointed, okay more than a little disappointed that I can't go on the Spring Fling beach trip. I don't have the money to go, Tessa offered to help with that. Theo promised his family that he would come home over break and help with their family landscape business. He's always doing stuff like that. It's why people like him so much and why I love him. He is completely selfless, always thinking of other people first. Or maybe I just love him for his sandy brown hair, dark brown eyes and megawatt smile.

It looks like Kelly is the only one gonna have any real fun. Of course, he's going on the trip. He is never one to miss or start a party. The rest of us have real work to do over the break and he will be *living it up* without a care in the world. Stupid military history major with the famous father, he pays younger students to write his papers for him. He tries just hard enough to keep a "C" average and not get kicked out of ROTC. But he doesn't really care, he knows that Daddy will get him some great job when he graduates. So, why bother?

Tessa does not like Kelly. But I like him even less. I remember the day I met him, straggling along behind Theo and Jackson like a little lost puppy. Except he wasn't cute like a little puppy- more like a mangy mutt that lived in the garbage dump. Kelly gave me a really tingly feeling all over and not in a good way. He screams *creepy* with girls and somehow Theo and Jackson just can't see it. Theo, I get- he thinks the best of everyone, and has never had an enemy. But Jackson? He's smarter than that. Raised by a single mom that cycled through loads of bad men, he should immediately recognize Kelly. But maybe because Kelly dresses up good, has money and a famous daddy, he is camouflaged. I've seen Kelly's type before, and if you're smart, you stay way away from them.

I am **very** curious about Kelly's girlfriend Kate. When Kelly starts getting on my nerves or being too creepy, I ask "when are we meeting Kate?" He usually makes excuses and walks away. But he is finally bringing Kate. He better not make me mad tonight or I may just give this Kate an ear full and tell her who her steady boyfriend really is. I feel sorry for her, because Kelly has tried to sleep his way through half the girlfriends of his Sig Ep brothers. They tolerate him, because his dad is famous and makes large contributions to their chapter. So, they let Kelly live to be creepy, another day.

There are so many social functions to go to that after a while, they all kinda blend together. Picking out the perfect dress and accessories is not as much fun as it used to be. Honestly, sometimes it gets to be a bore- especially if you don't have an unlimited clothing budget and are always scrambling to find something to wear that hasn't made a previous appearance. Tessa and I are not the same size. So, we can't trade clothes. I'm short, petite and pretty thin. She is taller and larger than me. She's not fat at all, just more solid and athletic looking. She's a size 8 but seems like a giant around me and some of her sorority sisters who are mostly smaller and petite. I think it bothers her that she looks different than the others, but she is beautiful, just the way she is.

Tonite, even though I'm not overly crazy about the black sequined dress I'm wearing with the statement huge puffy white sleeves; I am excited about Kelly bringing his girlfriend. He will be so uncomfortable. It will be nice for a change to see him squirm. He will spend most of the night avoiding girls he's hit on and their jealous boyfriends. I'm literally shocked he's bringing her. She must've ultimatum-ed him good. "Ha Ha," I cannot wait. It will be the most fun I've had in awhile.

The formal is taking place on campus in one of the new event spaces. They used to be off campus, at some fancy hotel with a ballroom. But the university administration realized all the wasted profits going off campus. Also, last year there were a few incidents, drunkenness, destruction of property, and other things that Student Affairs realized needed to be contained internally, on campus. I would bet my last dollar that Kelly Ryan was somehow involved.

Kelly flew Kate in from Indiana, and she is staying at the campus hotel. Convenient, I wonder who he is trying to impress? Her, or us? We are meeting them at the formal and I know Tessa is just as interested as me in seeing the midwestern girlfriend. I already know I won't like her. Anybody who really likes Kelly, can't be anyone that I would have anything in common with. She's probably just as classless as him.

We walk into the formal event space, Tessa, Jackson, Theo and me. Tessa looks beautiful in a strapless, emerald, green, sequined floor length dress that I talked her into wearing. It's a little out of her comfort zone, but it is perfect for her. The green contrasts so well with her dark brown hair and light brown eyes.

I wish I could say the room is beautiful too, but it is not. Well, I guess maybe it is. But after you've seen more or less the same balloons, netting, twinkle lights, and candles in glass pillars; at every event, you get a little jaded. There's usually not much budget for decorating, and sororities end up trading accessories around. You might see the exact same decorations at three functions. It's even worse at the fraternity functions, because they just don't care. Girlfriends come in and decorate and you see the same old tired stuff over and over again. I offered to help decorate this year. I had a few *off the hook* ideas that were different and pretty exciting. But the girlfriends of the decorating committee vetoed every idea and so here we are. Boring again! We will be eating undercooked chicken and overcooked steak, smiling, dancing and acting like we are having the time of our lives, again!

But this time, I'm all about the entertainment. And it's not the overpriced, snooze fest DJ that plays all the formal functions. I'm waiting for the main attraction, and they are late! Thirty minutes late. They only had to walk over from the hotel. It's a short walk. Kelly said the flight got in earlier today. I hope he didn't get cold feet and decide to ditch tonight.

I get Tessa's attention and point to my watch. She is uncomfortable. She doesn't like crowds or noisy places and tonight is both. I motion that we leave the room so we can find a quieter place to talk. Theo and Jackson are stupid-talking and doing secret handshakes with a couple of their brothers, they don't even notice we are gone.

After we get out of the noisy ballroom space, I pull Tessa into a quieter corner in the hall.

"You, okay?"

"Yes, I will be. Just need a few minutes. Thanks" she says, relaxing a little.

"They are late! The only reason I didn't consider faking a migraine and blowing this off, is the entertainment and they are late" I'm irritated about this.

"They'll be here. It's Kelly – always has to make an entrance" Tessa says, so sure of herself.

"How do you know, you having a vision or something?" I tease her.

"No," she laughs, "you know it doesn't work that way".

"So, what are you feeling right now", I ask her, curious about what she is picking up. She is an empath and being in crowded places with lots of people is sometimes overwhelming.

"Energy, lots and lots of positive energy. Happiness, fun, joy, craziness. It's all good. There's just lots - trying hard to block some of it", Tessa answers and smiles.

"Haven't sensed creepy Kel yet?"

"That's funny Mindy. Maybe our new code name, huh? We can call him CK for short", Tessa laughs.

"No, but he is coming".

"How can you be sure?" I ask her.

"Ego," she says quietly. "Kelly is full of ego. If he doesn't show up, he will never live this down with the other guys. They will say she's ugly".

"Is she?" I ask truly wondering that myself.

"No, I saw a glimpse of a picture, Kelly showed Jackson one day. She's pretty, maybe stupid, but she's pretty".

"We better get back in there. Don't want to miss any of the Kelly show. I've been waiting for this all semester. It's the only thing that got me through that awful math class" I say, grabbing Tessa's hand and dragging her back down the hall toward the loud ballroom.

When we finally see Theo and Jackson in a crowd of people, there is someone standing with them I don't recognize. It's a girl, a tall girl wearing a sky blue beaded formal with a shoulder wrap. She has short blonde hair and a thin model-like body. Whoever she is, I hate her already. Kidding, maybe. Then, as we get closer, we see Kelly off to the side, talking wildly with his hands to a Sig Ep guy I don't know. Kelly already looks a little drunk.

Theo smiles when he sees us. I love that his eyes always light up when he sees me. I hope they always will. We slide in a space beside Jackson, who is making small talk with this girl. Kelly is oblivious to everyone except himself and whatever stupid story he is telling. Theo introduces us.

"This is my girlfriend, Mindy" he says, putting his arm around my waist.

"And standing next to you, is Tessa- Jackson's girlfriend" Theo says.

"You must be Kate, Kelly's friend" Tessa says.

"Girlfriend," Kate says immediately.

"Yes, I'm so sorry, its loud in here. His girlfriend. It's so nice to finally meet you" Tessa says, correcting herself.

"We've heard so many nice things about you," I say pouring on the charm even though not a single word of it is true. Until this minute, we had no idea what Kelly's Indiana girlfriend even looked like. Why has he been hiding her? She is drop dead gorgeous. Bet she's been told a time or two that she looks like a midwestern version of Princess Di. She has just a little Midwest accent that is cute, instead of irritating.

She looks uncomfortable. Kelly is still talking away, no clue that he has left his girlfriend to fend for herself. "I haven't heard much about you guys. Kelly doesn't talk very much about school" she says almost apologizing.

"Please" do not apologize for him, I think to myself. I absolutely bet he doesn't talk about school much. Then he would lie about all the girls he does know or tries to get to know on a personal basis. What cornfield did she fall out of? If only she had any idea. He is generally not well liked. But somehow, between his dad's connections and his adoptive parents, Theo and Jackson, he has managed to hang on by his fingernails.

I consider kicking Kelly in the shins with my spike heels for completely ignoring this poor girl who came a long way to spend time with him. He continues to tell more lies, to his small captive, pathetic audience. I shoot Theo and Jackson mean looks, that I hope they interpret to mean "rein in your lovechild over there and get him over here" or something like that.

"So, you met Kelly at Purdue?" Tessa asks, trying her best at small talk which by God, is not one of her strengths.

"Yes," Kate says "at freshmen orientation week. We were in the same small group. I didn't know about him at first, but he is so funny. He just kept me laughing".

Tessa doesn't quite know what to say. I could rescue her but I'm hanging back to see how she interacts with real live people, instead of book characters. She needs practice.

"Um, yes, he can be very funny. Always the life of the party" she says, so carefully.

Well, she's trying. I guess she does need a little help before she steps in it and ends our fun with Kelly before it begins.

"So, what's your major?" I ask a basic safe question.

"Business management and finance" she says.

"Wow, you have something in common with Tessa. You serious, double major types. When do you have time for fun?" I ask her because I really do wonder that with these people.

"Do you have time for a sorority?" She sure looks like she would be in a top-tier one, but I really don't know much about Midwest schools.

She laughs. "Oh no, between my majors and part-time work at a bank, I'm busy. I also have to help my parents with their farm accounts. I am a member of Beta Alpha Psi, it's a business centered organization. We do fun activities" she adds.

"How about you? And Tessa?"

"Yeah, I'm Chi O, so was Tessa's mom. Tessa is Delta Gamma" I tell her wondering how much she knows about sororities or which ones they have where she goes to school. Greek life is so big in southern schools, I don't want to just assume that everyone else thinks so.

"Not Chi Omega too?" she asks Tessa, looking puzzled.

"No", Tessa smiles, "it's a long story for another time".

By now, Theo, Jackson, Kelly and a few other guys are standing around talking sports. Really? You're going to get dressed up, bring a hot date and then stand around in a circle doing the same stupid things you do every day of the week? Men? Who can understand them?

I look at the guy circle and roll my eyes. "C'mon," I say, grabbing Kate and Tessa's hands. "Let's go get some air, it is so boring in here".

We walk out on the back patio and sit down. I cannot believe the three brainless guys we came with would ditch us to talk sports. I mean look at us, we are totally *hot,* and they are totally stupid. Who needs them?

I reach in my black sequin bag and pull out a small flask, for emergencies only. This seems like a good emergency. I offer it up to Tessa and Kate. Tessa takes a sip and makes a face. It's vodka, good quality vodka. A sip for Tessa and that is it or by sip three, she will be dancing on the tables.

I hand the flask to Kate; she puts up her hands and waves it away. I take it back. "Okay," I tell her, "suit yourself. But Kelly is going hard, very early. From the looks of things, you might be wishing you had a little liquid courage".

Her eyes water and she pushes away the flask. " No thank you, someone else is drinking enough for all of us." I instantly feel sorry for this girl that Kelly truly does not deserve.

"Okay, let's go find our guys and get this thing started," I link arms with the two other best-looking girls in the place, and head out to reclaim our guys.

The night drags on. After the rubbery chicken and burnt steak meal, the formal portion goes fast, thank God. Then it's DJ time. All night Kelly has been mostly ignoring Kate and getting drunker by the hour. I don't know where he is getting the booze, but he is "in it- to win it". If this keeps up, he will either get in a fight with one of his brothers, get kicked out, or both. Kate looks extremely embarrassed and about to cry.

Tessa has had enough for one night. Never the life of the party, hell if you can even get her to the party. She must believe she really will turn into a pumpkin if she is not home, snuggled in bed, and lights out by midnight- latest. The noise, Kelly's behavior, shifting energy, the later it gets- and she is ready to leave.

Kate is sitting by herself, no Kelly anywhere. Tessa comes off the dance floor and sends Jackson over to talk to Kate. She doesn't want to dance. She looks miserable. I don't blame her; I would be super mad right now. Jackson comes and gets Theo in the middle of our dance. They head out into the hallway, looking for Kelly. Why does this seem so familiar? Every single time! Kelly gets drunk, he disappears, doing God knows what with God knows who, and Theo and Jackson always rescue him. If they can find him. Sometimes, he doesn't show up until the next day. For Kate's sake, I hope he is just somewhere passing around a bottle or even passed out.

I leave Kate with Tessa and make excuses about going to the bathroom. I look around in all the dark, hidden corners of the hallway. No Kelly! Then I hear Theo and Jackson, before I see them talking quietly to a loud and very drunk Kelly. He is in a back dimly lit doorway that looks like a janitor's closet or maintenance area. He's not alone. He has a girl backed up against the door. He is leaning heavily against her. She is a very drunk girl and not Kate. Her strapless dress is barely covering her boobs and Kelly has her dress hiked up way high on her thighs. He keeps grabbing her and saying, "Come on Kate, don't be a tease."

I am shocked still in place. Jackson and Theo are trying to get Kelly to quiet down and get off the girl. I'm not sure he recognizes them. They are being careful; Kelly has a bad habit of coming up swinging when he is this drunk. I've seen it before. Jackson looks up and sees me with my mouth hanging open, not really believing what I'm seeing here.

"Give me Theo's keys" he says holding up the drunk girl while Theo is talking quietly to Kelly.

"We will see who she came with and get Kelly home. Take Kate back to the hotel. Tell Tessa I'll see her a little later, sometime before I leave campus" he tells me, already formulating a crisis plan in his mind. He is a natural at this and unfortunately with Kelly, we get plenty of practice.

I run back down the hallway. Not because I'm in a hurry but because I want to get away from what I just saw, as quickly as possible. What do we tell Kate? I come up with a lie, or a half-truth, or what I think will get her back to the hotel and not worry about Kelly. What a damn mess!

"They found Kelly; he was outside getting some air. He felt hot and sick. Too much party. Someone gave him some moonshine and it was STRONG," I tell Kate hoping she buys my story. It is partially true; Kelly is drunk out of his mind. It's the rest, I'll leave out.

Kate looks up at me, so concerned. He really does not deserve her.

"Is he okay? Can I do anything to help?" she asks.

"Theo says Kelly is really, really embarrassed. They are going to take him back to the ROTC house, where he can sleep it off. We will take you back to the hotel and then Kelly will be ready to take you to Birmingham to catch your flight tomorrow. What time does it leave?"

I hate lying to her. Kelly is not embarrassed; he's so drunk he doesn't even know where he is or who he is with. Classic Kelly behavior!

"Noon" she says, starting to feel very uncomfortable at this embarrassing situation and having to depend on people she just met.

"Let's get you back to the hotel. Or, if you really don't want to stay by yourself- you are welcome to come home with us. We live just a few minutes from here. You can borrow some clothes and a toothbrush. We can take you back to the hotel first thing in the morning" Tessa tells her.

"No, that's okay, I'm fine to go back to the hotel if you don't mind taking me," Kate says looking exhausted.

"Not a problem, let's go. Are you hungry or want some snacks for later?" I ask her knowing good and well, she's not going to see Kelly for a while. That's if somebody can get him up in the morning. Theo paged me, they got Kelly back to the ROTC house and to bed. Theo was staying with him, just in case. Kelly had gotten so drunk a time or two before, that he left the house in the middle of the night and was walking around thinking he was bar hopping.

"I'm tired, I think I just want to go to bed. I have a long day tomorrow" Kate says staring out the passenger side window. She is quiet, I give her credit for that. I would probably be cussing Theo up and down, about now. But let's be serious- it wouldn't be Theo, or even Jackson. It's always Kelly.

Tessa drives us to the hotel. It is the longest, quietest three blocks of my life. The parking lot is crowded, but we find a space and park. We walk Kate inside and ride the elevator up with her to her third-floor room, even though she insists we don't have to. It's awkward, but we both give her a big hug. We had already exchanged phone numbers and addresses. We wait for her to open her door before we leave.

"Wait," Tessa says, as Kate is going inside. She turns around and looks at us.

"Listen, I get up early most days. Not because I love it, but I always have so much to do. And I'm not a night person."

I laugh, this is the understatement of the year. The only reason Tessa isn't already home in bed is because we had Kelly drama.

"Anyway," she says, rolling her eyes and shaking her head. "Why don't you plan on me driving you to the airport tomorrow? We are going home for break anyway and you won't have to worry about being late", Tessa tells her.

"Thanks, but you've done enough already. I can't ask you to do that. It's far and Kelly will take me" she says, trying to convince herself and us.

"It's no trouble, I promise. You have a pager, right? Just in case, Kelly oversleeps or is running late. You don't want to miss your flight and sit in the airport forever" Tessa seems to convince her.

"Just shoot me a message in the morning and I'll be right over to drive you".

"Okay." Kate gives us both a tired smile and goes in her room. We hear her turn the lock on the door.

On the way back to our apartment, I debate with myself whether I should tell Tessa what happened? She can be judgmental sometimes and has a definite sense of right and wrong. I decide to tell her, I don't want to keep that kind of secret from her. If Theo and Jackson don't want to talk about it, that's on them.

"Tessa, I need to tell you something and I don't want you to freak out, okay? Promise?" Since she is still driving and she drives like a little old lady, she likely won't go into freak out mode.

"What? Will this night never end" she asks me with a big sigh.

Sure, doesn't feel like it. Well here goes. We are parked now in our space by the apartment.

"You know when I went out to see what was taking the guys so long?"

"Yes," she says, wondering what is coming next. It's Kelly, you never know what you are going hear about him.

"I saw him in a back hallway, drunk, and feeling up a girl that he kept calling Kate", I just go ahead and say it. The shock on Tessa's face says it all.

"Excuse me, what? Don't play like that Mindy. It's been a long night."

Tessa sighs and puts her hands on the sides of her head like she has a pounding headache.

"I swear, I swear. I know it sounds unbelievable. But I saw it. Jackson and Theo did too" I say quickly, trying to catch my breath.

"Ew, Oh my..." Tessa starts, her eyes are very wide now.

"No, no, they weren't watching or anything. They found Kelly only a few seconds before I did. They were trying to pull him off, and not startle him. You know how crazy he gets sometimes" I remind her. We both knew some of the really crazy crap Kelly had pulled.

"But, in the hallway of a public building, with his girlfriend in another room and people possibly walking by?" Tessa is having a hard time wrapping her mind around this.

Me too, it was a new all-time low in Kelly behavior. "Gross, I know. Stupid jerk. He never knows when enough is enough. I guess the only positive thing maybe, is the girl was drunk too, she probably won't remember a thing," I tell her. Not that this thought is very reassuring.

"Kate, what do we tell her?" Tessa asks.

I knew she was going there. Jesus, I saw this coming a mile away. Tessa and her moral dilemmas and right and wrong. Sometimes, she could be so damn tiring.

"Shouldn't Kate know her boyfriend is bad news?"

"Don't you think she knows that?" I snap at Tessa. "After all, she was there tonight, and saw classic Kelly behavior. You think that just started when he transferred here?"

"I'm pretty sure I heard Jackson and Theo talking about Kelly getting into a lot of trouble at Purdue and having to transfer to avoid being kicked out of ROTC and school." I repeat this rumor. I don't know if it's true or not but based on Kelly's behavior since he showed up at Auburn, I don't really doubt it.

"Mindy, this is not about Kelly. It's about Kate" Tessa says, her voice getting louder.

"Really? You just met the girl. You know nothing about her. Why are you wanting to get involved in this? It's their problem, and they need to work it out."

"It doesn't matter how well I know her. She deserves to know. She seems like a good person, and she should know and then make up her own mind" Tessa is getting angry with me.

"No, Tessa. Stay out of it. You have no idea which way this might go. It's not one of your books where everything works out perfectly in the end. You cannot control any fallout from this. Meddling might come back to bite all of us. Just no." I tell her knowing that my hard headed friend will not be so easily convinced.

"Tessa, I mean it. Swear on your grandmother Esme's grave that you won't tell Kate", I know this is low, but it's the only way I am sure I can stop Tessa. Once she gets something in her mind, she's hard to redirect.

"No, that's ridiculous," she says.

"I mean it. Swear it" I yell at her.

"Okay, this is wrong. But okay, whatever" she gives in.

Tessa (Before)

Ugh, that alarm clock. It's a much earlier wakeup call than I would like to have on a Sunday morning after a very late Saturday night. But I promised Kate I would take her to the airport, if she needed a ride. Knowing Kelly, I fully expect him to bail on her, especially if he wants to make his ride to Spring Break week in Florida.

By the time I've showered and dressed, I have a pager message from Kate. No Kelly, imagine that. I let her know I'm on the way. A quick check on Mindy, she's still out cold. Mindy is **not** a morning person, but I thought she might want to ride along and keep me company on the drive. I message her to let her know my approximate return time. We are heading home to Lake James later today.

Kate is waiting in the lobby when I pull up to the entrance. She still looks tired. We load her things into the car and head for Birmingham. My mom's hand me down Volvo station wagon has sure been good to me during my years at Auburn.

I flip through the radio stations looking for something to fill up the space in the car. Madonna, Mariah Carey, Bon Jovi, Boyz II Men, and my current favorite *Kiss from a Rose* by Seal. That one is on every radio station, right now. So, not complaining!

Looking for some safe subject to talk about, I ask Kate about Spring Break plans.

"Are you on break this week too?"

"Yes," she says and that is it.

"So, you didn't want to go with Kelly to Florida? He's the only one of us that's going" I tell her.

She plays with the straw in her coke. I'm not sure she heard me.

"Um, no," she looks very intently at the cup in her lap. "He didn't ask me. He said no one else was going and I wouldn't have fun".

"Well, none of us were able to go," I say quickly, trying to make her feel better.

"Pretty sure Kelly signed up at the last minute, he's pretty spontaneous, sometimes" I tell her, trying to keep things light. What I didn't tell her was that it irritates me to no end, that the rest of us are up to our eyeballs in school and family responsibilities. Then there's Kelly, Mr. Irresponsible who ditches his out of state girlfriend and runs off for a week of partying at the beach. It is so unfair!

"Well, I couldn't go anyway. I have a ton of school projects coming due and I promised to help my parents finish up their farm taxes. Always too much to do- never any time for fun".

"Same, my new best friend" I say laughing and turning up *Kissed by a Rose.*

We drive on, eating our drive thru breakfast and sitting in awkward quiet. After about thirty minutes of driving and NOT bringing up topics that I swore I wouldn't; I can't contain myself any longer.

"Kate," I say, getting her attention. She has been looking out the window, deep in thought.

"Do you want to talk about last night? It's totally cool if you don't. After all, you don't know me" I carry on, sounding more and more like an idiot.

"Uh, that's nice Tessa. I appreciate that", she says nothing more.

Not sure if that's a "yes" or "no" I carry on.

"Sometimes, just talking about things makes me feel better or gives me some clarity. You're in the "no judgment" zone here" I say encouraging her to talk. Because "wow" Kelly's behavior was over the top and she doesn't even know the half of it.

She takes a minute, and it looks like she is trying to figure out exactly what she wants to say or maybe even how to say it?

"Kelly" she starts, "sometimes he drinks a lot, last night was not the first time I've seen him like that. He got in trouble at Purdue for drinking. I think his dad got him off and made him transfer schools to get away from bad influences" she shares.

This was not a huge revelation. We already knew this. Even though rumors that made the rounds sounded like it was more than just too much "party drinking".

"We almost broke up over Kelly's crazy drinking. I'm not opposed to drinking and having a good time but sometimes he goes so extreme- it's hard to deal with, you know?"

"Yes," I tell her carefully, "I've seen that a time or two myself". Please, please be careful here, I remind myself- thinking hard at Mindy's warning.

"It must be hard, having a long-distance relationship especially on top of you both having busy schedules. I don't see how you do it."

"Yes, it's hard but Kelly is so busy with school and all, we just do our thing and get together when we can, during breaks" Kate says.

It takes every ounce of self-control I can find and then some, not to tell this poor girl "what's what". The only things that keep Kelly busy are trying to get out of as much work as he can, and into as much trouble as possible.

"Kate, I'm sorry about what happened last night. Kelly should not have gotten so wasted. I know it was a special night for you," I tell her stopping just short of calling him an ass.

"Yes, not one of my best memories" she sighs.

I'm going for broke here, I did promise on my dead grandmother's grave not to tell Kate what really happened. But I did not promise to let this sweet girl walk away from this weekend thinking Kelly's behavior was her fault or that she had to accept it. Yes, I'm getting involved where maybe I shouldn't, but she should know.

"We've just met, and it is none of my business. And you can just tell me to be quiet and I promise, it's fine. But Kelly has a very serious drinking issue, that's not new. I'm sure you know that."

She waits to see if I'm going to say anything else. And I do.

"You are very pretty, smart, and seem to be a very kind, good person. You don't have to put up with Kelly's bad behavior. You deserve so much more than that," I tell her, hoping she won't get mad.

She looks at me with tears in her eyes. "He does this, he acts out so bad. Then he is sorry, acts better for a while. Then we start all over again" she says, in a hurt-filled tone.

"Is he worth it?" I ask her wondering if she has any idea that drinking too much is only part of Kelly's problems. There is something wrong with him, deep inside.

"Do you want to stay with somebody that doesn't respect himself or you? Is this the way you want the rest of your life to be?" I ask her. These are intrusive questions, and probably not right of me to ask them. Kelly is not the "one" for her. I'm not sure he is right for anybody, with his self-destructive tendencies.

Kate looks at her hands and then out the car window before she answers.

"Would you?" she looks at me.

"Would I stay with Kelly? Or do you mean generally?"

"If it was Jackson, would you stay or leave him?" she asks me. She is smart, she knows it's easy to give advice to other people when you can't imagine yourself in their situation.

I pause and then answer her. "Yes, I think I would leave. If Jackson had serious problems that he didn't try to fix. Yes, no matter how much you love someone else, you can't let them destroy you in the process," I say, knowing though that this would never be about Jackson.

"Look, I can't tell you how to feel or act. That's for you to decide. I've only known you a day and know that you deserve so much better than what Kelly Ryan is offering you. I would want that for anyone. Girls have to stick together, support each other. We have to be strong enough to show the world how we want to be treated," I say, not meaning to preach at her but doing it anyway.

She looks up and gives me a little smile. She doesn't seem mad but I'm not really sure what, if anything I said got through to her. It's not always easy to see what's wrong in our own lives, especially if we refuse to look too hard.

By this time, we are at the airport. I pull into the passenger drop off lane and help Kate unload her bags. I give her a quick goodbye hug and a wave as she heads into the terminal. I hope that our little talk gives her a chance to really think about her relationship with Kelly. I really hoped that she was able to read 'between the lines" and pick up on all the things I didn't say because of the stupid promise I made to Mindy. Well, I've either just made a new friend, or possible enemy and set into motion a bunch of stuff Mindy warned me against. Not sure which?

When I get back to school, Mindy is packed and ready to go for our week at the lake cottage. I'm surprised to see Jackson waiting for me. I thought we might catch up on the phone either today or tomorrow.

Mindy grabs my car keys and heads out to the store to get some road trip snacks. Jackson tells me they got Kelly off on his trip and Theo headed home ahead of the traffic. Jackson is leaving tomorrow, to spend a few days with his mom and sister. It bothers me that he wouldn't rather be spending the week or part of the week with me, but whatever. He gets very stubborn about his mom sometimes and I have to just let it go.

While Mindy is gone, we have one of the biggest fights ever since we've been together. Usually, the little fights revolve around Kelly's stupid behavior, or Jackson's mom, or how I am from a wealthy family (I am not) and don't understand everybody else. Well, today for some reason, we had to hit on all three at once. I don't know if it is lack of sleep, or Kelly's stupid bullcrap he pulled last night or school stress or what. But right now, I hate Jackson Carmichael and don't want to see his face for a long time. Maybe ever!

He leaves, Mindy comes back, and we leave campus. I am quiet, unusually so. Mindy knows something is up, but she's nice enough not to ask about it. Jackson can be so unreasonable, when he wants to be. My mind is spinning with what happened last night and my conversation with Kate.

Kelly Ryan is one of the worst things that has happened to us. I hope one day he just goes away. I really hope that Kate will kick him to the curb, sooner rather than later. He has made all of us miserable in some way. Maybe after graduation next year, he will get sent to some remote place and forget all about us. I sure hope Kate forgets all about him.

Tessa (2000)

We're not in Kansas anymore! Instead, we are in very hot Indiana, in the middle of July, surrounded by cornfields. The Invincible Six are getting ready for Kate and Kelly's wedding weekend at Meadowview Farm. Never in my wildest dreams did I ever think this day would come. I was sure after Kelly's awful behavior at our junior year Spring Formal, Kate would break up with him. Somehow, they weathered through that and more episodes of Kelly's stupid behavior and stayed together.

In spite of me wishing Kelly would move on with his life and leave us behind; here we are. The Invincible Six are getting ready to knock out the last of our weddings. Mindy and Theo married straight out of school, the month after graduation. They had a beautiful ceremony at Storybook Cottage with Mindy, us, Theo and his small nation of extended family. Jackson and I married the next year, while he was in a graduate engineering program. I also wanted to get married at Storybook but my mother, ever the defense attorney, argued (and won) the case for getting married in the large Methodist church in Lake James. My family co-founded the Lake James community and kept it going during WWII, so Claire Donovan Tanner thought it best to get married in town. You rarely argue with her and win.

If I'm being perfectly honest here, I never thought Kate and Kelly would make it this far. I hoped Kate would find some nice guy at Purdue or maybe even one of our friends in Alabama, fall in love and marry someone perfect for her. No, she stuck with Kelly. She became one of our closest long-distance friends. She is the perfect balance for my introverted *moodiness* and Mindy's *too muchness*. In the last two years of college, we spent as much time with her as possible. We wanted to keep Kate and ditch Kelly.

Kelly got into a lot of trouble on the infamous junior year Spring Break trip. It was bad enough that he was almost kicked out of his Sig Ep chapter and ROTC was threatening disciplinary action. I guess it finally shook him up enough to straighten up his act and get back on track. He didn't turn into an angel or stay completely out of trouble, but he did settle down quite a bit. It was a welcome change.

He was behind in school due to issues with transferring credits between colleges. He was the last of the Invincible Six to graduate. After graduation, he headed out to Army Reserve Officer Training. Kate stayed in Indiana, now working fulltime at her college bank job and helping her parents with their farm business accounts.

Mindy and Theo moved back to Theo's hometown. He manages the business side of his parents' landscape business which has grown quite large. Mindy, true to her word, opened an interior design business. She has an influential client list, including my mother and some of her friends.

Jackson and I are still in Auburn, while he is finishing up his graduate engineering program. I work as a feature writer at the *Opelika-Auburn News*. It's not a glamorous job, or high paying, but it is interesting. With Jackson in school full-time, I need to help with the bills as much as possible.

I would never tell Kate, but the rest of us had taken bets on if Kelly would ever propose marriage to her. He seemed content just to let things go on as they were, and Kate seemed mostly content to let him do so. Kelly always had an excuse, or a military school assignment or training to go to anytime the talk of commitment came up. It got particularly uncomfortable after they were the only unmarried couple.

But then one day, Kate conference called Mindy and me and screamed that she was engaged. Of course, Mindy asks "Who to?". Kate was in such a great mood, she let that slide. We were surprised at the very short engagement- three months. And here we are, marrying off the last two of us.

Kelly's dad offered up his farm for the wedding. Meadowview is a beautiful place. Acres and acres of cornfields surround a small white country chapel with an even smaller graveyard. At one point, this was the center of a small community of settlers that landed here in the early 1800's. At the edge of the property is a two story, white clapboard farmhouse that dates to the late 1800's. The house is in fairly good shape and has been updated. Ed Ryan plans to do a major renovation at some point. He intended Meadowview to be a retirement place for him and his beloved Ella. Life had other plans.

I think Kate's parents are both happy and relieved to have the wedding here. It is beautiful, practical and very affordable. Kelly's dad is a very well-known military officer who knows practically everyone worth knowing. He wouldn't let his only son get married without making a big *to do* about it. So, Bob and Cindy Maynard were more than happy to let Big Ed provide a venue and most of the wedding funds.

The wedding guest list got quite extensive at one point, completely freaking out Kate. Eventually, the list scaled back to a more manageable 200 – 250 or so guests. Not at all, what Kate envisioned. The small chapel would not accommodate so many guests, it would hold about fifty on a good day. So, Big Ed did the next best thing. He built an outdoor venue, adjacent to the small chapel. Big party tents were to be set up, portable bathroom trailers at a discreet distance away, generators, the works. It was going to be the biggest, private wedding this small town had ever seen. This did not help the bride and groom's pre-wedding jitters.

For the wedding, Kate chose a simple linen and lace, drop waist wedding dress. It has a Roaring Twenties, meets Little House on the Prairie feel and suits the setting perfectly. Well, until Big Ed and Ms. Cindy (our bride's mom) got carried away, buying up what looked to be half of the flowers in Indianapolis. Kate chose a simple wildflower garland for her hair. She will be a beautiful bride, straight out of a fairytale. I love her with all my heart because she picked simple spaghetti strap sage green bridesmaids dresses. Mine had to be tailored a little because we are expecting our sweet little Afton in October.

In his excitement, Big Ed has turned Kate's simple little wedding into a four-day extravaganza. Between the three of us, Kate is the one that wanted the least spectacle over getting married. And here is Big Ed, putting on the Ritz. I guess that's what happens when you marry the son of a famous person.

The rehearsal supper is supposed to be a small intimate affair with the wedding party members and immediate family. But it doesn't end up that way- not at all. After the wedding rehearsal, the catering company is ready to serve 100 of the couple's *closest* friends and families. My parents are here as Kate's guests. During college, she quickly became their third daughter. They are so pleased to be invited even if my mother can't stand Kelly. She loves Kate and is pretty taken with Big Ed, even if she won't admit it.

I have to admit, the spread is pretty impressive, especially in the middle of cornfields. With Ms. Cindy's vision and Big Ed's almost limitless budget, this supper will be talked about for years, in many social circles. Kate, Mindy and I compliment Ms. Cindy many times, giggling as we walk away. Two years ago, when Kate's older brother David married his Emily; the two wedding mamas got into a massive argument over the rehearsal supper menu. They haven't spoken since, which is awkward, because they attend the same church. I guess maybe, tonight is Ms. Cindy's revenge.

I am tired, it's been a long day. Being pregnant and out in the July heat is draining. We say our goodbyes, leaving the party early and head back to the newly renovated gatehouse next door to the farmhouse. Kelly and his groomsmen are staying at a small cabin tucked away further back on the property. Maybe Big Ed didn't trust Kelly enough to show up on time or sober for his own wedding.

We decided not to do anything outrageous for Kate's bachelorette party. She didn't want it and with me being pregnant, I'm not a lot of fun anyway. We will take a girls' trip later. But we do stay up awhile, eating snacks, drinking champagne (sparkling juice for me) and playing stupid Truth or Dare. This was all Mindy's idea.

"Okay, Tessa your turn have you ever lied to Jackson about something big?" Mindy asks me.

I grab the champagne bottle and pretend to take a drink. "Yes, Truth I say," knowing that my secret is safe with these two.

"What?" Mindy yells. "What have you been holding out on us? I am shocked, Contessa Donovan Tanner Carmichael" Mindy says my full name. She knows I hate that!

I roll my eyes at her and slap her lightly on the shoulder.

"This," I emphasize, "stays just between us." I point at all of us. "Swear?" They put up their right hands and swear. "I mean it! I will drop your asses so fast, if you breathe a word", they are surprised by me swearing and know it must be something good. They lean in expectedly.

"I didn't want to marry Jackson, when he proposed to me," I say watching their faces, to gauge their reactions.

"What? What in the Holy Hell are you talking about?" Mindy erupts.

"You didn't want to marry Jackson at all? Or you didn't want to marry him then?" Kate asks.

I gulp a little. "Y'all know that year I applied for the overseas internship for the *Stars and Stripes* with their London bureau. I got the internship. I had just found out and didn't have a chance to tell anyone yet. Jackson took me out to a fancy dinner. I was going to tell him that night" I say.

"Then, out of the blue, he proposed. You know the whole bit, flowers, fancy dessert with sparklers. He got down on one knee in front of everybody, the entire restaurant and asked me to marry him". I stop, replaying it all in my head.

"What happened next?" Mindy asks.

"I panicked. Here I was hoping to share news of the opportunity of a lifetime for me. Then he just up and springs this on me- out of nowhere. In front of Everybody. I couldn't think, I couldn't say no, I couldn't say anything. It was awful."

"I bet, poor Tessa," Kate says in an understanding tone.

"It wasn't that I didn't want to marry Jackson. That wasn't it at all. I had dreams, and goals, things I wanted to do just for me. Things I wanted to accomplish before I became somebody's wife and maybe one day somebody's mommy," I say patting my round stomach.

"That's hard," Mindy says taking my hand. "We all know how much you wanted that internship and how hard you worked for it".

"I was caught so off guard that I said "yes". Then immediately Jackson started making plans. We would stay in Auburn; he would go to grad school. I could get a job".

"Everything already planned out like I didn't have any say in anything. It never crossed his mind, that maybe I had my own plans. It made me angry that he just automatically assumed I wouldn't get the internship and that I would just do whatever he said. And he was right, I did" I start wiping away the baby tears that had gathered in the corners of my eyes.

"I was afraid of losing him, if I said, "not right now". So, I emailed the internship committee, turning down the internship. I asked Big Ed, if he could possibly make a personal recommendation for my good friend Trent James and I let that dream go".

Mindy and Kate are quiet, maybe because they are shocked or just don't really know what to say.

"Wait, you launched Trevor James' writing career?" Mindy, always the direct one, asked me.

I laugh. "Well, it appears that way. I helped a little".

It is quiet in the room. We are all trying to absorb what I have just shared. The silence stretches, and I grow uncomfortable.

"Well," I say, topping off Mindy and Kate's champagne glasses. "Who can top that?"

Mindy raises her hand, "I can," she says.

"Same rules, right? What's said here, stays here? Promise?" she asks.

"I don't know if I want to have any children" Mindy tells us with a pained expression.

"Theo and I talk about having kids, a lot. He wants four or maybe even five. Can you imagine that? Me, in charge of five dirty little screaming people all the time?" she shudders at the thought.

"I'm going to be the best interior designer in Alabama, how will I do that with a tribe of needy children? I know it's selfish, I'm selfish, but I just don't think I can" she says.

"Mindy, you may change your mind later. It's natural for Theo to want a lot of children. It's what he knows. Didn't you say, he's related to almost every single person in that hometown of his?" Kate asks.

We laugh because its true. In Theo's hometown, you can't walk down the street without running into a Greer or someone who's related by marriage somehow. Some of his relatives, who were very distant cousins when they got married, didn't even have to change their names.

"Sweetie" I hug her "it's okay to know what you want and it's okay to change your mind later. You would make a great mom, if that's what you choose" I tell her. I sense that some of her anxiety comes from being an orphan and growing up with her terrible Aunt Tisha who ended up going to jail for her mismanagement of Mindy's financial affairs.

"Our sweet Afton is not showing up with an instruction manual. No baby does. Jackson and I are going to do the best we can to raise a beautiful daughter. We will do that despite Jackson's terrible childhood and his poor excuse of a mother" I tell her. They both know my feelings about Jackson's troubled, man hopping, alcoholic mom.

"I just don't know, if I can" Mindy sighs and seems really upset by this admission.

"Mindy, you can. If you and Theo are meant to be parents, you will be. And you will be great at it. Look at Theo, he's already had so much practice with his brothers and small nation of cousins" Kate tells her.

We eat a few more snacks and finish our drinks. Kate stands up, yawns and stretches. "Alright, best friends, this bride needs her sleep if I'm going to be the most beautiful bride in Indiana", she starts to walk away.

"No, hello, get back here" Mindy tells her.

"Yep, nice try, we spill our guts, and you just walk away?" I ask her.

"Nope" Mindy yells.

"I'm the bride, it's my party. I can if I want to" Kate is acting like a spoiled six-year-old not getting her way.

"That is not the way this is going to happen. Sit back down and talk- Now!" Mindy orders Kate in her bossiest of tones.

Kate looks hard at Mindy and sits back down with a huff and a long sigh.

"You are so bossy," she tells Mindy.

"It is a gift" she sticks her tongue out at Kate.

I feel the air shift slightly in the room. Kate looks troubled. She feels troubled, I can barely sense, just around the edges of the room, something is not right. Whatever this is, whatever she doesn't really want to share is bad. Whatever it is, I am sure the minute she says it, I will regret hearing it. I want to just get up and go to bed now, but I can't because Kate is talking.

"If you two ever tell this to anyone, I will curse you straight to Hell" she says, her eyes show me that she is serious.

"After tonight, we never talk about this again and I mean never!"

I feel sick. Does she know about Kelly? Has she figured out his creepy ways and how he treats women? I do not want to know whatever is coming next. But my feet are glued to the floor, and I cannot make myself leave. This is such a bad idea!

Kate looks around the room and then back at Mindy and me. She takes a deep breath, lets it out and then she says, "I tricked Kelly into marrying me".

This was not what I was expecting. But still, what is going on?

"A few months ago, when Kelly finally proposed to me- it was because I was pregnant"

"What?" we both squeal.

"Why didn't you tell us?" Mindy glares at her.

"Because" she says, hanging her head. "I told Kelly, he was not excited at all. Said he needed to think about things, about us. Can you imagine how that made me feel?" She is so hurt by this.

"A week went by, and I didn't hear anything from him. I thought he was leaving me. He finally came back and said we should get married. But he didn't want to tell anyone about the baby yet. I agreed, even though I felt awful about that."

We listen quietly and she continues.

"Kelly thought a quick engagement was best. We've been together a long time, and with him in the military, people get married quickly all the time. We told our parents. They were so happy. Big Ed was "over the moon". I wanted a small ceremony. But, as you can see, Kelly's dad got a little carried away," she laughs and makes big eyes.

"Sweetie, people get pregnant and married all the time. We're in the 21st century now, you know" Mindy says.

"It's not that. I didn't get pregnant on purpose or try to trap Kelly into marrying me."

"Then what?" I ask her sensing there is more, way more to this story.

"Mom, Big Ed and I started making wedding plans. Kelly was not excited, but for once he had done something good. He liked all the positive attention he was getting."

"One morning, I got up feeling sick to my stomach. Cramping, headache, chills, felt like a period was coming on, except I was pregnant. Later that day, I lost the baby".

"I stayed in bed for two days telling Mom I had a little virus. She wanted to come over right away, but I put her off as long as I could. When she did come over, she was fussing over me and talking about wedding plans, so excited and happy."

"I couldn't do it; I didn't have the heart to tell her about the miscarriage. Worse, I couldn't tell Kelly. I wasn't sure he would still want to get married, with no baby" she starts crying.

"So, how did he take the news when you told him?" Mindy asks.

"I um, well "Kate starts.

Then it dawns on me. Oh no Kate, you didn't.

"You didn't tell him" I finish her sentence. "He still thinks you're pregnant?"

"Yes," she says in a small voice barely above a whisper.

"Jesus, Kate" Mindy smacks her forehead.

"What's your plan here, Kate?" I gently ask her. I think I already know, but I need to hear her say it out loud.

"Shortly, after the honeymoon, I will miscarry. Kelly has training in Arkansas right after we get home."

Mindy looks at me, a little shocked and then hugs Kate who is crying into her hands.

"Kate, do you really think this is a good idea?" I ask her.

"No, but what choice do I have now?"

Mindy shoots me a warning look and shakes her head "no".

"Everything happened so fast, and Kelly was cooling off on us. I honestly thought he would leave me at first. I didn't know what to do" she says.

"You could've talked to us," Mindy tells her.

"And get the reaction, you're giving me now? Tessa is sitting over there with judgment all over her face".

"Kate, that's not fair. I'm not judging you. I'm just trying to understand. I'm worried that starting your marriage with a lie is not setting a good foundation" I tell her, regretting it the instant I say it.

She looks up at me, with an angry expression, "You mean like not wanting to marry your husband but saying yes anyway, or maybe knowing you don't want kids but getting married to someone anyway that wants a lot of children? Yeah, it's so different!"

For once, Mindy is stunned into silence. This is not going well. Kate has a point, we weren't entirely truthful with our husbands, before we married them. Still, this feels different, way different. I'm not sure she will listen to anything I say, but I have to try.

"Kate, you're right. Mindy and I weren't honest before we got married. We should've told Theo and Jackson and then let things go where they would. You need to tell Kelly before tomorrow, or you will spend the rest of your life wondering if he married you out of obligation or love."

She stares at me hard, for a few seconds that seem like minutes. "I can't do that! And if you two care about me at all, you won't tell either, anybody" she is shaking when she says this. I know I can't push her anymore.

Mindy grabs her in a hug and motions for me to join in the group hug. I do.

"Your secret is safe with us Kate," Mindy tells her, even though I truly do not want to keep this to myself.

I go to bed, wondering how we got here? Kate is so blindly in love with Kelly she is willing to do almost anything to stay with him. What kind of hold does he have over her? Why can't she see the bad Kelly, the one that's always lurking just below the surface?

Wedding day is perfect despite the lies on which it rests. We pretend last night didn't happen. It's easy to do, seeing the joy on Kate's face. This is what she's always wanted. Even Kelly seems to be in good spirits, and not of the alcohol type. That must've been quite a job for his groomsmen, keeping the groom sober.

Kelly in his military dress uniform and Kate in her beautiful gown look like a couple straight from a Hollywood movie set. In the middle of their ceremony, I suddenly feel very lightheaded. On and off, during our stay at Meadowview, I've been having weird sensations along with some blurred vision and lightheadedness. I don't know if it's pregnancy hormones along with the heat or if it's something more. This land is giving off very strong sensations, it is very old. There are so many feelings and emotions trapped here that it is almost overwhelming. I've tried to block it all but it's a lot. Along with all the people and their swirling emotions, I think pregnancy has heightened my *gift*.

I glance at Jackson, standing with the other groomsmen and looking so handsome. I smile at him, trying to push down the sick feeling I have. He looks up in my direction. I smile wider, but then realize he's looking at Mindy. She must be doing something funny; you can't always trust her in public situations. From where I am standing, I can see both Kate and Kelly. She is radiating happiness, and Kelly, I can't quite read his expression.

Suddenly, it hits me and my knees buckle. Oh no, I'm going to pass out in front of all these people and ruin Kate's wedding. Someone catches me before I hit the ground. I expect to see Jackson. It's my dad, the surgeon. He leads me away from the front of the ceremony and gestures for the wedding to continue. He is walking me slowly to one of the tents, Mom meets us there.

Dad had been watching me and realized something wasn't right. He was standing right there, off to the side waiting. Mom told him I was sick. She must've felt it in that swarming sea of emotions. Yes, like me Mom has the gift. Most of the Donovan women do, to some degree. But Mom's is much stronger than mine. She can read people like nobody's business. It's one of the things that made her such a successful defense attorney. Most people don't have any idea how strongly the gift runs in the Donovan family. Several of our early ancestors paid a terrible price for their gifts and were burned at the stake as witches.

After some water, and a cool cloth on the back of my neck, I start feeling better. Maybe the heat, it is hot as hell, pregnancy hormones and lack of sleep have gotten to me. My parents are worried about me. My dad is checking my pulse, pupils and skin resiliency. They force me to eat something and drink a gallon of water. Just sitting in the shade with a cool drink and cool air blowing across my face makes me feel so much better.

I hate that I've ruined the wedding. Dad assures me that I did not. He got to me quickly and it continued without missing a beat. Mom reminds me it will be a funny wedding memory down the road. Dad wants to give me an IV infusion just to be safe, I refuse to go to the hospital. No need, he brought supplies with him, just in case. Of course, he did.

By now, the wedding party has done the recessional and are gathering in the VIP tent to wait for photos. Mindy, Kate and Jackson rush over to where I'm sitting. I assure them I am fine. Dad says he and Mom will take me back to the house for an IV treatment and some rest. Jackson offers to go. But I want him to stay and enjoy the reception. Big Ed's farm manager drives us back to the farmhouse and offers to stay with us. Dad refuses and sends him back on his way. We have Big Ed's farm truck keys or one of the waiting limo drivers to take us back to the reception when we are ready.

Dad sets up the IV treatment for me in one of the spare bedrooms and heads downstairs in search of some food. Mom sits with me while we wait.

"Mom, was I a complete idiot?"

"No, no Honey, not at all. Everyone is just worried about you. It's so hot out there. Who in the hell gets married in the middle of a cornfield in July?" she asks, shaking her head.

"The Ryans?" I laugh.

"I've been to some fancy things in my time. But I have to admit, this is the fanciest party I've ever been to in the middle of crop fields", she says bursting out laughing.

"Shh" I raise my finger to my lips. "We don't want Ms. Cindy hearing us. She might not ever speak to us again."

"Well, that wouldn't be the worst thing, ever" Mom says over a fit of laughter.

"She's been something, all right" I agree.

Mom takes my hand. "Are you sure you are, okay? Nothing more than just the heat and wedding excitement?"

This woman knows and feels everything! You can hide very little from her. My poor dad.

"Yes, no, I don't know" I start "Being here is hard. Out there at the chapel and cemetery there's so much energy just rushing around. It's overwhelming" I admit to her.

"You will learn to control that, with time. But that's not all, is it?" she looks at me closely.

"No," an involuntary chill rushes through my body.

"Maybe I imagined it, its hormones, its my biased feelings about Kelly, I don't know"

"What about Kelly?" she sits up straighter on the bed. "What did he do?" It's no secret my mother does not like Kelly at all.

"When I was looking at him today, with Kate, standing up in front of God and everyone, I felt something that I have never, ever felt before" I tell her, closing my eyes.

"Can you describe it?" she asks.

"Did you feel anything off during the wedding?" I ask her.

"No, nothing other than you, I felt you being out of sorts. And Kate, I sensed how happy she was. But there were so many emotions and feelings there- nothing other than these really stood out for me, why?"

"I felt evil there today. It was a strong presence, overwhelming. When I looked over at Kelly, I really couldn't see his face. And I couldn't really sense any of his emotions. You know I'm not very good at that. Not with people anyway. But I was slammed with a strong sense of *badness* I tell her.

"Badness" Mom questions?

"I can't really describe it. Um intense anger, fury, coldness, badness. I don't know."

"It scared me, and I didn't want me or Afton anywhere around that. Do you think she sensed it too?" I ask the thought just occurring to me. I hope she didn't feel that.

"No, probably not Sweetie. I have no idea if the gift is present before children are born or even what babies can actually feel "in utero". No worries, your mother instincts would automatically protect her from anything bad," she reassures me.

"Mom, please don't tell Dad, I don't want him to worry".

She leans over and hugs me on my side. She lays down on the bed with me. She doesn't even question why. She knows. She knows that one of my deepest fears is that if I don't learn how to manage this so-called *gift* I've been given, that one day it might drive me to craziness.

"You rest, sweet girl. Let's get you better, so we can get back to the party. After all, Big Ed has gone to so much trouble to impress us and all" she laughs.

After a bit, Dad checks me out and declares me party ready, with restrictions of course. We head back to the reception that is in full swing. Big Ed sure knows how to throw a party. It is the cherry on top of a gala celebration that people will be talking about for a very long time. Before the night ends, Mindy requests a friend song from our DJ. She grabs me and Kate and guides us out on the dance floor. Just the three of us, the music starts its "Kiss From A Rose" by Seal. This song defines our relationship. It played on loop that Sunday the day after I met Kate. We played and sang it so much in the next two years that everyone around us was sick of hearing it.

This is the absolute most perfect time, with Jackson, my family, my friends and soon with our baby Afton. If only everyday could feel exactly how I feel in this very moment. For now, in this one small perfect moment in the universe, it is all good, so very, very good. I hang on to this feeling cherishing it, because somehow, I know, somewhere deep down, I know. We will never be this happy again.

MINDY (2007)

Four miscarriages in five years. Four little angel babies gone to Heaven before we could love them completely. Maybe, I was right after all, and I didn't want children because they weren't allowed to be mine.

I have tried, the Good Lord knows I have tried and tried. Theo so desperately wants to have children. It's become almost all we think about, talk about and try to make happen. Maybe I am being punished for saying out loud that I wouldn't make a good mother and didn't want to find out. Maybe, it was wrong of me selfish even, not to want to carry on Theo's legacy. It's not that exactly. Theo would make an awesome father, **will** make an awesome dad.

It's me. I don't think I'm cut out for motherhood and Nature knows it. I like kids, it's not that. Afton, Reagan and little Jason are my heart. Theo's million plus nieces, nephews and little cousins are fine too. I just can't remember all their names.

If my parents had lived, and Aunt Tisha had not; my life would've been different. Growing up with her was such an awful experience that I would never, ever want another child to go through that. Theo would be wonderful, and I would try so hard. But what if I'm bad like

Aunt Tisha? What if no matter how hard I try, I am still a bad parent? What then? That would shatter Theo and I just can't live with that.

Theo and I have had our private parts, poked, prodded and stared at by so many doctors. Every expensive specialist has said the exact same thing. There's nothing wrong with either one of us. I can get pregnant; I just can't seem to stay pregnant until the baby is viable on its own. The last two pregnancies almost made it out of the danger zone. Our last sweet baby Gregory Theodore, almost lived long enough to breathe on his own and then he didn't. They all hurt; each one took a little more of us with them. But this last one, Theo's legacy, I think he may have broken me.

We've talked about adoption. But unless we do a private adoption, it's nearly impossible to adopt children here. There's something very wrong with that. We've explored surrogacy. I'm not really comfortable with that, although I'm not completely opposed to the idea. Tessa sweetly offered, but that's a lot to ask even from a close friend or family. We've started a fund for in vitro fertility treatments. After the last pregnancy, doctors are hopeful I could carry a child to term with a lot of special care.

The only reason I'm even considering this, is because it's so important to Theo. Even though he doesn't say so, each loss tears him completely apart. What if we do have to mortgage everything we have and scrape together almost $75,000 to go through with this- only to lose the baby again?

I agreed to starting the fund. Theo's family offers to loan us half of the money for the treatments. While we appreciate their kindness so much, I don't think it's fair to Theo's three brothers. So instead, we take an advance on Theo's portion of his parents' company. We had hoped maybe to use that one day to finance our own vacation rental company. Right now, I guess this is more important, at least to Theo anyway.

My interior design company *Mindy By Design* is doing well. I want to use some of the profits to grow my business and hire some damn help. But we agreed, that if Theo was going to use his family business assets, then I would need to divert some of my expansion profits. It only seems fair.

I've been seeing a new therapist lately, an older lady, who has suggested my pregnancy issues *might* be connected to my unresolved feelings of trauma with my parents' deaths and the Aunt Tisha tragedy. She seems to believe that my mind is rejecting the babies because of my own feelings of abandonment. The mind **is** a strong and powerful thing, but I'm not sure I buy her theory.

Even so, Tessa's offer to carry our child appeals to me. We ran the idea by Jackson, for his input, and he was weirdly opposed. Not because there could be issues of boundaries, but because it was not a good time for Tessa to be pregnant. When exactly is a good time to be pregnant?

The fertility clinic in Atlanta called today and left a message. We need to decide soon about moving forward with treatment. I so don't want to do the wrong thing. If we use all this money trying to get pregnant and it fails; we will not financially be able to start our dream business or expand my own.

I have a client in the Lake James area, one of Ms. Claire's friends. I haven't seen Tessa's mom in a while, so we make a lunch date for today. The restaurant is a cute local lakeside place called Crosbys. It's not that much to look at, but the food here is fabulous. I'm already seated at a lakeside table when Claire Donovan strolls in ten minutes late for lunch. This woman always knows how to make an entrance. I could pick up some pointers from her.

She kisses my cheek before sitting down. Claire is a beautiful lady; she doesn't seem to age. Our server Josie believes Claire is my mom. It's an honest mistake that happens often when we are together. I don't know if it's the similar hair color, or closely matched blue eyes; but we look more alike than she and Tessa. It used to bother Tessa a lot, but we laugh about it now.

"Looking lovely, as always, Sweet Girl" Claire looks at the menu even though she doesn't really need it.

"Same, Ms. Claire," she hates that I drop that "Ms." in front of her name. But I try to remember good manners and show respect. She is older than me, after all. She won't let me call her mom even though she's the closest, I've come to having one in a very long time.

"How's my favorite designer doing?"

"Good, busy, busy. Theo is insanely busy right now," I tell her knowing that she's not talking about business, but I intentionally sidestep her question.

I pick at my salad even though Crosby's cobb salads are the best, anywhere. Ms. Claire didn't suggest lunch with me today, because she has been missing these spectacular salads. So, I wait for her to get to the point.

"Goodness yes, Finn and I have been so busy in the office. Everybody is selling real estate right now. Not complaining, it's a good busy. We need to get you set up to stage some commercial properties for us", she says talking fast. Claire is always thinking fast and planning the next thing. I wait, before responding because this still isn't what she wants to talk about.

I nod my head "yes". "Of course, absolutely, just let me know. Any excuse to see that dreamy nephew Finn is a win in my book". I tell her. And it's true! If Theo wasn't my soulmate *forever guy* Finn would be a close second. I think I might have a *teensy* crush on him. If I ever find myself alone in the future- watch out Finn.

Ms. Claire gives me the *look*. That *watch yourself sassy pants* look that she has perfected by now. "How are you doing really?" she asks, placing her hand on mine. There, there it is. I knew it was coming. But how do I answer? Do I tell this lady, who can practically read minds, a lie? It's okay, I'm okay, we are fine. Or do I tell her the truth – that I will never be whole again. Losing Gregory Theodore before we even got to know him, broke my soul.

"Everything is fine, we're fine" I say trying to sound convincing. Yep, go with the lie and see how far it will run.

She looks at me with a very steady look- probably one of her courtroom faces. It's the one designed to make a witness on cross examination feel uncomfortable. It works! I stare back with my best effort, knowing I'm not winning the staring game, but right now, it's all I got.

"Are you really going to sit there and lie to me? To me? I know you well Melinda Grace and you are **not** okay" she tells me firmly.

I let out a long sigh and tell myself not to cry. No, I'm not okay even though the world expects me to be. Somehow, I 'm supposed to just carry on, even though there is a giant size hole in my heart.

"Mindy, did Tessa ever tell you she had a little sister?" Ms. Claire asks me. The surprise on my face gives her the answer.

"Maybe she doesn't remember. She was about four, almost five years old when it happened."

"I had two miscarriages before Tessa was born. Then along came Tessa- our *miracle* baby" Claire says dabbing at her eyes with the linen lunch napkin.

"William and I were so happy and so thankful for her. Tessa made our little family complete. Then when Tessa was three, she started talking to an imaginary friend Steve. We didn't think much of it, lots of kids do this. Esme even suggested it might be the Donovan gift manifesting itself in a different way. Who knows? But Tessa was intense and obsessed with Steve, she babbled to him all the time. We finally figured out, she was lonely and needed company."

"After a lot of thought, and some prayers, we decided to try again and give Tessa a little brother or sister. The pregnancy went well until the seventh month. Our Hope was born too early with heart failure and the doctors couldn't save her" Claire closes her eyes briefly, pain written all over her face.

"Even after all these years, the pain is still here. Know that you haven't done anything wrong. Or that it wasn't meant to be or it's God's will or any of those things that people say trying to comfort you. It just happened and you do the best you can, every day to deal with those losses. But you don't have to forget about them or pretend they didn't happen or just move on because it's easier for other people for you to do so."

"Do you understand me?" she asks, looking directly in my eyes.

"Yes, I do," I say.

"You get to decide when you want to let go of the grief. You get to decide who or what you want to be. Don't let other people define that for you, okay?" she pats my hand and changes the subject.

I am glad she does, because I am a few seconds away from telling her that I don't want to have a baby and I'm about to break Theo's heart.

"Have you talked to Kate recently? I've been meaning to call and have been so busy, I can barely remember to eat every day."

"Yes," I say, "I talked to her a few days ago. She seems fine".

"Is she happy?" Claire asks, she's made no secret of her intense dislike of Kelly.

"Well," I say tactfully, "It is Kelly, you know. That's always a crap shoot", shrugging my shoulders.

"Hmm, yes." We let that thought linger in the air between us.

Claire has finished eating and looks at her watch. "Oh, where does the time go? Fun and good company are time stealers, for sure". She reaches in her oversize Coach work bag and digs around, pulling out different things until she finds an envelope. She pulls it out and casually hands it over to me.

"Oh, here's a little something for you. Please use this to expand your business or for your fertility treatment plan if you and Theo go that route. It's a gift, use it for something that brings you joy."

"No, Ms. Claire, I can't accept this," I tell her, sliding the envelope back across the table.

"Were you not raised with good manners, dear?" she asks with a smile on her face.

"Yes, you will accept this. It's from my mother's fund. It's no secret that she blessed William and me, tremendously. She wanted me to use part of the trust money to help women in need. You've heard the stories. She believed in helping women be independent and follow their dreams."

"But Ms. Claire, there are other women more deserving."

"No," she stops me. "If you don't take this money and put it to good use- I will be mortally offended. I can hold a grudge for a very long time. Don't test me!" she says then winks at me.

She gets up, gathers her bag and walks away from the table. She turns, comes back, gives me a hug and whispers, "tell that beautiful daughter of mine, I should not have to make an appointment to see her and my fabulous grandchildren. You hear?"

She straightens up, looks at her watch again, "I really have to go. Good lunch, please stay and enjoy some dessert. Lunch is on me. Love you Sweetie", she says and makes a graceful exit, before I can say a word.

I really wish she would have stayed because I would've told her "I'm afraid". I 'm afraid of trying again to have a baby, afraid I may be a bad mother, and afraid of terribly disappointing Theo if I tell him "no" on the baby plans.

Later that night, after supper, I talk to Theo about my feelings. The check Ms. Claire gave me was overly generous; fifteen and some zeroes as in $15,000. It was a mistake to tell Theo. He immediately wanted to schedule fertility treatments without even listening to any of my concerns.

We argue, it is the worst argument we've ever had. My usually calm and laid-back Theo turned into something else entirely. I really had no idea that he was so set on having a baby, even after the miscarriages-even after losing Gregory. He doesn't know how many times I heard him sobbing in the garage, so he wouldn't cry in front of me.

I am not going to be bullied into getting pregnant again just because it's his life dream. We can build a very good life together, children or no children. I believe it is true, if men had to be pregnant and deliver children; humans might be an extinct species by now. I'm not against having children, I'm not. But I cannot lose another. If I do, I will lose myself in the process.

I don't know why Theo can't understand this. I will tell Theo there is a very long waiting list for treatment, at least six months long. Then I will call the clinic and cancel our slot. I will deal with Theo, when the time comes. What am I getting myself into? Please, please let this be the right thing for me.

Jason (2016)

Mom and Kelly (formerly known as Dad) are getting a divorce. It's about time! Probably about 10 years too late, if you ask me. Why do parents think they need to stay together for the children? I bet if more parents asked what their kids really thought, there would be more divorces and more happy kids.

Yeah, yeah, people are always saying it's better for the kids if Mom and Dad work out their issues and stay together. Bull, that only works if Mom and Dad don't hate each other. Or in my case, Mom is stupidly in love with Dad, and Dad could care less.

Maybe Kelly was different before, and they really loved each other. But I wouldn't know. All my memories are of the *other* Kelly, after Aunt Tessa's lake house burned. Then it all went to hell.

Aunt Mindy got burned and Kelly got hurt trying to put the fire out in the boathouse. My nightmares started, after that weekend. Something about that fire messed me up. I started dreaming about red-headed monsters with fire faces and started wetting the bed again. Everything, even my favorite foods, made my stomach hurt. I got paranoid about sleeping in the dark and begged Mom to let me sleep with her every night. Some mornings I would wake up curled up in a ball outside of Mom and Kelly's bedroom door.

The worse I got, the more the parents fought. Kelly thought I was just acting out for attention. Mom started taking me to a lot of different doctors. Later, I ended up going to a head doctor because none of the other doctors could find anything really wrong with me.

The more Mom worried, the madder Kelly got. He yelled a lot! Sometimes he would get in these crazy moods that just being in the same room set him off. It was worse, way worse when he was drinking. Kelly was a world champion drinker, probably the best in the world. The more he drank, the louder he got. Sometimes, I was sure the neighbors down the street could hear him. When he got crazy like this, I hid in my closet. He scared me so bad. A few times, I would wake up the next day wondering why I had slept in the closet. Then, I remembered.

Mom tried hard not to set yelling Kelly off. If she saw that he was in one of his *moods,* we usually left the house for a while. If he was drunk when we came back, we would go to Grampa and Grandma Maynard's house. If it was a school day, Mom would send me to my room and tell me to lock the door. We had a secret code word for when I could come out. I learned how to call 911, very young.

When he totally lost it, he would break things and scream. He would get so worked up, I hoped he would fall over dead with a heart attack or stroke out. Usually, he would slam the front door so hard it rattled, heading out to the detached garage. Who the hell knows what he did out there? We tried hard to stay out of his way. Sometimes, if we were lucky, he just passed out and we had a peaceful night.

Mom tried so hard to convince me he wasn't hurting her. I never saw him hit her. But so many times, he grabbed her hard when he was mad at her. She had bruises on her wrists, arms, and shoulders that she tried to hide. It didn't always work.

The best times we had as a family, were when Kelly was gone with his Army job. The house was quiet, it was what normal could look like. Mom and I waited for these trips and counted them on the calendar.

Kelly was gone more and more. We didn't complain. He started spending nights at work and away on trips a lot. It made me so happy. Even though Mom was glad he wasn't around, she got sadder and sadder.

One day, I got home from school and Kelly was already there. It was my 12th birthday this week. Mom promised I could invite friends out for pizza, and ice cream. She was taking us to see the new *X-Men Apocalypse* movie. We didn't plan on Kelly being in town.

He was quiet and left me alone. He sat staring at CNN until Mom got home early from work. She was surprised to see him. We got ready for the movie, Mom invited Kelly to come along. He said "no" and went back to watching tv. Whatever. We met up with Matt and Chris at the theater. Mom fed us and gave us our movie tickets. She watched some dopey romance movie in another theater. *X-Men* was cool- we waited for Matt and Chris' parents to pick them up. Then, we headed home.

It was a school night, and Mom wanted me in bed at regular time. With Kelly here, who knows how he will act? When we get home, he is still watching tv, this time four empty beer bottles are on the side table.

Mom sends me upstairs. I brush my teeth and hear Kelly yelling even over the running water. I feel like I'm gonna puke. Perfect, what a way to end a good day, Not! What an ass! Can't he just chill for one day? Just once- can I have a good day that he doesn't try to ruin? I feel bad for thinking that. He's down there giving Mom a really hard time and I shouldn't only be thinking about myself.

I stand out in the hallway so I can hear what he is so bent about. Something to do with Melissa, female soldier, something, something, discharge. I can't really make out everything cause Kelly is starting to slur his words. I hear a loud crash that freezes me in place.

Mom has always made me promise that when Kelly starts throwing things that I won't try to stop him. She's afraid I will get really hurt. Like I could stop him. I'm just a skinny kid. He's a grown ass, big man. But sometimes, sometimes when he starts this - there is this rage that builds up in me, so big I see red. When it does, I just want to go down there and kill him. If that's not possible, at least get in some good hits before he beats the hell out of me.

I hear the front door slam and I run and get in my bed. Mom comes to check on me. She looks upset but okay otherwise. She tucks me in, even though I'm too big for that. She leans down messes up my hair and kisses my cheek. I'm too big for that too, but I still like it.

In the morning, I wake up and get ready for school. The house is quiet, either Kelly left, or he's passed out somewhere in the house, sleeping off the booze. It's my birthday, Mom made me pancakes with a birthday candle. Grampa Ed sent a card with a big check. Sweet! Mom takes the check to put into my savings account. I usually ride the bus to school but because its my birthday, Mom drives me.

On the way to school, she lets me pick the songs on the radio. Most of the time, she does not. She doesn't like hip-hop music and monitors it at home **a lot**. She doesn't like the lyrics but today is okay. Chance the Rapper's *No Problem* is playing. I sing along (mostly, except the parts she won't like). It's a good morning!

I ask about Kelly. Probably not a good move, but I do it anyway.

"How long is Dad in town for?"

She doesn't answer me right away. "Well, it's going to be awhile this time".

She doesn't say anymore. Not sure what the hell that means? A week, a month? A year? C'mon woman, need a little more detail here.

"Mom, how long? A week, more?" I ask her, I have a right to know.

"Well, it's complicated" she starts. Anytime you hear that word, you know it's bad.

"Dad is changing jobs soon and going to be home for awhile until he finds another one" she says trying to sound positive, for my sake, I guess.

"How do you just change jobs when you're in the Army? Is his time up? Can he just do something else?" I ask, because I really am curious, now.

"Jason, your dad is changing careers and that's all you need to know right now, okay? It's stressful for him, so let's do everything we can not to antagonize him alright?" she asks me in that *Mom* tone of voice.

I let it go. If something happened with Kelly's job, he is going to be major pissed and that just means trouble for Mom and me. I try to stay away from him, but Jesus, sometimes just breathing too loud makes him mad.

He is home, when I get home from school. Still sitting in the den with the same stupid news channel playing in the background. I slip quietly upstairs being careful on the two stairs that squeak. Honestly, judging by the number of empty beer bottles in the den, he probably wouldn't hear me anyway.

Mom gets home later, and the front door slams again. I hope that means he is gone for the night. Mom says Kelly went out and won't be home until late. That's good, it means we can eat in peace and maybe watch *MacGyver* together. I pick up some good tips from that show. This is the way I wish it always could be. Just peace and quiet, a mom (maybe a dad) and a kid just hanging together, no drama, no yelling, no hurting. It's not too much to ask for- right?

I had the dream again; it's been a while. I thought maybe they went away, maybe I'd outgrown them like my head doctor thought I would. This time it was different. There were many fire monsters with blue eyes chasing me and Mom in the house. It was like a video game- every time I killed one, two more popped up in its place. The whole fucking house was overrun with these things. They were like indestructible! I tripped and fell, hitting my head. I lay on the floor trying to not see double of everything. Then all I could see were the fire monsters closing in on me. Yep, I was a goner. I closed my eyes waiting for death.

Then the dream changed. I was at Aunt Tessa's cottage, Storybook- it was summertime. It was that summer, when the boathouse burned. I saw everyone, except they were all younger. I guess I was watching everything. I saw Aunt Mindy go into the boathouse, then the boathouse went up in flames, like an explosion with no sound. Aunt Mindy and Kelly ran out of the boathouse, Kelly was on fire. Aunt Mindy was screaming, then everyone else is screaming.

I look around and Storybook is on fire, burning to the ground. They head to the lake and the lake is now on fire. Everything is burning now, if it wasn't so scary it would be cool. It looks like the end of the world , the Apocalypse. What a cool video game graphic except it isn't cause everyone I love is burning up just like the fire people. I can't do anything except watch it happen.

I wake up in a heavy sweat after that dream. It was intense, the worst one ever. Probably won't be any going back to sleep after that. I pick up my copy of *Invisible Man* that I dropped by the bed last night. It's on my summer reading list. It's a hard book to read so I guess it's going to take a lot longer than I thought. I won't just be able to half ass read it a few days before class.

I guess I am really tired because a few pages into the chapter, I fall asleep.

I sleep until 10:30. Maybe it's the smell of bacon that wakes me up. Mom always makes a special effort on the weekends cooking up breakfast feasts. It makes her happy making pastries and cooking up big meals; I don't mind.

Or maybe it's the yelling that wakes me. Kelly is back in the house, in a big, loud way. I hear loud noises coming from the kitchen. Then, heavy footsteps are coming upstairs. Is he drunk already or still drunk from last night? I pretend I'm asleep, maybe he's headed to the bedroom and will pass out again.

My door flies open and the next thing I know there is dragon breath breathing heavy on my face. He shakes me, his bloodshot eyes and red face all up in my personal space. I'm scared!

"Get up now- lazy ass," he roars.

I'm frozen in place; I don't know what is going on. But I don't want to make him any madder than he already is. So, I open my eyes like I'm just waking up and look at him. It is hard, he stinks and is furious. He goes to my dresser, opens some drawers and starts slinging out clothes. I watch him not believing what I'm seeing right now.

"Lazy ass, NOW! Get up, get dressed and get your piece of shit self, outside- front yard," he barks and heads out the door. Is he having some kind of Army flashbacks, or is this fraternity hazing or what? I do what I'm told though, cause he is already mad as hell, and I don't want him to get any madder.

Mom stands on the front porch, watching and not knowing what to do either. Dad is wearing the same wrinkled stinking clothes from yesterday and now is wearing boxing gloves. He points at the ground and tells me to pick up the second pair and put them on. Not again. We tried this boxing thing when I was ten. I hated it! Mom made a compromise with Kelly and put me in karate lessons, those were pretty cool. Until Kelly made me quit.

Then Kelly starts swinging at me. Are you kidding me? I'm still trying to put on these stupid gloves. Kelly is yelling "mama's boy", something about being spoiled, "discipline" "be a man" all while he is hitting me in the stomach. He gets angrier and angrier. Mom is crying and telling him to stop. She comes off the porch pulling on his arm to stop. This just makes him madder.

I'm trying to defend myself from the punches. Mom is crying, Kelly is getting louder and louder and then I hear a snapping sound. I fall to my knees; everything looks a little blurry. I can barely see Mom, Kelly, the neighbors that are now out in their yards watching. I taste blood and spit out a tooth. Mom pushes Kelly and gets me up. I guess being a man means it's okay to hit kids, but you don't hit your wife in front of the neighbors.

Kelly is laid out on the ground, talking to himself. Mom doesn't look back. We go into the house; Mom stops in the kitchen and grabs an ice pack from the freezer. She tells me to go straight upstairs and lock my door. She doesn't want me to open the door until she says so. She gives me her phone and tells me to call 911 if I don't see or hear her within 15 minutes.

I go upstairs as fast as I can, my heart is thumping out of my chest. My head and jaw hurt but I don't have time to think about that right now. Mom knocks on the door and calls my name. She comes in the room, carrying one of my extra duffel bags already packed with clothes. She has one for herself too.

"We are going away for a while. Pack important things you need. Anything else, we can buy. Hurry, we have to get out of the house before Kelly comes upstairs" she is strangely calm right now.

I nod, and pack a few things, and as I'm heading out the door, I pick up the *Invisible Man* book. Mom is serious, she is standing by the door with her stuff. She slowly opens the door and looks outside.

Kelly is still laid out in the yard just like we left him. She waves for me to come outside. We quietly step on the porch and take our bags to Mom's Jeep. She looks again at Kelly and at the neighbors still standing outside watching and gets in the car. She backs it out of the driveway and heads down the street looking straight ahead. She doesn't give a second look to Kelly or the neighbors staring after us.

This morning was so weird and wild that we sit quiet in the car for a while. I see we are headed out of Fort Wayne, but I have no idea where we are going.

"Mom, where are we going?" I finally ask her.

"Meadowview," she says still staring ahead at the highway.

"Grampa Ed's?" I'm surprised we are going there. Usually when we need a cooling off period, we go to Grandma Cindy and Grampa Bob's farm. It's closer to where we live.

"Yes," Mom is still not talking much.

"Does he know we are coming? What will Kelly do, he won't just show up there, right?" I ask her worried that he might. She doesn't even blink at me calling my dad by his first name. I guess you lose that status by beating the crap out of your kid.

"No, I don't think so. Big Ed will help us" she says trying to control the tears coming down her face.

I take that as my cue to just shut up. Mom is dealing with a lot right now- trying to hold it all together. She doesn't need any extra stress from me right now. Besides, my jaw hurts when I talk. Mom turns the radio to a 90's hits station. This is some old school music- but it makes her happy. She starts singing along and telling me about the songs. There is some song playing, she says it's "Kissed By A Rose' by Seal. Yeah, the guy with the scars that married the hot model. It was the theme song for one of the Batman movies that bombed. Mom tells me it is *their song,* for her, Aunt Mindy and Aunt Tessa. I guess it was popular and they played it so many times for a year that it made everyone around them, hate it for life. She laughs at that!

"When we get to Grampa Ed's, we'll see if Doc Smith can take a look at your face. Then we can head to the ER if we need to. We will have to see a dentist after we figure out what is going on with your jaw," she is having a hard time not crying.

It's fine, Mom" I tell her "it barely hurts". I'm lying, it hurts bad, but I won't tell her that. I pop two extra strength Tylenol and close my eyes. I've tried reading my book, but the lines keep blurring, and I can't concentrate on anything anyway. All I keep thinking is how if there was a big branch, shovel, baseball bat, anything laying around in the yard that I could've used: I probably would've killed my dad.

"Mom, do you think anybody called the police? There were a lot of neighbors outside" I ask her.

She doesn't answer right away. "I don't know. I don't think so"

"So, everyone just stands around and watches a grown ass man beat up a little kid and they don't say or do anything?" I feel myself getting mad.

"Maybe someone did call the police. We weren't sticking around to find out."

"But, all those times, Kelly screaming, slamming doors, breaking things. I know the neighbors heard and no one thought to call the cops. This has been going on a long time," I say not understanding why.

"Sweetie, people have the tendency not to get involved. They see something, they turn away. They go about their business if it doesn't directly impact them. This morning though, that was the show. It's like the train wreck you see coming and you just can't turn away from it" she says wiping tears.

Then immediately it hits me, and I ask before I can even think about it.

"But why have you never called the cops? Dad could have killed us today."

"Because I couldn't" she says in an almost whisper. I can barely hear her.

"God, I did not ever want to tell you this. Your dad told me if I ever went to the cops, he would take you away from me. He threatened to make me lose my job too," she tells me, sounding so pitiful right now.

I slam my fist hard on the book in my lap. "Damn him, he can't do that. He is the bad dad and terrible husband. Nobody would ever believe him," I say, so angry right now that I can't see straight. My head is pounding, and my jaw is hurting again.

"I know Sweetie, I know. Yes, they would believe him. Your dad has spent his whole life using his family name to get him out of trouble. This wouldn't be any different."

"But, Jesus Christ, that's so unfair!" I yell to no one in particular.

"Jason, it's probably hard for you to understand. I wanted to leave your dad a long time ago, but I couldn't. I should've but I couldn't, because of his threat. I had to wait. As long as it was just me, he was taking it out on, I could live with that."

"I had to wait until he lost his temper enough that he did something that others saw. I never expected what happened this morning. I'm so, so sorry!"

"Mom, its..." I tell her.

She interrupts me. "No, no, it's not okay. Please do not say that!" she says loudly.

"It's not okay, but this morning people saw the real Kelly. The one he hides from most people. His family name is not going to shield him from that craziness this morning. "I'm so sorry and will never forgive myself that he hurt you. I should've stopped this long ago" she sounds so angry. I've never heard her like this.

I don't know what to say. Instead, I think of the feast she made us, sitting in the kitchen. My stomach rumbles. I hope she turned the stove off. I imagine the drunk idiot stuffing his face full of my food and wondering where everyone is. I ask Mom if we can stop and get something to eat. Maybe I can eat, if I chew carefully on the other side of my mouth.

We stop at McDonald's; Mom sends me in to get food. She needs to call Grampa Ed and maybe Neil, his farm manager if Grampa is at his swanky house in Virginia. The *workplace* house, he calls it. I bring out the food and we eat in the parking lot. We are both hungry. I can eat almost everything, if I'm careful and only chew on the left side of my mouth. The whole right side of my face hurts. Mom tells me that I'm going to have a spectacular *shiner*. Great!

Meadowview is a little over an hour from our house. Grampa Ed is home, but he's out doing horse stuff. He knows we are coming, Neil his farm manager tells Mom the new gate code and gets Grampa's housekeeper busy making the house ready for us.

"Mom, what will Grampa think?" I ask her a few minutes before we get to the farm.

"I don't know Jason, but he is the only one that can protect us from your dad now."

This doesn't really make sense to me. It's his son, and he wouldn't want him to get in trouble. And this looks like big trouble. I trust Mom, if she thinks this is the right thing to do- then I do too. Hopefully, it means that he is gone, this time forever.

Mom gets me settled in my bedroom at the farm. She makes me rest even though I really feel okay, other than pain in my jaw. She goes down to the kitchen and waits for Grampa Ed to get home. I hear her talking to the housekeeper, who is also a great cook. I hope we stay here awhile.

I guess I fell asleep, when I wake up it feels a lot later. The alarm clock on my desk says its 4:30. Damn, my jaw hurts! I hear voices downstairs, sounds like maybe Grampa is back. I head downstairs but stop about halfway down when I hear Mom and Grampa talking about Kelly. Maybe one day, I should consider Special Ops or something in the military. I sure like this stealth mode. Practiced it a lot, creeping around when Kelly was home.

I hear Grampa talking, he is agitated. Mom is responding and it sounds like she is crying.

"Doc Smith will be here in a few minutes, he was on a fishing trip," he tells her.

"Damn if that boy's jaw is broken, I will kill Kelly myself. What the hell was he thinking?"

"I've never seen him like this Ed. I think getting in trouble with his command and dishonorable discharge coming up in conversation sent him over the edge" Mom tells him, surprisingly calm, considering everything that has happened.

"Drinking heavily again?" Grampa asks her and sighs loudly.

"Yes, and so angry at Jason and me, all the time. I knew he was having an affair with that soldier. But I did not bring it up, not once."

"I can't live with him anymore, Ed. Mistreating me is one thing, but I cannot allow him to be around Jason. I won't allow that. I don't care if he does try to take him away from me."

"Calm down, Kate. He won't do that. It's a bluff, he's trying to bully you," Grampa tells her.

"And it's worked. For so many years, he threatened to take Jason and ruin me. He is sick and needs help. But we can't be his whipping post anymore" Mom tells him and starts crying.

"Kate, you and Jason are precious to me. I will not let anything happen to you," he says.

"Dear God, woman why didn't you come to me a long time ago?"

Mom waits before she answers, "He's your son, you've always protected him."

Grampa lets out a little roar. "I've spent Kelly's whole life fixing things for him. I will fix this too. But I swear to you, on Ella's grave, my son Kelly will never hurt you or Jason again. I promise that." I hear Grampa Ed crying.

I debate going downstairs but decide not to. I think that if Grampa sees my face right now, he may lose it. I feel sorry for him, and I don't want to cause him any more pain. So, I turn and head back upstairs to wait for old Doc Smith. He is one of Grampa's old friends and his best hunting buddy. I sure hope he hurries up cause this jaw is hurting like hell now.

Well, Doc Smith doesn't think my jaw is broken but we are going to go get x-rays in the morning, just to be sure. It will be sore for a while, and I can't eat hard foods on the right side of my mouth. I'll be getting expensive dental work to replace my missing tooth. I will have my first black eye for a while. My head and jaw may hurt for weeks. He says it was a good lick. This makes Mom cry, that and looking at my ugly face right now. The one good thing is he will leave some pain meds, just in case I need them. I need them, they are the only thing that keeps the fire monster dreams away.

Grampa keeps his promise, and *fixes* things. I will be spending most of the summer out at Meadowview with Grampa and Neil. Then I'm going to spend some time with Aunt Tessa and family at the lake. Aunt Mindy is taking me to Uncle Theo's family beach house too. Mom says she needs to get back to work and I can spend this summer doing fun things. I think it's more to keep me away from Kelly.

Nobody called the cops back home or if they did, Grampa made it go away. Because Kelly was messing around with one of his soldiers, he had to leave the Army Reserves. He was allowed just to resign his commission, and avoid a dishonorable discharge, also probably with Grampa Ed's help. Grampa sent a moving crew to move Kelly out of our house, had all the locks changed and installed a home security system.

In exchange for not getting in huge trouble, Kelly promised to go to a high-end rehab center in California where Aunt Kimberly lives. He will then go to a veterans' in-patient treatment center. Aunt Kimberly is the yoga and wellness instructor there. She can keep an eye on him. If he leaves treatment or gets into any more trouble, then he's on his own. No more help from Grampa Ed.

After he gets out, then he will live on the farm property in the restored cabin. Grampa plans to let him work in his consulting service. If that doesn't work out, Uncle Jackson has offered him a job with his search and rescue drone company.

Mom and Kelly are legally separated and will be getting a quickie divorce. Grampa Ed has taken care of everything. Mom and I get everything, and Kelly pretty much gets nothing. I think Grampa is trying to make up for all the shitty things Kelly has done. I don't care what happens to him. I just want him gone, and out of our lives, for good!

— · —

MINDY (2021)

This is the absolute worst day of my life. Finding out I was an orphan at age 10, living with crazy Aunt Tisha, the miscarriages, losing sweet Gregory, the fire summer, NONE of it is as bad as today.

Today, I want to die! Part of me already did. I'm sitting in Lake James Memorial Hospital waiting for a Covid test result and permission from some administrator to go see my dead husband. How ironic is that? I can't infect him because he's already dead. The hospital staff are suited up looking like scientists in some alien movie- so they're probably good too. This hospital bureaucracy is ridiculous. If I don't get to go back soon- heads are going to roll!

Theo is gone. I can't quite wrap my mind around it. Is this just some sick joke that somebody's playing on me. Theo isn't dead, he just had some bad ingestion and a mild case of Covid. They have him mixed up with some other poor guy. They won't even let me go back past the waiting area to straighten this mess out. I'm the only one in the waiting area. Finn is here somewhere; he's out making calls to family. They didn't want to let him in either, until he mentioned he was my family attorney. He is family and an attorney; so technically he's not lying.

I was working when I got the call, Theo collapsed in his office. He usually works from home. Business is so light with all the Covid restrictions. There was some paperwork he needed at the office. It's a good thing, he was in the outer office, or he might've laid on the floor in his inner office, suffering for who knows how long. Just the thought of it makes me sick.

Apparently, he was making copies of paperwork, clutched his chest and fell to the floor. A local ambulance company happened to be down the street from Theo when the call came in. They were on lunch break and empty, so they took the call. Finn and I were out at the lake looking at some potential rental properties. I didn't get the messages from the hospital until we came back into better cell service. By then, it was too late.

Theo had what they call a widowmaker heart attack. Very few people survive this. His crew called 911 and the response time was very quick. But it didn't matter, they couldn't revive him. I guess if it's any consolation, he went so quickly he felt very little. No, it's not any consolation, not at all. The very little the hospital has said is that he died almost immediately from the heart attack and complications from an asymptomatic Covid infection. That's not true! Theo died from a broken heart, Jackson and I killed him.

This past weekend, Jackson, Finn and Theo headed out to the lake for a weekend of fishing. Everyone is going stir crazy staying at home. So, they decided to spend some lake time together. All had negative Covid tests before they left, and none of them had been anywhere with crowds of people. Theo complained a little of being tired and seasonal allergies but nothing more. A good weekend of fishing and he would be right as rain again.

Theo came home Sunday night with an ice chest full of fish, sun-tanned and rested. All seemed well. I made his favorite meal; it was a rare comfortable June night with no humidity. We eat in the backyard garden that we had just redesigned last month. Co-owning a busy landscape company means you rarely ever get around to your own work. But this summer, work on the residential side was slow. So, we finally got caught up on our long overdue projects. It was good to finally see it get done. It also helped keep Theo's crews employed so he didn't have to lay any of them off during this lean time.

I pour a California merlot into the wine glasses and mix a whiskey sour for Theo. He brings the steaks and potatoes to the table. I serve our salads and bread. We taste our food, enjoying the newly decorated space and the weather, which is almost perfect today. Theo is quiet, but he had a full weekend. He's probably still a little tired from the early mornings and long days on the water. Jackson is serious about all he does and likes to go hard with any activity.

I try carrying the conversation small talking, mainly to myself. Theo eats a little but mostly pushes food around on his plate. It's his favorite meal and the steaks are cooked just the way he likes them, medium rare. Not the burnt variety, I usually grill. I don't understand his behavior.

After a few more minutes of me making silly talk and him not paying attention I test him.

"Hey, guess what. I've been waiting to tell you this. I'm so excited-I bought a lottery ticket when I was up in Nashville and guess what? We WON! We are gazillionaires."

His expression doesn't change, and he keeps pushing his food around on his plate.

"That's nice, Mindy."

"Hello, Earth to Theo," I say snapping my fingers, trying to redirect his attention.

"Did you hear anything, I just said? Are you okay honey? Feeling, okay? You don't look so good" and he doesn't. His skin is blotchy red, and he has tight lines around his mouth.

He looks at his plate, pauses for what seems like forever and then finally says, "Mindy, I need to ask you something and you need to tell me the truth." Whatever this is, it is most certainly not going to be a good conversation.

"Last night, when we were having drinks on the deck, Jackson said something I couldn't believe. I thought I misheard him maybe or misunderstood what he was saying. You just need to clarify things for me, okay?" he asks looking up at me, so troubled.

"I don't even know how to say it right," Theo says obviously trying to find the best way to say whatever it is that needs saying right now. "That summer the boathouse burned, did something happen between you and Kelly?"

Here it is. Damn Jackson, he cannot handle the bourbon. After a drink or two, he just goes shooting off his big mouth, with no filter. All these years, he's been the one so insistent on keeping the secret and now, without my permission, he blows it all up.

I take in a breath, hold it and let it out slowly. I have to play this so carefully. I have no clue what Big Mouth has said and will likely have to pull it out of Theo and then, maybe, be as evasive as possible. Why now- Jackson Carmichael? Are you trying to ruin my life even more?

"Theo," I take his hands in mine. "You know what happened that night. I went in the boathouse to get lanterns for the tables. Some of the oil spilled, it was dark in the boathouse. I lit the lighter so I could see, and it sparked the fire. Kelly saw the fire and tried to help me put it out," I lie through my teeth with a pretty smile pasted on my face.

"Jackson said something about Kelly hurting you, and him hurting Kelly and honestly none of it made any sense," he tells me looking intently at my face trying to catch any twitches or other telling signs that I'm lying.

"Jackson must've really been drunk, was he drinking bourbon? He gets wild on that stuff'" I'm trying as hard as I can to deflect Theo. I can tell he's not letting it go that easily.

"Mindy, tell me the truth. Did Kelly hurt you? I think you are lying to me right now," he says banging the table. It startles me, his face is clenched in anger. This is a new look; I've never seen on Theo, and it really scares me. I have no idea what to say, so I stick with the truth.

"Yes Theo, he hit me in the boathouse," I so don't want to tell him this, especially not after all this time "Kelly was being his usual, drunk ridiculous self. He had the babysitter cornered in the boathouse. He was scaring her. I came in to get the lanterns and she ran out. I made a rude comment about her being too young for him and got the lanterns out of the storage closet. Kelly shoved me against the closet and hit me. I dropped the lantern, and it was so dark in there with the shades down. I clicked the lighter, it fell and started the fire. Kelly pushed me down and headed for the door. I got out somehow, that's all I remember, really." It's not, but looking at Theo's face, he can't hear the truth. It will crush him.

He sits quiet for a minute, processing what I've told him. Then when it sinks in, the anger comes. "Damn that sorry ass, I will go up to Virginia and kick his ass all the way back down here," he says in a low, quiet, hate-filled voice. "Why Mindy? Why did you keep this from me? Am I the only one that doesn't know?" He is so angry now.

"No, Theo please calm down. Kate doesn't know either. And Tessa, doesn't really have all the facts."

"So let me get this straight. You, Jackson and Tessa just decided on your own to keep this a secret. Is that right? Without even considering that we should know or that Kelly should get what was coming to him. Why is that, Mindy? Help me understand that".

I do not see a clear or easy way out of this mess. "For the record, Tessa wanted us to tell. She has wanted us to come clean, every year since it happened" I tell him gently hoping to diffuse his anger a bit.

"And you said No? Jesus, Mindy the man assaulted you. That's not something your husband should know?"

"Theo, I know it sounds crazy but it's more complicated than that. We weren't thinking clearly at the time. Everything happened so quickly. That night was chaos, you remember" I say hoping I don't have to tell too much but feeling I will need to, anyway.

"Kelly had the 15-year-old babysitter trapped in the boathouse. Caroline, do you remember her? A sweet girl, she always babysat for Tessa in the summers. He was saying inappropriate things and standing way too close to her and wouldn't let her leave. I don't know what he said or did before I came in, but she was scared. That little girl was scared," I tell him, still seeing her face in my mind.

"Did he .."

"Touch her? I don't know. All I know is that Jackson took her home. Caroline never babysat for the Carmichaels again. To this day, they don't know what really happened."

"Theo, don't you see? It wasn't just that night or the alcohol. We called Kelly "creepy Kel" for a reason. He hit on me and Tessa so many times, we lost count. Your best friend. As a prank, one of the sororities handed out warning posters with Kelly's picture and hung them in all the sorority bathrooms. If she breathed and was female between the ages of 18- 45, Kelly thought it was fair game" I say not wanting to hurt Theo, but surely, he was not this clueless.

"You do remember the first night we met Kate and Kelly's drunken exhibition, right?"

Theo is deep in thought. I have no idea what he is thinking or what direction this conversation is headed. But we are having it anyway.

"Mindy, Kelly has serious issues, things he needs to fix. But that is no excuse, to lie to me about something like this. Keeping this from me and Kate just let Kelly continue his bad behavior. Or did you forget about all the bad years with Kate?" he asks me and he's not wrong. I've beat myself up every single year since we made that very wrong decision to keep quiet. I will never forgive myself for all that Kate and Jason went through with Kelly.

"I don't know. It was stupid, incredibly stupid. We got caught up in the fire, and somehow, I guess we thought that was bad enough. We didn't know what Caroline would do, and I guess I thought down deep that maybe when Kelly sobered up and realized how badly he acted, it might scare him back on the straight path. I was very wrong" I admit.

"Let's go back to the root of this. You, and Jackson lied and drug Tessa along with you in the lie. My best friend and my wife. My wife for God's sake lied and continued to lie about this. You don't think I needed to know? Lying about big things is not protecting me, Mindy. What else have you protected me from? Didn't think I needed to know about? This is a real trust issue, and I just can't handle this right now" Theo throws down his napkin, pushes his chair back and stomps inside the house.

Right now, if I was with Jackson and Kelly and had a gun; it's a strong possibility I would shoot both of them right between the eyes. I am in an impossible situation. Even after coming clean with Theo against my will, I am still holding on to the biggest secret of my life. The truly crazy thing is that I can't tell another living soul. If I do, I will surely lose everything and I will not do that.

Theo sleeps in the guest bedroom on Sunday night. He is furious with me and probably more than just a little disappointed too. Trust, and honesty are a big deal to Theo, and I've blown that. He leaves early on Monday, doesn't return my texts or calls. I get aggravated with him and decide to ignore him too. Two can play that game. Eventually Mr. Perfect will get over being mad and remember people are human and make mistakes. This is hard for him; he is very driven by values and morals and never seems to struggle with doing the right thing. It always seems to come easy for him.

Tuesday morning, I get up before him. He slept in the guest room again. Finn and I have a busy day in the Lake James area and frankly, I can't take anymore of Theo's judgement right now. He will just have to sulk and get over himself at some point. I leave a note on the kitchen island, letting him know my travel plans. I'm still mad so I just sign it "Mindy". Not feeling the mushy feelings today.

Hours later, it seems like an eternity, I'm still waiting to see my newly dead husband. Finn finally makes some headway with the hospital staff, and they allow me to go back to a special room. They have set it up so I can spend a little time with Theo and say goodbye to him. Finn waits just outside the door; in case I collapse or something.

I look at Theo, who has already started turning shades of grey and blue and see nothing of the handsome boy I fell in love with at age 20. Neither do I see my husband of almost 25 years. What I see instead is the Theo's hull. He is gone. I see someone who will be a Covid statistic even though he had a massive heart attack. His death certificate will still say Covid death.

But Theo didn't die of Covid or even a massive heart attack. He was collateral damage, killed by a lying wife who was, and still is keeping the biggest secret of her life. I will never forgive myself for being so petty the last few days or with my obsessive need to be right and have my way. I didn't even tell my husband that I loved him after we fought; even though he is the greatest love in my life. I will always regret that!

Finn comes and gently leads me away. It's time for them to take Theo. Tessa is waiting at home for me to help with what I need and help me prepare for a life without Theo. I've lost nearly everything today to that damn secret. Watch out, Kelly Ryan and Jackson Carmichael. You know what they say, People who have lost everything are willing to do just about anything to even the score.

TESSA

I splurged and booked a suite at the Gaylord Opryland Hotel for a few days. Yes, I lied to Jackson about a meeting with Annie (my editor) and the Twisted Oak owners. I do have that meeting but it's later in the year. Annie scheduled me for a week of compassionate leave to deal with the Kelly mess. It was good timing, if death can ever be considered good timing? Past early summer until right before Halloween, we usually hit a publishing lull. That and the fact we are very short-staffed, and I have been regularly putting in close to twelve hours, sometimes seven days a week. I think she senses a coming burnout and is trying to head that off. Do more with less- it seems to be everyone's motto these days.

Originally, I planned to stay at Meadowview and give Kate a break with Jason. The construction crew at Honeywood is on a two-week break and our dogs are boarded at our favorite kennel for nine days. Somehow I stupidly thought that maybe Jackson and I could spend a few days together reconnecting. But now, spending time with Jackson is the very last thing I want to do.

Between Jackson's apathy and the crazy scene with Mindy and Kate, I had to leave there. Big Ed's farm has always been a hard place for me with all of its residual energy. Add in Kelly's death, memorial service and Mindy's truth bombshell and you have all the mixings for an Irish car bomb. It is too much for me! More importantly, I couldn't stay any longer in the same place with Kelly's killer. Someone at that memorial service had something to do with Kelly's death.

I have to take a few days to clear my head and sort out what was real and maybe what my own emotions conjured? What are facts and what are my own biased opinions? I know just the person to help me do that; Trent James, my long-time Auburn newspaper friend. He is now an award winning celebrity journalist. Thankfully for me, he is home-based in Nashville and will happily grab supper with me to catch up with each other.

Trent James, I've known him almost as long as Jackson. We worked closely together on the Auburn student newspaper and crossed paths often at Sig Ep events. He took the overseas internship, I turned down and the rest is history. Trent has done super well for himself, and any success is well deserved. He is one of the best feature journalists out there. It doesn't hurt that the camera loves him, and he is just as comfortable in front of the camera making video documentaries as he is writing award winning *Rolling Stone* articles. He just signed a deal with Netflix to write and star in a limited mini-series on homeless Afghanistan war veterans.

I don't know Trent the celebrity, I haven't met him yet. I know Trent the friend who has supported me and offered good advice for many years. In the early years, he would come to our famous summer gatherings at Storybook whenever he was in town. The more success- ful he became and the higher his star rose, the less I saw him.

For some reason, Jackson can't stand him. I don't exactly know why. But I think it's some long standing slight that goes way back to their fraternity days. Jackson has never said I shouldn't be friends with Trent, but I know he'd rather I wasn't. I've tried finding out the reason but neither one will say. So I just ignore their behavior and let it be. Trent is devilishly handsome with his sandy brown, long wavy hair and green eyes. He has a strong jaw, good height and a soldier's athletic build. He could easily be an actor, if he chose that career path. It's not jealousy between he and Jackson, they are both handsome and successful. I think it has something to do with Kelly- but what doesn't anymore?

Trent has a brilliant mind and his deductive reasoning is off the charts. He knows all the characters in the Kelly saga well. Even though he ran in different social circles, he still spent time with all of us. He has at least passing knowledge of Poppy Hawthorne Ryan and has interviewed General Ryan multiple times through the years.

I'm excited and a little nervous to see my old friend. It's been a few years since we've been together. The *girly* girl in me wonders how different I will look to him now. I know, that's completely ridiculous. But I am getting to the age that I'm sensitive about looking *old* even though that's sexist and stupid.

He offered to take me anyplace in Nashville. He has enough status he can now get in anywhere, anytime. There are some great places I would love to try out. I actually have a list on my phone somewhere. I've been hoping Jackson would be home long enough that we could do a Nashville weekend together. Well, that's not happening anytime soon. But I just don't feel right doing the town with Trent. As a semi-famous person, Trent is photographed all the time now. The very last thing I need is a photo floating out in the world of me having a good time with one of Jackson's sworn enemies. That wouldn't help our relationship at all.

I counter with an offer of *eat in* just like we used to do in our young newspaper days. Besides, a noisy restaurant with interruptions for autograph signing will not allow me to pick Trent's brain over my current puzzle. He thinks it's a great idea and offers to bring take out from Nashville's best Asian fusion restaurant. Crisis averted!

I dress carefully for my very casual supper with Trent. Not too much, but a lot of prep to make it look like I just tossed on a linen flowy tunic and wide leg pants in purple (my signature color). Some small classic jewelry, hair back in a headband and lots of makeup, expertly applied to get the no makeup look and I'm done- an hour later. And yes, I do look in the mirror and roll my eyes that I am trying too hard.

Right on time, the room doorbell chimes. I look in the peephole and see Trent standing there in all his gorgeous glory. He has hardly aged. He is holding two large take out bags. How many people are we feeding? I let him in, take one of the bags and give him a giant hug. I've missed my friend so much.

We head to the living room area. I have already set up our table and open the French doors looking out over the small balcony and atrium. It is always so prettily lit up at night. Trent reaches in to give me another hug. A small part of me does not want to let him go.

"You look great Tessa, haven't changed a bit," he says sitting down and pouring two glasses of the expensive white wine he brought.

"And you, my old friend are still a terrible liar." I laugh and take a small sip of the wine. It is exquisite, like tasting Heaven if that's even possible.

"Well my famous friend, I am honored and a little surprised you have time to fit me in your schedule on such short notice. You've made my week and I'm very appreciative!"

"When I got your message, I was so happy to hear from you and more than a little intrigued by your need for my help. You were so cryptic on the phone. And I've been meaning to get down to Honeywood to visit you. The place sounds wonderful and I have really missed you. But all I do is work anymore. No time for any fun," he says running a hand through that beautiful hair of his. Jackson is very lucky I take my wedding vows seriously. Right now looking at Trent, I can see why he is so popular with female viewers and gets unsolicited marriage offers.

I laugh, mentally slap myself and refocus on the real purpose of our visit. "Trent, I am so incredibly happy for you and so very proud of all your success. It could not happen to a better person," I say, raising my glass in a toast to him.

He blushes a little which only makes him that much more charming. He grabs my hand. "Tessa, any success I have, I owe it all to you. That *Stars And Stripes* internship cemented my future. You giving it up and making sure I got a quality recommendation; it changed my life."

"Trent, **you** changed your life. You've worked hard for everything you've gotten. You would've been super successful even without that opportunity," I tell him. "Besides, how do you know about the recommendation? That was a secret. Did Big Ed tell you? That man should know how to keep a secret better, he's had years of experience doing just that," I say shaking my head and laughing a little.

"Yeah well, anyway. Let's dig in before this all gets cold. I didn't know what you wanted so I got a little of everything. I hope you like it," he opens containers and starts serving my plate. It's such a sweet gesture that doesn't go unnoticed.

As we eat, drink that delicious wine and catch up on our lives; there is an easiness I haven't felt in a long time. I miss male companionship and intelligent conversations. I used to have that with Jackson. Being here with Trent and picking up right where we left off years ago, makes me miss suppers with Jackson. I can't even remember the last time we sat down and had a nice supper together.

Trent tells me he ran into Afton and her husband Gage at a Nashville gala fundraiser a few months ago. Afton didn't mention this, although she probably didn't realize that Trent and I used to be close friends. He also mentions following Reagan's husband Jonas on Instagram. Jonas is an adventure blogger and is apparently quite popular on social media. Trent generously offers to connect Jonas with adventure oriented national sponsors. Trent moves in big circles now; everyone wants a piece of him. I message him Jonas' contact info. Jonas will be absolutely thrilled.

We small talk some more about his work (mostly) and a little about mine at the publishing house. He encourages me to think about moving beyond Twisted Oak and not continue wasting my talents there. Funny, in the past two years, I've had exactly the same thoughts. My friend knows me so well.

I get up, clear the supper dishes and get my notebook. I've been making notes since Kelly's death trying to collect my thoughts. Over a chocolate cheesecake to die for and a bottle of Dom Perignon that I took to Indiana to share with Jackson; we work out the details of Kelly's death. It reminds me so much of our late-night sessions at the *Plainsman* trying to get the latest edition to print on time.

"Okay, I do feel a little guilty dragging you into the Kelly mess. I need help though trying to figure out if I'm onto something. Or is it just all our emotional baggage and years of dealing with Kelly? Maybe Jackson is right and my imagination is working in hyperdrive right now? I don't know. Help me please!" I look at him helplessly.

He pulls out his reading glasses, puts them on and starts rearranging my notes, marking on them in the margins. He takes a few minutes reading and absorbing them. You can see the wheels turning in his mind. He leans back in his chair, takes a sip of the champagne and picks up one of my scribbled note pages. "No, no you are not crazy

Tessa Donovan. The facts do potentially point to foul play in Kelly's death," he says, looking at the notes again. It does not go unnoticed that he addresses me by my Auburn byline "Tessa Donovan". In college, I was Tessa Donovan Turner. I shortened my byline for the newspaper because our sports guy was named Turner too. It cut down on confusion for the newspaper staff.

"What makes you think this is a homicide and not just a freakish accident? Do you have any sixth sense feelings about it – or does its just seem off"?

I take a long drink from my ice water. This explanation is going to take a bit. Trent is patient and knows me well. He knows I tell roundabout stories, so he just waits me out. "Okay, a little of both. The facts don't really line up with Kelly's more recent behavior. Well the nanny does, but we can address that separately. And yes, when I was at the memorial service- I got a **strong** feeling that someone there was hiding something about Kelly's death. That is a little more complex because the level and number of emotions on that day were intense."

I look at him for confirmation. He is following along, so I continue. "According to Poppy and all other reports, Kelly had quit drinking, two reasons probably. (1) his life worked better when he didn't and (2) I'm fairly sure AA was a real major sticking point for Poppy. I heard rumors that it is part of their pre-nup agreement. He goes back to drinking..."

"He loses everything, the supermodel, access to millions, and more prestige than even the Ryan name brings him," he finishes for me. Trent is fast, this is precisely why I need his help.

"Yep, exactly. Why would he be willing to give up all of that over some cocktails? Something happened that put Kelly over the edge, or someone intentionally tempted Kelly into drinking again. The question is who or what caused this falling off the wagon?"

I go on, "Why was Kelly driving the nanny and where was she going? The Hawthorne-Ryan family has chauffeurs available around the clock. Why was the nanny still at the mansion? Poppy took the twins on her trip and didn't require the nanny to go along. If the nanny had a trip scheduled (1) Poppy would know about it and (2) wouldn't the nanny have left as soon as Poppy did to maximize all her free time?"

Trent is watching me and taking it all in. "The third thing that troubles me is the luggage issue. Why did Kelly and the very young, attractive nanny both have luggage? Only the nanny was supposedly going on a trip. Then Kelly apparently told the house manager that he might head out and surprise his dad at the farm. Only, Big Ed had just seen Kelly the week before. Why would he fly out to the farm? Big Ed and Kelly worked together and could see each other anytime they wanted- if their schedules lined up."

"So, I hear you saying the nanny had a trip lined up that no one seemed to know about, and Kelly scheduled an impromptu trip to see his dad that he had just seen. Sounds like Kelly and the nanny were up to something while superhot mama and little bear cubs were away," he says, with a smirk on his face.

"Exactly, even though I probably wouldn't have put it exactly like that, but yes. It does appear that Kelly was at least up to some of his old behavior. But was it an impromptu hook up thing or something more long-term? I'm sure that famous pre-nup also includes clauses about infidelity, etc."

"Yep, keep the zipper zipped Kelly, or lose everything" Trent says.

"Um, something like that. Why risk everything over a fling when you are married to a supermodel that sweats money? It doesn't make sense. Except, maybe it does. I don't know how much you really interacted with Kelly or knew of his *ladies' man* reputation in college."

"You mean creepy Kel?" He laughs. "Yeah, I overheard you and Mindy talking about it once. Fits him perfectly. Everyone also knew about the warning posters plastered in the sorority houses" he tells me. I am a little surprised his fraternity brothers knew what girls called him. Then again, maybe not, Greek life is a small society and rumors travel fast.

"Yes, Kelly had quite a reputation back then. He seemed to settle down though with Poppy and leave that bad behavior behind either out of love for Poppy or love of money. I don't know which. So, I guess the nanny angle surprises me a bit."

"What about the nanny's family? Are they still planning to sue Poppy for wrongful death?"

"I'm not sure. I overheard Jackson, Big Ed and Hawthorne talking about it being "handled". Whatever that means. But with both big guns involved, I think it will go away. But I'm just not sure. They were very careful with their talk there. Considering the occasion, it makes sense." I tell him, now wondering what they really did talk about out at the horse barn. Finn was there and I can always ask him.

"So, what does your journalistic gut tell you?" Trent asks.

"Truthfully, I think there's something more to the story. Minimally, Kelly was suddenly doing a lot of crap that he hadn't been as far as anyone close to him knows about. I think that's the main reason Big Ed and Hawthorne have really tried to squash the story and make it go away. Even though that plan is not working well. I saw a short clip on TMZ that looked really incriminating for Kelly."

"Once the trash outlets get ahold of a story; it usually grows legs, as you know. There's no doubt Kelly was doing all the wrong things, but the question is why? Switching gears, what does your superpower tell you?" he looks at me and winks. Dear lord, women have sold their souls for less than that little gesture. This man oozes charm.

"My **gift**," I say seriously, "you know, that's all over the place. It's not always reliable with people. Ed's farm has so much stored energy that I'm not sure if what I experienced was in current time or something lingering from the past. I really don't know," I tell him. Truthfully, I am confused by it.

"Tessa, I trust you and your instincts- both the journalistic and the *woo-woo* ones. What is your *gift* showing you? Trust yourself."

I hesitate a bit before answering, "I think there is good reason to believe that at least one person and maybe more, wanted Kelly dead. Mindy shocked Kate and me with some information about Kelly that blew me away. I'm still processing it. I can't tell you right now-even though I trust you. But I will say, she's still not telling the truth. She's not telling everything. That I do know."

"Wait, is this about the boathouse fire? You always had a lot of unresolved questions about that."

"It is and after all these years at Kelly's memorial service; I find out that people I love and trust have been lying to me. It's not so much what they said, it's what they left unsaid. In the middle of all that grief, in unguarded moments, I felt a lot of dishonesty beneath the surface, from multiple people. It's very upsetting to find out people closest to you have been keeping so many secrets that you had no idea about."

I've said more than I intended. I trust Trent, he's always acted in my best interest. He is level headed, reasonable and like me is a *truth seeker*, whatever those truths may bring. He knows some about the fire, and at least a little about Kelly's past. I'm hoping his voice of reason and clear head will be exactly what I need to fill in the gaps of the fire summer and solve a murder case- Kelly's murder.

"Wow, that's a lot to think about. I'm heading out to California in two days to finalize talks with Netflix folks. Let me think a few days. Do you mind if I take your notes with me? When I'm done there, I'll come to Honeywood or meet you here and we'll come up with a plan. Do you mind if I reach out while I'm in California? Two things, (1) I think we have a mystery to solve and (2) I want you to be very, very careful and not say the murder word to anyone. Not even to Jackson, okay? Kelly was connected to some well-known high-power people who know people. You know Hawthorne is connected to Anthony Marconi, even though they both deny it" he says in a serious tone.

My eyes get big. "Anthony Marconi, New York Mafia?" I ask.

"The same, see what I mean. Jackson's boss Martin Land has been making public connections with powerful high rollers. General Ryan is a powerful man. Hawthorne owns the communications technology world and has connections with the New York mafia. You don't want to play with these people or get on the wrong side of them. You promise, Tessa?"

"Yes," I squeak.

We say our goodbyes and I walk him to the door. He hugs me tightly and kisses the top of my head. It would be so easy, to entice Trent to stay and let happen what will. We have always had an undercurrent attraction to each other. No, I will not, no matter how lonely I'm feeling right now. Trent has always been a good friend to me. In the current situation, I need all friends in my corner.

I close the door wondering if I just imagined this whole day. Supper with the very charming Trent James, intelligent conversation and one of the biggest mysteries of my life to solve. I just didn't count on mafia connections, power hungry men, infidelity, and whatever other craziness Kelly Ryan may have brought into his life. Hopefully, I have not opened Pandora's box, but it's done now. There is always a chance that Trent will pursue the story on his own, with or without my permission. I guess I really didn't stop to think that solving the mystery of Kelly's death might mean implicating someone I know, maybe even my husband. Am I prepared to go that far for Kelly who did nothing but cause his friends and family misery and pain?

The next day, I check out of my suite at Opryland and meet Annie for lunch. I don't come into the city often, so it's nice to spend time with Annie that's not in a meeting setting. She has been a wonderful mentor and friend for years. It makes me sad to think that one day soon, I will be leaving her. It's time for a career change and that's not a matter of if, but when.

We eat at a sweet little bistro in Brentwood, Annie's favorite. I really think of this place as the original, southern take on Panera's – lots of soups, sandwiches and light fare but with a southern twist. It's very popular with the locals, but Annie has a standing reservation here. It's her favorite *get out of the office* place, and she brings many author clients here too. She has a thing for sweet potato biscuits and collard salad, which is a lot better than it sounds.

We make an unusual pair, Annie and me. She is tall, willowy, and ebony with long hair that she usually keeps coiled around her head. She carries herself regally. Then there's me, the shorter, full figured, pale faced brown eyed girl who's always somewhere else in her mind. Our backgrounds are also vastly different . Annie grew up in South-side Chicago, with dreams of going to college and getting out of the cesspool. After college, she moved around a lot working for many of the major newspapers in the Northeast and Midwest hoping that someone would take a chance on an African American female editor.

Eventually on a visit to some cousins in Nashville, Annie saw an advertisement looking for copy editors for a new regional publishing house. On a whim, she applied, got hired and worked her way up to Senior Editor. I love her spirit and determination so much! She inspires me.

"So, what's new with you, Ms. I Never Slum In The Home Office Anymore. Other than the whole Kelly mess- of course," she asks stirring her hot green tea.

"Yes, I know you are dying to know all the details about Kelly's memorial. I will share the little that I can, in a minute. But guess who I had supper with this week?"

"Who, who? You better tell me right now and don't beat around the bush with one of your long winded stories," she says her eyes twinkling.

"Trent James, super attractive celebrity journalist."

"No, you did not. Girl why are you kidding me like that?" she says playfully slapping my hand on the table.

"Yep, at the Opryland Hotel," I say winking at her.

"Hotel? Tessa ,Honey, are you sure you sure even be telling me this? It sounds scandalous."

"Ha, no not that kind of supper. I was in town and haven't seen him in a while, so I called and asked him to supper. We didn't go out cause he's famous now, and people snap his picture everywhere. And Jackson kinda hates him, so not a good idea to pick up a newspaper and see your wife out with a guy you don't like. No matter how innocent it might be."

"Yes," she says nodding . "I see your point. The last July 4th party at Storybook that Trent James showed up for; Jackson was a very unhappy man."

"See, I knew I wasn't imaging that and neither will admit the truth. So, I don't know. But I do know he is just as gorgeous as ever, oh my Lord", I say, fanning myself and we both burst out laughing.

"That sure is one handsome friend you have there. Lucky girl! So, spill the tea on Kelly Ryan." Annie being a former investigative reporter is not one to let a good story get by her.

"Ok, so because of the non-disclosure agreement, I really can't say much. I'm kidding, not much, but I am kidding. It was small, weird, kind of crazy, I don't know surreal, I guess" I say, wondering if anything I said makes sense.

"Poppy Hawthorne Ryan is one of the most ridiculously beautiful, most put together, kindest people I have ever met. I hate her! No I don't, but you sure could if she wasn't just so sincerely nice. She and the twins are coming to Honeywood when more of the renovations are done," I tell her wondering how weird this sounds.

"So, Kate and Poppy- was there a catfight or some high drama, anything?"

"You will NOT believe this. I think Kate and Poppy are actually friends. With Kelly gone, I think they could be good friends. Can you imagine that?"

Annie shakes her head in disbelief. "So do tell what the supermodel was wearing out in the middle of the midwestern cornfields."

"Were you there? How did you know? She had on the most perfectly inappropriate Katherine Hepburn inspired outfit. It was so beautiful, a black silk dress, long black gloves, pearls, sky high Manolo Blahniks, glam dark sunglasses and a black hat that shaded half of Indiana. No kidding, she looked straight out of the pages of a photo shoot. Her makeup was flawless and her manners, impeccable" I tell her, still holding the visual of Poppy that day fresh in my mind. I will never forget it.

"That Kelly was one lucky dude," Annie says sipping her now cold tea.

"Until he wasn't," I immediately fire back. We can't talk more about the memorial service because I am trying to be respectful of Big Ed and Poppy. I also cannot say much more because Annie is very perceptive and might pick up on my uneasiness about the whole affair. I also remember Trent's warning. So, I let it drop.

We chat on a little bit longer, talking about the latest office gossip. I make her promise to come out and spend a weekend with me at Honeywood or out at the lake in the fall, when the leaves turn. We hug, wave goodbye and go our separate ways.

I check my phone. I have two missed calls from Finn. A missed call from a number I don't recognize, text messages from Afton and Reagan. I have appointment reminders, sales notifications but nothing from Jackson. I'm going to have to deal with that eventually. I also have to figure out the best way to reach out to Mindy and Kate. We left on such unsettled terms.

I guess I will start first with Finn . He is insistent that he needs to see me soon. We plan lunch for tomorrow. This gives me a chance to get home and resettle the dogs before he comes. I wonder what could be so important? He has been pestering me for a while now. I hope everything is okay with him.

It will be nice to spend a Wednesday afternoon not in the editing grind. Just hanging out with my favorite cousin Finn, who is more like my little brother. He is perfectly on time, unlike Jackson who is always at least ten minutes early for anything. On time is late in Jackson's world. It's a nice day so we decide to have lunch outside by the pool. It's a little overcast so not too hot or humid and there are no infernal banging noises coming from my construction crew. There will be peace and quiet at Honeywood for a few more days.

"Wine with lunch or are you working this afternoon." I offer.

"Yes please, red. I'm meeting Aunt Claire to do a walk-through on a property and then heading home."

By home, he means my childhood home. He rents our house in Lake James since Mom and Dad got a wild whim and moved to Boca Raton last year. They weren't sure they would stay, so Finn offered to rent and keep up the house for them while they were away.

"I know little Finn, it hasn't been that long. You only like red wine preferably a Cabernet. You know that's the only reason I keep that stuff in the wine cellar," I tease him. He hates when I call him Little Finn.

We eat our fancy salads and artisan bread, talking about nothing important. The weather, Southerners always have to talk about the weather. Our relatives, Finn's parents are thinking about moving to Florida too. I predict our parents would be back home in a year. We talk about the upcoming Auburn football season. Lately, there hasn't been too much to get excited about there. He asks about plans for a Labor Day get-together at Storybook. That's news to me- must be Jackson's idea. Then finally, he gets to the point.

"You know, I've been trying to talk to you for awhile now and you keep avoiding me."

"Well, next time Kelly can schedule his death at a more convenient time. How does that sound?" I say this in a snarkier tone than I mean.

"Tessa, you have no social graces anymore. It's all this living so isolated," he says throwing his napkin on the table and draining the rest of his wine glass. "I have something important to discuss with you, okay? Let's check the flippant attitude for a bit."

I listen to him, he being testy with me is unusual. We joke, kid around and pick at each other all the time. But this is different. Oh no, what is wrong?

"Jackson asked me to Kelly's memorial to discuss business. I thought it was strange timing being invited to Big Ed's farm. I wasn't close to Kelly. Hell, I was his replacement after he and Kate divorced."

This is true, once the Invincible Six parted ways, Finn became the *stand in* for guy activities. He, Jackson and Theo started spending a lot of time together.

"Go on, spit it out," I encourage him.

"It's been no secret that you and Jackson haven't been spending much time together. You never seem to be at the same place at the same time other than Kelly's memorial service. You didn't spend much time together there either. Anyway, Jackson asked me some vague, odd questions about real estate law," Finn looks troubled by this.

"Yes Finn, Jackson and I have hit a little rough spot. It happens in marriages sometimes. We'll figure things out. What do you mean odd questions? On 8th grade reading level please," I laugh, trying to ease the tension in the air.

"He was asking about using property as loan collateral, deed questions, splitting up properties in separation/divorce settlements. Of course, these are all questions he could've emailed me or just Googled himself. But I really don't get why he was asking me this? Is everything okay?"

Is everything okay? I've been asking myself that same question for over a year now. It doesn't feel okay. Life with Jackson hasn't really felt okay in a while. If I'm being honest with myself, it's really been more like eighteen months since I felt we were "okay".

"Define okay? Everything else seems okay. Jackson and Tessa, not so much," I tell him picking up my wine glass and sloshing around the contents. This is a hard admission for me, it's the first time I've said it out loud to anyone other than Jackson.

"I don't know Finn. Jackson is so distant and remote. At first, I thought it was work and all the stress with trying to grow the business, but now, it feels like something else. Do you think he's carrying on with Mindy?" I ask him, sharing my deepest fear.

Finn sputters, and almost chokes on his wine. "What? Are you... No, no I'm not saying he's not involved with someone or thinking in that direction. Look at the questions he asked. But Mindy? No, it's not her, if there even is another **her.** Why would you think that?" he looks at me with the lawyer face on, trying to sort the facts from the emotions.

"They were both giving off some weird vibes at Kelly's memorial. Mindy said something about me needing to pay **close** attention to Jackson. That I had been too caught up in other things and not really noticing him? It was a strange thing for her to say."

"Tessa, I think you are reading this wrong. If, and I mean a BIG if Mindy and Jackson were getting together, do you think she would tell you to watch Jackson closely? That would be the very last thing they would want you to do. Use your mind, and not your heart," he says pouring himself a second, half glass of wine.

He takes a sip and puts his glass down. "This wine is very good by the way. Look, I agree with Mindy on this. Start paying attention to Jackson. Get him home, find out what's going on in that mind of his. Use that famous Donovan gift you have if you need to. Whatever it is, there is a sense of urgency surrounding Jackson. You don't bring a lawyer out to a memorial service to discuss business unless you are getting ready to make some big decisions."

"I know you don't want to hear this. And I don't want to say it. Asking the property questions he did leads to two possible conclusions. Either he wants to use your personal properties as collateral for a large loan or he's thinking of leaving you and trying to figure out what he gets to keep," Finn seems upset telling me this.

"Has Jackson talked about needing big loans for ADT or having any issues in the company."

"A couple years ago, he and Martin were talking about wanting to expand the company and needing a large amount of money to do it. Jackson approached me about selling Storybook or cashing out the rest of Grandmother Esme's trust fund. I told him "no". It was my family's legacy, and I wasn't doing it. We had just bought Honeywood, so we had no real equity there either. You know the huge money sink this Old Girl has been," I tell him smiling and waving my arms around like Vanna White.

"But the company, as far as you know is solid? No major issues?"

"Finn, you know Jackson doesn't talk much to me anymore about ADT stuff. That's his baby, more like his mistress in the past five years. I'm not an owner, so other than supplying cash influxes when he needs them, I'm a non-player in anything to do with ADT," I tell him and I'm a little embarrassed by this.

"That's probably good. Honestly. So,trying to respect your privacy here, but I need to know; who owns Honeywood? Are you still the sole owner of Storybook?"

"This feels like cross examination little brother," I tell him. "Yes, I'm the sole owner of Storybook, just like Esme wanted it. Jackson has tried for years to get me to sell that place. Honeywood is a bit more complicated. Jackson was insistent we buy this place, even though with the company debt and most of our available money going to fund Afton and Reagan's college experiences and weddings; we were not flush with cash. So, Mom and Dad gave us the down-payment for the farm with the stipulation that they were on the deed with me as co-owners."

"I'm surprised Jackson went along with that deal."

"I was too, at the time. He fell in love with the idea of living in this place. My parents gave us the down-payment money and a starter renovation fund as an advance on my inheritance. To save Jackson's pride, they insisted we could buy their share of the house. When ADT took off, we could reimburse them a small portion of the money they fronted for us to buy this place."

"It seemed a strange arrangement to me and I didn't think Jack would go for it. He was stuck on getting this place though. Then he got so engrossed in ADT, spending every moment trying to grow the company quickly. I guess he just forgot about my parents owning half of our home, or he just quit caring about it."

"Bookworm," he calls me by my detested childhood nickname. "That may be one of the smartest things your parents ever did for you."

"I don't understand, what are you saying?"

"Aunt Claire is a living, walking genius. Do you know what this means Tessa? You are independent of any bad decisions that Jackson is thinking about. You have a trust fund, and two valuable properties in your name. And no real tangible connection to ADT. I have no idea what Jackson is up to. It's your job to find out and then when you do protect yourself, Afton, Reagan and those little hellions Chase and Scout. You understand?"

I'm still trying to process what he is saying but underneath it all, I **do** understand. Even though I very much do **not** want to understand. Jackson is possibly having an affair and thinking about leaving me. Or something major is going on with the business, that he's not telling me. Either way, he's keeping secrets that may very well be the end of us.

Finn looks down at his watch, "I need to get going. Take a raincheck on that cheesecake?" he asks.

"Oh, before I forget. Is everything okay with you, Min and Kate? I walked into something intense at Big Ed's farm. I called Kate to check on her and Jason and she was very tight lipped about why you left so early. Care to share?"

"No, love you but no I do not. You are worse than gossiping old women, Finn. I may be able tell you someday, but not now. Trust me, we are not okay, right now. But we will be," I tell him hoping this is true.

I pack up most of the cheesecake to send home with him. I walk him to his car, the sporty red Corvette that is his one vice. He leans down and kisses the top of my head. "It's all going to be okay, Bookworm, I promise. Get Jackson home and let's figure this out," he says and gets in his car throwing up a wave out of the window as he carefully drives down our gravel potholed, tree canopied driveway.

Well, that lunch date didn't go as planned. What am I going to do? Have I really been burying my head in the sand like Mindy has suggested? Have I missed the signs of Jackson's restlessness? It's hard to tell when you just don't see someone. You can't pick up on body language clues or tone of voice, when that person isn't around. Did I make it too easy for him to stay away from home, and get involved in whatever he's doing? Maybe, I made the mistake of being too comfortable and taking our relationship too much for granted. Yes, I need to have a difficult face-to-face conversation with Jackson. I dread it more than anything in this world.

Later, I finally sit down for a few minutes with my laptop. I'm so used to my work routine I really don't know what to do with free time anymore. Work has filled the lonely void and without it, I feel a little lost.

I open Gmail, the one I use for junk stuff. There are over 100 messages here. I rarely check this account. Scrolling through, I delete a lot, probably don't have time to read through all of them encouraging me to buy something I neither want nor need. Two messages catch my attention. One is from a local bank First Federal, (we don't bank there) and the second is from a large national lending company. Both have loan application documents attached, encouraging me to complete the loan process so home appraisal appointments can be scheduled. We aren't borrowing any money; and certainly not using either home as collateral for anything.

I call both companies, and confirm that yes, loan applications have been started by my spouse Jackson Carmichael and as the owner of properties offered for collateral, I need to cosign. Like hell I will. Jackson, what in the world have you gotten yourself into? Why didn't he talk to me at the memorial service? It was important enough to bring Finn in to ask abstract questions but not important enough to tell his wife, who owns these properties? I feel a red-hot anger creeping up my body. This is an unusual thing for me. It's usually other people's anger I feel.

Oh Jackson, we need to have a serious conversation sooner rather than later. I pick up my phone to text him, trying to tamp down the anger and send a tactful, friendly message. My phone rings, it's Mindy.

"Hey, there you are. You busy?" she asks.

"No, no, not really," I tell her even though in my mind, I'm plotting possible ways to murder my husband and get away with it.

"You left so fast, and we didn't get a chance to talk. I just wanted to make sure, you're okay?"

"I'm fine Mindy," I tell her, even though I'm not fine. Not fine about the way we left things, not fine about whatever is going on with my secretive husband. But I say what is expected of me.

"Listen, I know that whole thing at Meadowview was too much for you. Kelly, the memorial service, just being there, me losing my mind. Are you sure you are okay?" she asks a second time.

I pause before I answer her, not wanting to burden her but not wanting to lie either. "No Mindy, I'm not okay. That was intense- I had to get away from it all. I will be okay though. I'm feeling better, being at home. Annie gave me some time off (bless her), so I can recharge."

"Are **you** okay? That was quite the revelation you dropped on Kate and me. Especially after all this time."

"Yes, no, I don't know. The timing was terrible; I know. But you know me, never let a dramatic moment go to waste," she laughs a little trying to cover the seriousness of the moment.

"Listen, that's what I want to talk to you about. Can I visit? You up for company right now? There's something I need to tell you in person. Could we meet at Storybook?" she asks. I'm surprised at the location and instantly I'm overwhelmed with a sense of dread, but I agree. Better to face this head-on and get it over with.

"This weekend? You have any plans? We could do lunch on the deck, maybe watch the sunset together? How does that sound?" she doesn't give me a chance to say no.

"Okay, I'll plan a picnic menu. Will you want to spend the night or head back to Clearview? There's plenty of room if you want to stay?" I tell her even though I am not overly excited about sleeping over at Storybook. Ever since the fire summer, I haven't stayed out at the cottage overnight by myself again.

"No, don't go to any extra trouble for me. Let's have lunch and take it from there. I have some great food gifts from grateful clients that I've been waiting to share with someone. We will have the feast of feasts and enjoy the day together," she tells me, keeping her tone light and friendly. Hopefully this means no more terrible bad news. I don't think I can deal with that right now.

We plan to meet at noon on Saturday. We say goodbye and hang up. I forgot to ask how long she stayed at Meadowview. Or how Kate, Jason and Ed are doing? I've been so caught up in my own crazy headspace, I really haven't thought of anyone else this week. I also ignore the thought of Jackson and Mindy possibly spending the week together. No, "*next thought*" I just can't go there, not yet.

My mind spirals in many different directions. It's going so fast; I can't seem to slow down any of my thoughts. What does Mindy have to tell me, on top of the fire summer confession? Is there more to the story- yes, I believe there is. Why now? Is she involved with Jackson and finally feels guilty enough to come clean? Or does she know what else might be going with him? They seem so close these days. I hope, hope, hope, she is coming to tell me some good news. I keep telling myself that but I know I'm just kidding myself.

MINDY

Well, the Mindy *truth* tour is coming to an end. After Tessa abruptly left Meadowview and me shooting off my mouth at the very most inappropriate time; I felt obligated to stay and try to fix what I had done to Kate. It's something I should've done a long time ago, way before the boathouse fire. If I had just listened to Tessa right after we met Kate, maybe we could've all been spared a lifetime of pain known as Kelly Ryan.

Dumping this on Kate just after Kelly's death, and after all these years is pretty crappy. Sometimes though, you have just got to yank off the band-aid, feel immediate pain and move the hell on. There's no easy, gentle way to tell your best friend that her husband raped you and you kept it from her, all this time. Rape, what an ugly, violent word. It's that thing that always happens to someone else. You know those who knew better, who were sexually teasing someone, who were maybe asking for it. Yeah, those women, it's never us. We don't like to say the word because women are afraid that speaking it out loud, either brings it to your door or is somehow shameful.

I don't know why now, of all times, the secret reveals itself. Except maybe, I just somehow got tired of protecting Kelly. Yes, protecting the rapist- how sick is that? I didn't care about Kelly Ryan. I loved everyone else enough to keep a secret that let a rapist go free. Who was

I really protecting? Myself, our loved ones? In the end-I only ended up protecting Kelly. The guy who deserved to rot in Hell for what he did to me, that sweet little babysitter, his soldier Melissa and only God knows how many other women that he might've hurt.

Kate didn't want to hear what I had to say. Who can blame her? It's not every day you hear that your former husband was acting inappropriately with a 15-year-old child, raped your best friend and started a fire all while so drunk, he could barely stand upright. This happened while she and her son were in the same place, celebrating. I spared her details of that night even though they play on a continual loop in my dreams. Just the knowledge that it happened is enough to permanently hurt her.

I was more or less, expecting her reaction. I was blown away by her own confession that Kelly had sexually abused her for most of their marriage. It got worse after the fire summer. This, I was not prepared to hear. All these years, we thought we were protecting Kate, and damn if we didn't abandon her right into the monster's arms. I feel so sick at this news, I can't stand it. She also tells me the real reason she finally left Kelly. She walked out the day Kelly turned his abusive rage on Jason. I have such a hard time processing all this. For the first time, in a long time, I wanted a drink, multiple drinks. In fact, I wanted to drown in vodka. But I knew taking that first drink would be my undoing and there would be no coming back.

Now on to the second stop on the *truth* tour. This one is even worse, if that's possible. The last one was awful. I hate being me right now! Tessa deserves to know the truth and I still have to tell her about Jackson. I don't know which revelation is going to hurt her the most. After today, she will never be the same.

I meet her at Storybook Cottage around noon. I know she's wondering why here? Storybook is central to the bad news I'm bringing her, and she needs to face this directly. She's been avoiding spending much time out here because of the fire, and everything after. But she needs to address her fears and stomp them, so they don't consume her. I don't know any easy way to do this, and I hate myself for what I'm about to do to my best friend.

I show up late, as usual, with arms loaded full of food gifts. In the trunk, I have some small gifts for her and the little boy tornadoes that I don't see nearly enough. I knew Afton and the boys were coming to Honeywood soon for an overdue visit.

Tessa has the deck set up for lunch. The lakeside deck is one of my favorite places. This house has a *money* view of the lake. One of the best, in my opinion. We spread out the feast. It's eclectic, but so yummy. I've put this off about as long as I can. I hate this SO much!

"I'm sorry for springing the boathouse truth on you and Kate the way I did. That was not well planned out, at all," I say, making big eyes at her.

"It's okay, Mindy. Sometimes, things just need to come out. You don't always control the perfect situation for how that happens. It was probably a relief for you to finally share that," Tessa says, in a forgiving voice. Why do I suddenly feel like I'm in a therapy session?

"Yes, and no. You probably know and just didn't say, I didn't tell y'all everything that day. I couldn't do it. That's why I'm here today. To check on you, of course. But I need to come clean with all of it. I've already told Kate and now you need to know what really happened that day."

She waits patiently, her face is unreadable. I wonder how much Tessa may have already guessed or maybe her sixth sense had already filled in the gaps. She will hear the rest, as much as I can possibly bear to tell her.

"You were right again." I shrug my shoulders and roll my eyes. "There was a lot more that happened before the fire. Afterward, it so chaotic and I couldn't think. Then it just got easier to try and forget. But you kept bringing it up and trying to get me to fill in the blanks. You knew, mine, Jackson's and Kelly's stories weren't lining up. I regret every single day of my life not listening to you. Not respecting your gift, or trusting you. You ,Tessa, were our moral compass and we did not listen to you. Can you forgive me?"

Tessa looks at me and reaches out her hands to take mine. She is puzzled and has no idea what I am about to dump on her.

"I went in the boathouse to get lanterns to set up for our fireworks watching area. Caroline was in the boathouse and so was Kelly. He had her pinned up against the storage cabinet, it was a little dark in there. I couldn't see what he was doing, I called her name. It startled Kelly enough that he backed away from her, and she ran out of there. Tessa, you should've seen her face. She was terrified," I tell her, shuddering a bit, reliving that scene in my mind. I still can't get that little girl's scared face out of my memories.

"Mindy, are you sure you want to talk about this?"

"No, I am not," I say dabbing at the small tears at the corners of my eyes. "But I have to. I cannot let that monster win anymore."

I compose myself and continue. "Kelly was drunk, drunker than I thought. You know me, I made some sarcastic comment, about her being too young for him, typical thing I would say."

"I walked over to the cabinet to get the lanterns. I had my back turned to Kelly. I had forgotten he was there. Thought he was embarrassed and slipped out the door, hoping no one would notice him. Then I felt pain in the back of my head. He hit me with something. I don't know what. He spun me and hit me several times across the face. I fell down," I'm having a hard time telling her this, my heart is thumping so fast.

"I was so shocked; I didn't think to fight him immediately. I just kept saying his name thinking he would snap out of his drunken stupor and leave me alone. And then" I have to take a very deep breath to calm myself enough to get the words out. "He raped me, Tessa. When I came back into my right mind, I fought him with everything I had. I got him off of me enough to try and run for the door. Kelly was faster than me. He blocked the door. An oil lantern overturned in our scuffle."

Tessa is staring at me intently, waiting to hear the end, even though I know she truly did not want to.

"Kelly lit one of the matches I brought and threw it on the oil. I screamed and begged him to let me out. He didn't listen. No one could hear us. Everyone was up by the house and the band was playing loudly. He hit me again, hard in the stomach. It brought me to my knees. I don't know exactly what happened next except I think Kelly was dousing the room in oil and setting more fires. I don't know if he meant to burn us both up or just me. The smoke was starting to get bad. I thought I was going to die in there, Tessa. I was so scared."

"Do you remember what happened next?" she asks amazingly calm considering what I just told her.

"Not really, someone grabbed me and carried me out of the boathouse. I remember wondering where Kelly was. I think it was Finn that took me up to the house. I don't really remember anything more. It was so crazy and chaotic, and the burns were hurting something awful."

I can see the wheels turning in her head. My dear sweet Tessa, she's so transparent. "Where was Jackson and Kelly? Did you see them after Finn got to you?" she asks.

"I don't know, really. That's all mostly a blur. I thought Jackson took me from the boathouse. I remember him being so angry with Kelly. Kelly was so drunk; he couldn't stand up. I believe Jackson was beating him and saying terrible things to him. I was laying on the ground, Jackson leaned down and told me not to tell anyone what happened in the boathouse. He would take care of it. I didn't know what he meant, exactly. I was so shocked out of my mind, and in pain with the burns. I thought maybe I had imagined the whole thing. I couldn't make sense of anything, so I did what he said," I tell her not feeling any better that I had finally told the truth. It did not set me free.

Tessa comes around the table and wraps me in a hug. I am now shaking so hard that we are both trembling. She just continues to hold me until the shaking stops.

"I am so very, very sorry, oh my lord Mindy. What terrible pain you have carried for so long. If I had any idea, I would've brought Kelly Ryan to his knees a long time ago," she is so angry right now.

"I know."

"Does Kate know everything?" she asks me with a heavy sigh.

"No," I say quietly. "I only told her the bare minimum. Conveniently left out the part about her husband trying to kill me," I laugh sarcastically.

"But Jackson, did he know? Why did he protect Kelly?" She's so confused.

"Sweetie, I don't know. He saw the blood; he knew Kelly hit me. The rape, he may have guessed. He knew something had happened with Caroline. Kelly locking us in the boathouse, no he didn't know that part."

"I don't know why any of us gave Kelly the benefit of the doubt. Except that maybe exposing him would tear us all apart. Telling the truth might send our friend to prison. Maybe we stupidly thought that when he hurt one of his own, it was enough of a wakeup call to get help?"

"Instead, we sent the monster home with Kate and Jason," she says after having the lightbulb moment.

"Tessa, we did that a long time ago, back in college, Kate, said I could share with you if I wanted to, but she doesn't want to talk about it ever again. After the fire that summer, Kelly started abusing her. She finally left Kelly after he hit Jason. For years, he threatened to take Jason away, if she left him," saying this out loud makes me want to vomit.

Tessa walks over and picks out a deck chair and slings it across the deck yelling "Damn it, I knew that was going on. That worthless excuse of a man." I've never seen Tessa react like this; she is scary looking right now.

She calms herself and sits back down by me. "Why, Mindy, why? Why didn't she tell someone? Us, her parents, Big Ed, my mom, or someone at work?"

"The same reason none of us tell. The shame of it. She believed Kelly meant what he said. For years, she's watched him use his family name to get out of all sorts of trouble. How would this be any different? Except she had everything to lose."

"I hate the very day; I heard the name Kelly Bradley Ryan and saw his awful face. I should've broken up with Jackson, if he wouldn't drop Kelly. I never understood why guys protected him through the years. Damn that "bro code" and look the other way crap," Tessa's outburst is so unlike her. I get it though, years of pent-up Kelly problems. He changed every single one of us, and not in good ways.

"Well, let's put that on the back burner for a while. Kelly problems never seem to go away. There's something else we need to talk about and it's not good either. But this problem is more up-close and per-sonal, and we need to handle it immediately," I tell her and silently ask Jesus to give me the courage to break my best friend's heart in order to save her.

Tessa takes a big drink from her wine glass. "Do I even want to hear this? What could possibly be worse than Kelly?"

"No, but it must be done. There's something about Jackson that you need to know. Jackson is ..." I hesitate trying to find the right words, they aren't there so I just say the very thing my best friend would never want to hear.

"Jackson called me about a month ago, told me he was out here. Asked if I could meet him one afternoon, he had some questions about the house, and he needed my advice. Sure, I said yes. Thought maybe he was going to surprise you with some renovations or some-thing. I met him, we talked about the house. Then he started asking money questions about the house. The appraisal value, a good selling price, real estate market questions. I thought it was weird, but maybe you had decided to sell again. I know you have been uncomfortable with this place since the fire."

I look at Tessa trying to gauge her expression. She knows nothing about what I'm telling her which is going to make this so much worse. Jackson Carmichael, you are such an ass!

"Then he asked me to strongly encourage you to sell the house. He knows I've advised you to keep the house. It's worth a lot of money and it's meaningful to you. Has he said anything about selling," I ask her, knowing he probably hasn't.

"No, but it's odd you are telling me this. This past week I got emails from two lending institutions with loan applications and house appraisal permission documents attached. Finn told me Jackson is asking him questions too about real estate law. What is going on?"

Here goes, This is going to hurt. I can only hope Tessa believes me and her gift is glitchy or I will never pull this off.

"Jackson seems desperate for you to sell Storybook or maybe use the lake house and maybe Honeywood to get a big loan or settle some debt. Do you know anything that may be going on with ADT, any trouble?"

"No, Finn asked me the same question. I have no involvement with the operational side of the business. In fact, I don't have anything to do with the business. I'm a beneficiary, if something happens to Jackson, but that's it. He never wanted me to be involved in any way. I think he didn't think I was smart enough to understand it or something," Tessa says, raising her hands and shrugging her shoulders.

"Tessa, Jackson is cheating on you," I blurt out.

She looks at me, a little startled. "With you? You told me you weren't involved Mindy. How could you?" She is hurt and lashing out.

"Sometimes, you are so dense. No, I swear on your grandmother's grave, it is not me. No! There is no one else for me. Theo was it. Maybe if I didn't want to blow up my successful business, I'd take a turn with Chase. In another time, I'd look twice at Finn, that sexy cousin of yours. Jackson, absolutely not! We are friends, we were close until the whole fire thing. Jeesh Tessa, Hell No! Give me some credit, okay?"

Tessa eyes widen, she's waiting for the ball to drop. Good, her spooky, spidey senses aren't working well. Please let it stay that way, until this is done.

"Not who, what. Jackson is committed to one thing only- Jackson. I think he's become so obsessed and so deep into growing ADT, becoming a *mover and shaker*; he's lost all sense. At this point, I'm not sure what he's willing to sacrifice or how far he's willing to go, to get there. He's like a man possessed, anymore," I tell her these things because they're true. I don't recognize the man Jackson has become and I haven't in a very long time.

"He's so different, Mindy. I don't know who he is either. I have no idea how to fix things between us. We feel so broken, and I don't even know exactly how or when it happened," she says,beginning to cry a little.

"What I'm about to say is going to hurt you deeply and I am so sorry for it. You can't fix this, Tessa. It's not you, the girls, your life here. It's Jackson. And he's gonna have to fix himself. He is spiraling downward and if you don't let him go, he will pull you straight to Hell with him."

"What is he involved with? What am I not seeing?" she asks, pounding her fists on the lounge chair arms.

"Jackson is rumored to be hanging out with some powerful people who aren't afraid to do almost anything to get what they want. His name keeps coming up with some of the luxury rental guests. He and Kelly had similar networking connections. He's either deep or thinking about getting deeply involved with some people that you do not want coming to the barbeque," I tell her hoping that she is reading a little between the lines without me having to give away anything else.

"Mindy, tell me. Is there another woman, is he being blackmailed by somebody? Is he involved with the Mafia? What is it? I will go crazy if I don't know."

"Damn, don't make me do this. Jackson doesn't love you anymore. He treats you like he's already moved on in his life and you are yesterday's news. Yes, he's into something with the business, whatever it is, and you want no part of it. Cause when it falls apart, and it will, Jackson won't come away unhurt," I see her flinch and hate myself for it.

"Tessa, please get Jackson home immediately. Tell him whatever it takes to get him here. Then for the love of Jesus, use that Donovan superpower and figure out the truth. If he's lying, you have to leave him Tessa. You have to."

She's quiet for a long minute. I don't know what's she's thinking or feeling. Anger flashes across her face, then it's replaced by something that looks like resolve. "Okay" she says softly.

There's one last thing we have to do. I know when I leave today, my best friend may hate me. I owe it to her though, she's always been there for me through everything. I need to take a chance today and help her face one of her biggest fears and survive, intact.

I reach for her hand, lead her down the dock to the boathouse. She starts protesting immediately. "Mindy, the boathouse is locked. I don't have a key. We can't go in there." She is tugging on my hand and trying to pull me back toward the house, away from here.

"There's a key here," I reach down into the flowerpot and pull out a key box. Jackson used it last month. I put the key in the lock and turn it. This is the first time; I've been inside since that night with Kelly. Last month when I was here with Jackson, I just stuck my head inside the doorway. I was afraid to go back in there.

Today, Tessa and I will go in together. I grab her hand and pull her into the space. She does not want to be here and neither do I. Looking around, I can see the scene replaying in my mind, smell the smoke, feel the fire. I have to blink hard and take several deep breaths to clear it all away. Tessa is trembling, she has a wild look in her eyes. She is feeling all that happened here, and it is overwhelming her. Caroline's fear, Kelly's sickness, my pain, Jackson's anger.

She almost collapses with the heaviness of all that went on in this little space. I brace her, grab her face with my hands and try to get her back into the present time, where none of that is real.

"Tessa," I say sharply, her eyes still glazed. "Tessa," I say again more firmly this time. Her eyes return to normal; her breathing slows a bit. She can support her own weight.

"Look at me, look into my eyes," I tell her trying to get her to focus. "We are okay. All of that, everything that happened that night. It's over. It ends here, today. That monster Kelly has no more hold over us. Not me, you, Kate or Jason." I run over to the door and open it wide. "Get out, Kelly Bradley Ryan. Get out of our lives and stay out! Say it with me, Tessa."

"Get Out," we both yell over and over again until we are nearly hoarse. Thank god, there are no close neighbors. We help each other out the door. Tessa takes the key, locks the door and puts the key back in the flowerpot. We walk down the dock, toward the house without a backward glance. We don't speak. That was so draining, we don't have the energy or know what else to say. We gather up our picnic food and carry our things out to our vehicles. I give Tessa the gifts and wrap her in a tight hug. She is limp, all wrung out. It's been an awful day for her.

"I love you and will do everything I can to support and help you. You know that, right?" I hate to be the messenger of so much pain for her.

"Yes, I know," she says like speaking is almost too much effort right now.

"Day or night, if you need me, call?"

"Okay," she says, opening her driver's side door. She sits a minute staring hard at the cottage. Then she puts on her sunglasses, checks her rearview mirror and pulls out. I wave as she passes. I pull out right behind her. She has a lot to think about on her drive home.

Hurting Tessa, made me physically ill. I told her as much as I could. I knew it would gut her. But even though I promised myself, I would not lie to my friends again about big things. I did not tell her, could not tell her about Jackson. Not about how four weeks ago, Jackson and I stood on her lake deck and Jackson kissed me. Or that I slapped him hard across the face. And I can't ever tell her his stupid profession of love. That jackass is willing to leave his wife and the life he's made with her, if I would only say "yes" and run away with him. Where did our friendship go so wrong? I can't even tell her that Jackson knows if he breathes a word of this to Tessa, I will ruin him. And he knows I can do it, too. It's too late to save Kate and Jason from Kelly. But I can fix things for Tessa. Maybe, I can fix things for all of us.

I have one last stop on this truth telling tour. There is one last person who needs to know what Kelly did. I don't want to do this either. Big Ed Ryan has been like a father to me. He has cared about me, helped me and loved me like one of his own. Telling him will devastate him.

When I was staying out at his farm, I needed extra towels. Kate and Jason were out at the stables and the housekeeper was in town, grocery shopping. Even though I knew I shouldn't, I ducked into Big Ed's bathroom and borrowed some towels. Also, shouldn't have, but I took a peek in his medicine cabinet. Those tell a lot about a person. There was so much medicine in there. That cabinet should really be locked with Jason in the house.

Ed is sick, very sick. I recognize some of the medications from when Theo's dad was in chemotherapy and dying with cancer. I don't think he's told anyone, as far as I can tell. I will keep his secret; he likely doesn't have long to live.

Being sick doesn't excuse him from the burden of knowing his only son Kelly, his legacy, was an abusive sociopath who hurt everyone who tried to care about him. This news will break him, but Ed Ryan shielded this monster and looked the other way. He needs to see the consequences of his failure to get help for his son. And I will not be merciful- he will hear every single detail about his rapist son. I hope he never forgets it- I never will!

TESSA

I guess it is a good thing, the drive back home from Storybook is only a couple of hours. Or maybe it isn't. At least the drive keeps me busy enough that I don't feel the urge to destroy everything in sight. Finally, Mindy has told the truth, as ugly and vile as it is. I don't even know what I'm feeling right now. What must Kate be going through? I knew this secret was going to blow up in our faces.

I am still so unsure about what happened with Caroline. And that kills me. I knew she was upset when she asked to go home early that night. With the chaos from the fire, Jackson took her home. She knew Jackson and felt comfortable with him. She never worked for us again. Her mother made many excuses and eventually I let it go.

I saw Caroline in town one day, about a year after the fire. She was walking with friends. I waved, she put her head down and ignored me. I caught up with her and tried talking with her for a few minutes. She responded but looked uncomfortable, not the friendly Caroline from before. I later asked Jackson if he remembered her saying anything the night of the fire? He didn't remember anything and said she was really quiet on the ride home. I asked Mindy, all she said was Kelly had said something inappropriate and likely embarrassed her. That poor girl, none of us really have any idea what happened in that boathouse. I'm so sorry that I brought her into Kelly's orbit. But being sorry doesn't fix or do anything for her. It's just another one of my many Kelly regrets.

First, Finn and now Mindy have broken my heart, telling me my husband is a liar and possibly a cheater too. I confess to being angry with them, in the first minutes. Why were they doing this to me? To me- who loves them both so very much. Then after the anger settled down a bit, I realized they were speaking the truth. Truth, it's a hard thing to swallow sometimes, especially when you are on the painful receiving end of it. Mindy though, she didn't tell the whole truth.

I've lost Jackson to Mindy. He loves Mindy, maybe he always has. It was swirling around them at the memorial service. I've seen glimpses of it through the years and just pretended not to see. Mindy is being truthful when she says she and Jackson aren't close anymore. She has not taken their relationship in a different direction. Today, when she was speaking about him, there was a feeling of loathing emanating from her. I'd love to believe she feels this way out of loyalty for me. No, it's not that. It's something more, and it's likely another one of the mysteries that goes unexplained.

I call Jackson again and leave a message. That makes three this week. Along with two text messages that I've already sent. There were another three that I deleted. The messages are being delivered; I'm getting silence in response. I will ask Finn to check in with him, just to make sure Jackson is okay. He's probably just ignoring me.

My relationship with Jackson imploding, I haven't had time to think much about the possibility of Kelly being murdered. After Mindy's revelations today, I am more convinced than ever, Kelly's death was intentional. Kate, Mindy, Jackson and even Jason have good reasons for wanting Kelly permanently out of their lives. But could any of them actually commit murder?

I feel so lost and alone right now. I don't know who to trust or how to reclaim my life. Or, as it turns out, possibly starting a new life. One without Jackson in it. Where did I go wrong and get to where I am today? I thought I was doing all the things I was supposed to be doing. Look, where it has gotten me. I have a husband who's keeping secrets and maybe about to leave me. A possibly murdered former friend, a terribly expensive dream home renovation and a career that has stalled and brings me zero joy anymore. I need help figuring out how to tackle this huge mess called my life.

I call the only person I know who can help me fix things.

She answers on the second ring. "Mom, I need you. Can you please come as soon as you can?"

Mom flies in on Monday. Finn offers to pick her up from the airport. She declines and rents a car service instead from Nashville. I'm sure it was crazy expensive, Claire Donovan never does anything halfway. Most of the time, her grand entrances and taking over my life, annoys me. Not this time. I need her steadying influence and cool head to help me get through all the things that are trying to crush my soul right now.

I've taken an extra week off from work. Annie encourages me to take the time while things are slow. I'd planned to save vacation time and spend it with Jackson. He would rather hang out in remote locations, living in primitive conditions than spend any time with me. That tells me pretty much everything I need to know about how he feels about us these days.

Mom settles in easily and begins taking over for me, which is so Claire. But it is exactly what I need right now. Afton and the boys are coming for a long weekend. Mom is excited to see them and I am too. I realize it's been a few months since I've seen Afton or Reagan and their families. Mom believes I've been isolating myself because of the situation with Jackson. I counter that work has been insane. Wise Claire suggests I'm using work as an excuse to retreat from my problems. She's not wrong. Dealing with Jackson is about the last possible thing I want to do.

It's Tuesday morning, Mom and I are sitting out on the terrace enjoying the only cool of the day before the late July heat gets cranking. My phone rings. It's early for a phone call. I know the number.

"Good morning, Jackson," I say as pleasantly as I can manage.

"Tessa, sorry it's taken me so long to reach out. I'm in a remote area with spotty cell service."

"Yep, work is very busy then?"

"Insane! These wildfires in California are intense," he tells me.

"Oh California, I saw something about that on the news." I had no idea he was there. I haven't really known his whereabouts for over six months, other than Kelly's memorial service.

"Jackson, I need you to come home as soon as possible. It's not an emergency but we need to take some time and sit down together. Work through some things. Figure out where we're heading in our relationship."

"Tessa, I really don't have time for that right now, later maybe. I can come home in November for the holidays. I'll take a lot of time off then," he says. I can see him running his hand through his hair, it's his irritated reaction.

"Jackson, you aren't understanding me. I need you home now. You have time to go behind my back and open loan applications without telling me. You have time to spend days in Indiana consoling Big Ed. You have time to come home and figure things out with me." I am trying to keep the anger I'm feeling out of my voice.

"Tessa, I can't do this right now. I talked about the loan applications with you. I need seed money for investors that are coming on board.

We discussed this. I can't believe you've forgotten. Please sign the paperwork and get it back ASAP. I need to move forward with that quickly," he tells me in a dismissive tone.

"No, what you need to do is come home, Jackson. I'm not signing anything until you come home and we can talk through things."

"Why do you always have to be dramatic and difficult? I am busting my ass here to provide nicely for you. It's never enough. Can't you ever just be supportive and trusting without giving me the third degree all the time? I'll come home when I'm damn ready to and you aren't going to guilt me into it."

His response unnerves me. How did we get here? I don't quite know what to say. "I guess I'll see you whenever I do. Stay safe and stay in touch. Goodbye." I disconnect the call not trusting myself to say another word.

Mom is looking closely at me with a guarded expression.

"That didn't go well. Jackson is not a morning person?" Mom asks, smirking.

"Used to be, but I don't know what he is anymore. I do know we did not discuss any loan paperwork or using the properties as collateral for loans. I am not losing my mind. We've talked so little in the past six months; I would definitely remember that conversation." I tell her, rubbing my temples.

"Sweetie, it sounds like Jackson has made his mind up about a lot of things without your permission," she says, carefully.

"Funny, you're the third person to say that this week. I guess it's time for me to see the writing on the wall and accept that this marriage is probably over."

"Honey, I'm so sorry you are going through this, but you will get through it. I promise." She goes back into the kitchen and pours us some more coffee. We sit on the terrace a little bit longer until the heat kicks in. Mom shares the name of one of her colleagues. She is one of the best divorce attorneys in Alabama. She recommends filing for a legal separation to let Jackson know just how serious I am. We can always go back from that, but it doesn't leave us in eternal limbo. I share Finn and Mindy's concerns about Jackson. Mom wants me to see her friend immediately to protect myself and the girls. It's a hard decision to make, but I do it.

Trent calls later in the day. We catch up for a few minutes. His Netflix deal is going well and he hopes to be home next week. He invites himself to Honeywood for a visit and I accept. Maybe, I can't figure out Jackson but I can figure out what happened to Kelly.

I enjoy Mom's visit. By the weekend, she knows about Mindy and the fire. She isn't shocked. I don't know if she intuitively knew Kelly or her years as a defense attorney had prepared her for almost anything. I share my feelings about Kelly's death. She isn't surprised about that either.

We talk about Honeywood and maybe reopening Storybook for a Labor Day party. She tells me about Boca Raton and how Daddy feels a little lost and out of place there but he's too proud to admit it.

On Friday, Afton and the human tornadoes came to visit. We hoped Reagan might be able to get away for the weekend, but she had out of town plans with Jonas. He was participating in some sponsored endurance hike. So, maybe we will see them on Labor Day weekend.

The weekend went so fast. I've missed having family in the house. Those two little bundles of energy, Chase and Scout kept us busy and laughing the whole time. I now know why Afton is exhausted all the time. It is a happy tired though. I hated to see them drive away on Sunday. The house got entirely too quiet.

Mom plans to go home next week. Daddy is lost without her even though he won't say so. She is afraid he will ruin all their laundry. That man hasn't washed a load of clothes in at least forty years. Having her here has been good for me. I've been alone for too long.

On Tuesday, Finn drives Mom to the airport. She wanted to hire a car. But he insisted on spending time together so they could discuss all their many ongoing side hustle projects. I'm back in my work routine and trying to find a new normal. Although I dread my consultation later in the week with Mom's lawyer friend, moving forward in this process is necessary. At least, I have Trent's visit to look forward to. It will be nice to think about something other than Jackson and our problems for a while. With the new fire night information from Mindy, I think Trent and I can begin to unravel the mystery of Kelly's death. At least, I can keep my mind occupied instead of spending countless hours wondering why Jackson has abandoned me and if he ever loved me at all?

The younger version of me, the *truth seeker*, would've burned down Atlanta and not looked back. The older me knows better. Truth will come out in the open, eventually. Sometimes, you just have to be patient enough to see it through.

Based on my new attorney's recommendation, we serve Jackson with legal separation papers. I've told Afton and Reagan; they aren't entirely surprised. They've both guessed, more than I've let on, of the seriousness of our marital problems. Jackson has always been a great dad and grandfather. He keeps in regular contact with the girls. Just Not Me. I've gotten angry text and phone messages from Jackson. He's reached out more times in the past ten days than he has in the past year. He has to figure out his life and no matter what, I'm not signing away either one of our homes. Any financial trouble will be his alone to fix. He didn't inform me and went plunging headfirst into whatever he's gotten himself into. I will not be on the backside to bail him out of problems. Real relationships and partnerships don't work that way.

Trent and I have met several times since he's come back from California. As promised, he's done some background digging for me. I'm happy to pick up our friendship again. Through the years, I made an effort, but Jackson disliked it so much. Trent and I agree to a very late lunch at Honeywood to catch up on our Kelly sleuthing.

Summer is holding on with a vengeance here in Tennessee. Today is another very hot and humid day without a raindrop in sight. Trent and I eat in my writing room out on the sun porch. The ceiling and floor fans are going at top speed and it's still a little warm. He surprises me with my favorite chicken from Hattie B's in Nashville. They are the undisputed hot chicken champions. On Trent's request, I serve up the very popular Donovan potato salad. We also have fresh tomatoes from the garden alongside my neighbor Clancy Jones' bread and butter pickles. We finish our meal with the famous Donovan chocolate chip cookies and Toomer's Corner lemonade sheet cake. It is a fine meal with good company.

Trent asks after Kate and Mindy. Kate is working remotely from Meadowview making sure Jason goes to counseling sessions and doesn't relapse. She's also looking after Big Ed who's staying home more and working less. He's been so unwell since Kelly's death. I think Kate is really worried about him. Mindy is super busy accommodating Poppy's friends with her luxury rentals. She is also conferring with Mom and Afton and is looking for a second location of *Mindy By Design. This location* features a home store. I think her struggle in finding the perfect location is that she's also looking for a Mindy II and that's not possible. God broke the mold on that one.

Trent asks about Jackson. I knew he would. I don't want to talk about Jackson, but I owe Trent the truth. Or at least some of it, anyway. I briefly tell him about our unofficial separation followed up with the legal separation papers, which he still refuses to sign. I mention Finn, Mindy and Mom's warnings to distance myself from him. I don't mention that Jackson loves Mindy because I still find that hard to believe myself. This part of the conversation is awkward, but I better get used to it. In the future, there might be a lot more uncomfortable moments involving Jackson.

"So, I have interesting news. Should I go first, or you?" he asks me.

"Definitely you," I tell him. I want to put off the fire night revelations as long as possible.

Forever would be great.

"I did a little checking on ADT; Jackson has been working hard on expanding the business. He's been very busy trying to get big name investors onboard. That's not all that surprising or interesting really. What is interesting though, Martin Land (Jackson's business partner) is a registered agent for a new LLC in Delaware. It has nothing to do with any of his other business interests and doesn't seem to really make anything or provide any services. It's newly formed, about a year old and has substantial assets."

"Forming an LLC in Delaware usually means more lenient tax obligations and privacy surrounding the LLC members, right?" I ask. I know this because I just read about controversy surrounding so many out of state businesses being registered there.

"Yes, companies do it all the time. Usually,it's no big deal. But, with Martin and Jackson so aggressively chasing business expansion and getting exclusive government contracts, it caught my eye. Sometimes, those limited liability companies are shell companies used for money laundering, kickbacks and all other kinds of bad business," he tells me.

I look at him strangely (probably) trying to connect the dots. "Are you telling me, Martin and Jackson might be involved in something illegal?" And here I was just thinking he was in love with my best friend, that's all.

He hesitates, drumming his fingers on the table before answering. He looks at me a few seconds before saying, "Yes, I think it's possible. I hope not. But Martin and Jackson have been socializing with *big boys* in political and business circles. Did Jackson do that before?" he tactfully asks me.

I let out a big groan. "No, I don't think so. Until the past eighteen months or so, Jackson was always either out on a work site or here at home. He and Martin would meet here or the lake cottage to talk business. I believed Jackson had been out on work sites all this time, not out gallivanting around the country socializing with *important* people. Or at least that's what he told me." I feel angry now, just another part of Jackson's life that he has hidden from me.

"Let's not jump to anything, just yet. This is a "watch" situation. I'll get one of my trusted research guys to put together a list of people, places, times; then we'll see if some pattern emerges, okay? I agree with the advice you've already been given. Jackson is withholding information from you. **If** he's involved in anything illegal, you need to be far, far away from that."

"What's your share? No illegal activities, I hope," he teases me.

I take a big breath and blow it out, rolling my eyes at the same time. "Well, actually it does," I tell him mentally calculating how much I can say while protecting Mindy's privacy but still giving him enough details.

"It's the fire night, I was right that Mindy, Jackson and Kelly were lying about it." Even though I so desperately wanted to be wrong about that. I give a very short summary (for me, anyway) of Mindy's revelation. I tell him about Caroline, Kelly's drunken rage, the assault, Jackson beating Kelly, and the different accounts that my husband and two friends told about that night.

Trent sits very quietly for a minute or two. It's a lot to take in at one time. Then he asks the very same question I've been asking myself for almost 14 years now. "Why didn't y'all tell someone? What the hell? Kelly is inappropriate with a minor and rapes his best friend's wife and no one tells. That's insane," he says, shaking his head in total disbelief.

I can tell he is really struggling with this information. I reach out and take his hand to calm him a little. "It's crazy, I know. When you say it out loud, it's utterly ridiculous what we did. Mindy didn't tell, Jackson may have guessed and protected his friend and I just did not know the full extent of what they were hiding. I live with the consequences of this every day." I tell him, not really wanting to acknowledge these things.

"I spent almost 14 years trying to get one or all of them to come clean about what really happened. I knew there was more but none of them would tell the secret. Foolishly, I believed Kelly had just been inappropriate with Caroline and Mindy. She didn't want to say anything because it would be awkward and strain our friendships." I put my head in my arms on the table, trying to hide from the shame of what we had done.

"Tessa, there's something I don't understand," he says, laying his hand gently on the top of my head. "Why did Mindy not tell for so many years?"

I lift my head and look at him, with a deep sadness reaching all the way down to my bone marrow. "Trent, you know there's great shame for rape victims. Mindy, Kate and others, are conditioned to believe, in some way, that they deserved what happened to them. Mindy didn't tell because she couldn't make herself believe it actually happened or what she did to cause it. Then if she did, she couldn't handle all the fallout that would happen. Kate endured years of intimate partner abuse because she believed Kelly would take Jason and her career away from her."

"The most horrible thing, my husband possibly, unknowingly supported a serial rapist for years. His best friend that he protected for almost 30 years. He watched Kelly year after year, embarrass, intimidate, harass females and it was all laughed off as stupid Kelly behavior. "That's just Kelly, hitting on everything that moves. Hide your girlfriends and sisters." It was all just a big stupid joke to them. Kelly embarrassed a lot of girls and made them uncomfortable. He terrified others. He slept through Auburn's Greek society. He raped two of my friends and a girl at Purdue. But somehow, we all just looked the other way and let him get away with it." I am shaking by now, and feeling so overwhelmed.

"Tessa, it's no secret that Jackson and I don't get along. I've never said the reason why, but back at Auburn we got into it one day. Since that day, we haven't been friends. Gonna spare you the details, but it basically had to do with Kelly and how he treated girls. Jackson's protection of Kelly was wrong, but I'm sure it doesn't extend to him assaulting women. Especially if those women are people he cares about."

"You're right. I'm so close to all of this, I can't think straight. But Trent, I am now convinced more than ever, someone I know had something to do with Kelly's death. I won't protect people I love a second time, not if they did this."

Trent picks up his beer glass, drains it and sets the glass back down on the table. "Okay," he says, "I'm going to need a second piece of that cake, a handful of cookies and some tea, if you have it. We have a murder to solve and I'm hoping not to have to pull an all- nighter. I didn't bring a toothbrush," he smiles and winks at me.

We work out a *potential* murder suspect list. It doesn't take long. Mindy, Jackson, Henry Hawthorne make the list. Kate and Jason are *maybes*, Poppy (for now), Big Ed and Kimberly (Kelly's sister) are *throwaways*. We wrestle with the possibilities of some jilted boyfriend/husband finally taking revenge. Or a scorned woman-like Melissa, Kelly's former subordinate who lost her career over Kelly. Or maybe it's somebody entirely different. It's Kelly who always seemed to attract trouble and anger people wherever he went. There's also the outlier possibility that some other woman Kelly might have assaulted took justice in her own hands.

Because of emotions I picked up on at Kelly's memorial; we focus on the attendees. As much as I don't want to, we need to focus on Jackson and Mindy. They have motive, Jackson maybe finally realizes Kelly raped Mindy. Mindy has years of pent-up rage against Kelly. He hurt her, Kate and Jason. But why now? After all these years- why would either of them go after Kelly?

Henry Hawthorne is a highly probable suspect. It's no secret that he terribly spoiled his only child Poppy. He never remarried after Poppy's mom died. For years, it was just him and Poppy. I was more than a little surprised he even agreed to Kelly as a son in law. But Poppy wanted it. And what Poppy wants, Poppy gets. Of course, Kelly's marriage to Poppy likely came with one of the toughest prenuptial agreements ever. Henry Hawthorne loves his daughter and will protect his assets. If he found out that Kelly was back to his "pre-Poppy" bad behavior; he would take care of the problem.

But as Trent pointed out and I had already considered, there were much easier ways to get rid of Kelly. Ways that did not include killing him or the nanny whose family is causing a lot of trouble and bringing bad press on the Hawthorne/Ryan names. It's been rumored for years that Hawthorne is in bed with the New York Mafia. But Kelly's death was messy and amateurish. Doesn't seem like the work of a British gazillionaire or New York Mafia who don't actively seek out trouble. Not eliminating him from our list just yet, but the sloppy murder doesn't quite vibe right either.

Kate and Jason, have pretty solid alibis and also every reason in the world to end Kelly. Neither feels exactly right though. They were at Meadowview farm, as far as we know. Their alibis are each other. Though no one else has confirmed their whereabouts around the time of Kelly's death. Big Ed was in Virginia at the time it happened. I remember hearing that Neil Frasier was away on a horse prospect trip at the time. Jason's home health nurses change depending on availability. Celia, the housekeeper, is a day employee. She has her own family to take care of. Also, she usually does not work every day when Kate and Jason are staying. Kate insists on her taking well deserved time off. Trent doesn't think Kate or Jason should be considered suspects. I agree but will follow up on confirming their timelines.

This just leaves Poppy. Trent also thinks Poppy is a throwaway. I wonder if it's because she's rich, and incredibly beautiful with a doting daddy. Or as he sarcastically reminds me, she was out of town. It would take a lot of planning to do all of that. Poppy does not seem like the calculating, vengeful type. Yes, he's met and interacted with her a few times. Same large social circles and all that. I wonder if it's possible instead of the kind, thoughtful persona she projects; maybe she's really a psychopath instead? I get a well-deserved eye roll from Trent.

Well, you never really know about people. Sometimes, it's the very one you least expect. However, I did not sense anything but sadness and grief from Poppy at the memorial service. She really loved Kelly;

those emotions would be difficult to fake. Not impossible, but not very likely. I'm just going to keep an open mind here.

We keep circling back. I wish I could know for sure, who was giving me the murderer vibes. Mindy was filled with rage that day and Jackson has been so evasive and secretive. As much as I could justify it being one of them, nobody else is completely off the hook, either.

Trent needs to get back to Nashville. I load him up with leftovers and a promise to get together again soon. He has some connections that he's going to tap into to dig a little deeper in Jackson's business dealings. As much as I hate to admit it, Jackson's problems, whatever they are, have much greater impact on me right now than Kelly's death. Kelly is gone and hopefully his days of hurting people are done.

I won't completely give up on my murder theory just yet. I need to call Kate and check on her and Jason. Somehow, I need to figure out if they were both home during Kelly's murder. Not sure how that is going to happen, but I will try. Next, I will reach out to Poppy and see if I can get her and the twins out to Honeywood. A visit would be great and the perfect opportunity to see if I can discover any other facts that might make solving this murder just a little easier.

In the back of my mind there is a small voice that whispers insistently, asking if I really do want to solve this thing? Am I married to someone who's maybe breaking laws, definitely in love with my best friend and very possibly a murderer too? I don't want to think about this, because if I'm truly being honest with myself; I'm not sure I really want to know. And this scares me even more than the fire nightmares that I've started having again.

We are here at Storybook having Jackson's Labor Day weekend get together, minus Jackson. He is elsewhere, choosing not to attend. I haven't put eyes on Jackson since Kelly's memorial service. Avoidance is the new normal. He's very angry with me, if his barrage of voice messages and text messages are any indication. When I return his calls, no matter what time of day, they always go to voicemail. It's clear he doesn't want to talk to me in real time. So, we barely communicate, via back-and-forth terse messages. It is a new low in our relationship. Sometimes, I feel like we are going to be stuck in an endless time loop- never moving forward and never able to go back.

The End of Summer party at Storybook is a good idea. Slowly, we are trying to put the painful past behind us and move toward a new beginning. Only my new beginning will not include Jackson. It is a small gathering this time, so different from the large 4th of July parties we used to have. Annie comes and brings her mother Ida. She is a precious woman; I instantly see where Annie's strength and quick wit comes from.

Mom and Dad are here, they are back taking care of some business in Lake James and helping me with some renovation decisions here at Honeywood. Dad is a quiet man by nature, but he sure knows how to handle construction crews. I think it's a throwback skill from his military days and managing hospital surgical teams. His knowledge and directness is most appreciated right now.

Mindy comes and I am thankful. It's been a little awkward between us since her last visit here. I want her to always feel welcome here or at Honeywood. Places where we have so many memories, and so much history together. Trent surprises me and shows up. I thought he would be much too busy doing celebrity things, but he's here enjoying being just Trent, a longtime friend and avid Auburn fan.

Our daughters, Afton and Reagan have their own family activities and I miss them so much. Afton, Gage and the littles are attending a work sponsored family event. The kind where you need to put in an appearance, for the bosses. Reagan and Jonas are out on another product sponsored hike followed up by a charity concert to save Asheville's natural habitats. It's a work weekend for both of them.

I invited Kate, Jason and Big Ed. Poppy and the twins were also included in the invite. They are all out at Meadowview tending to Big Ed. His health has declined quite a bit after Kelly's death. It feels almost like he is giving up on life. I need to go out and visit him soon. Kelly's death has been so hard on all of them in very different ways. My traitor cousin Finn is also out in Indiana, apparently helping Ed with some of his horse breeding. Finn, gentleman horse breeder has a nice ring to it.

I hired a local high-school modern country band. They are good, and with time and experience could be very good. They need the gigs, and I thought it would be fun. I pay extra for them to DJ exclusively 90's playlist hits. They don't mind even though they think the music is lame. Trent brings enough Hattie B's chicken to feed a small army or most of Mindy's inherited Greer relatives.

Dad and Trent are trying their luck fishing from the dock. The fish are taking a break today too and aren't biting. It is a peaceful, good day, ending with fireworks over the lake. This little party feels so different from the other one. That one wrecked our lives. This weekend was just what I needed to transition into that in-between space, in the middle of Before and Soon.

Two weeks later, after I've heard nothing from Jackson, a Fedex driver shows up with an envelope. With shaking hands, I open it and pull out the documents. It is the separation papers with Jackson's bold signature across the bottom. No note, no nothing. So, this is how we move to ending a marriage of almost 27 years. With signatures, and other than our daughters and grandchildren, it vanishes, like it never existed at all.

I try to stay busy, keeping my mind from going down too many rabbit holes. Between the separation, Kelly's murder and a growing dissatisfaction with my career; my mind is spinning all the time. Mom and Mindy keep me focused on the renovations at Honeywood. They are coming along nicely. Thank goodness for parents who pay forward their legacies early. I may be in debt to my parents forever, for their generosity. Without them, I would lose my home.

I've taken on a new challenging project at work. Agreeing to work with a brilliant, yet difficult new author keeps my mind from straying too far out into the weeds and the "what ifs". I am working on this pain in the behind project on an unseasonably cool, late September morning when Kate calls. I haven't spoken with her on the phone in a few weeks. I hope it's just a catch-up call and not bad news, even though I think it might be.

Big Ed passed away. I'm so sad at the news, especially since I didn't take the time to go visit like I said I would. I had no idea there wouldn't be another opportunity. Kate seems to be holding up okay, so far. Jason, who knows? Sometimes, he's calm and other times he has melt-downs over bad news. This will hit him hard. It's just a matter of time before he explodes.

Because of General Ryan's rank and status, there will be an official funeral mass at the famous Basilica of the National Shrine of the Immaculate Conception in Washington DC. I guess this location was chosen because of seating capacity. Big Ed's networking connections are vast and wide. Security will be a nightmare at this invitation only event.

Kate, Jackson, Poppy and children, and Mom will go. Big Ed earned a spot in Arlington Cemetery, but his wishes are to be buried out at Meadowview with Ella and Kelly. Mindy, Jason, Kate's parents, and I will be attending the smaller intimate service out at the farm. I cannot be around all the pomp and circumstance and hordes of people at the public funeral. Kate understands and does not expect me to go. Surprisingly, Jackson and Finn will be accompanying her per Big Ed's final requests. The Maynards will stay with Jason until Kate returns home. I don't feel good about going back out to Meadowview. That place holds bad memories and lots of suppressed negative energy in the land. But for Big Ed, I will do it.

I watch parts of the public funeral on television. The local news outlets in the Beltway area carry the service live. Other outlets around the nation pick up sound bites that play well on the evening news. Shortly after Lt. General Ryan's respectful funeral, Kelly's sordid death details begin to surface again. First, in the tabloids, then it hits the mainstream media. Suddenly Kelly is primetime news again, overtaking his father's somber and honorable funeral service. Even in death Kelly becomes a problem, impacting everyone around him.

TMZ runs a short segment on the Hawthorne/Ryan's' nanny. The reporter interviews some of Dana Smith's friends. He also emphasizes pending 'wrongful death' ligation by the nanny's family. He ends his segment by hinting Dana Smith was not just a certified nanny who loved children and was working to earn money toward a master's degree in Early Childhood Education. He hints at her other employment at a porn website, and an erotica blog ghostwritten by Dana.

I believe very little in the TMZ reporter's credibility. But as a former journalist, I do know where there's smoke, there's usually fire. There's something to this, hopefully Trent and I can pick out the truth.

Trent has been busy working on his Netflix documentary. He's still working on our case, through his informants and professional investigator that owes him a few favors. I've offered to pay for the help, he's refused saying he owes me for saving him in our Auburn newspaper days. I gratefully accept the assistance.

On September 30th, I receive a large envelope hand delivered by a courier. I expect it is something from mine or Jackson's lawyers regarding the separation. It is so much paperwork to *uncouple*. I don't recognize the law firm and quickly open the packet to see what's next in the Jackson and Tessa drama. Only the paperwork is not from Jackson, it's from Big Ed's longtime personal attorney, Brooks Douglass. The cover letter is from Douglass, basically telling me the enclosed document was written by General Ryan and is for "my eyes only". Do what I will with the information but destroy the document after reading. Sounds a little like a scene from Mission Impossible . Of course, I start reading immediately.

August 2024

My Dear Tessa,

I'm writing this letter to you, because I trust you. You are one of very few of the very many people I have met in my lifetime, that I do trust. I am dying, Tessa. I've known for months, I'd planned to tell Kelly and Kimberly, but I could not find the right words somehow and then Kelly died, and it did not seem to matter much anymore.

When you know you are dying, you unwillingly do an evaluation of your life. I have done this at several important junctures during my long lifetime. This one, however, is different. This is the final pass and review with no opportunity for correction.

For all the many important things I have accomplished in my life; I failed at what mattered most. I was a miserable father to my children. I let the pain of losing Ella, pride, ambition, power, reputation, I let all of these worthless things take priority over raising Kelly and Kimberly properly.

I have come to realize, much too late that I raised a sociopath in Kelly. I tried for years to correct his behavior, then I spent years covering for his behavior. At the time, I thought I was acting out of love. I now realize

I was acting out of guilt for being an absent parent. I want to believe that Kelly's issues were a result of losing his mother entirely too young. Perhaps, it was having an absent, distant father, when he desperately needed help. Or, letting myself off the hook, maybe Kelly was destined to be exactly what he was, no matter what intervention I could have provided.

The real cross I must bear until my dying breath is I knew Kelly needed help of some kind. Instead of stepping up as a responsible parent, I hid his behavior and "fixed" things for him in hopes that he would adjust on his own. Maybe, I did not create the person Kelly became, but I enabled him to grow into someone who raped three women, possibly more. With his pattern, I am disgusted and shamed beyond repair, there may be even more women out there in the world that suffered greatly because of my son.

Living with the reality of this has crushed me. I can never repent enough for what I have done. If this cancer, which is faster, stronger and tougher than me, was not already killing me; I would have taken matters into my own hands. Yet, I could not bring myself to do that because of Kimberly, Kate and Jason. They have suffered enough because of my blind spots with Kelly.

This next part of my dying confession may shock you, but it is necessary. I apologize in advance for any turmoil which it may cause you. I thought Poppy was the one to straighten out Kelly, the answer to so many unanswered prayers. And she did, for some time. However, Kelly reverted back to his subversive behavior and crossed the line, again. By this time, I had enough of rescuing him. Most of his life, I have been pulling Kelly out of the gutter, dusting him off and making his transgressions go away.

I finally had enough and informed Henry Hawthorne of his son-in-law's actions. I'm ashamed to admit, I sold my son out to a man with long reputed Mafia connections. I am even more ashamed to admit, at the time, I did not care what happened to Kelly. Only that Kelly could not run roughshod over the world anymore and suffer no consequences.

As you may have already guessed, Kelly's death was highly unlikely a simple accident. I asked no questions because I did not want the answers. Hawthorne and I went into battle management mode in handling the aftermath of his death. Hawthorne wanted to protect his family name and Poppy from embarrassment over the situation. We discovered the nanny's sordid past including pornography and attempted extortion of other wealthy families. I wanted the attention to disappear, because I know Kelly's death was not accidental. I very possibly killed my son, with exposing his terrible deeds. I will carry this guilt to the grave.

There is something else, on top of this terrible disclosure you must know. I love your husband Jackson, as a son. In many ways, he has been the son I never had. However, I am warning you most urgently. Jackson has gotten in way over his head, in a situation that threatens to blow up his entire life. I have tried to counsel him and strongly suggested he take a different path. He did not listen. I care deeply about him, and you. You had no choice in his actions, and I do not want to see you become collateral damage because of his poor decisions. Please heed this advice, if you have not already disengaged yourself from Jackson; do so immediately!

Jackson is potentially in danger with people you do not take lightly. He is also on the radar of law enforcement agencies. I cannot say anymore, please be very careful around Jackson. I have tried to protect him as much as possible. As my time is coming to an end here on Earth, he will be on his own to face the consequences of his poor decisions.

Tessa, thank you for taking care of Kelly's family when he would not. You are the moral compass with the biggest heart in your inner circle. The way you have always taken care of others and fiercely protected them has both impressed me and warmed this old man's heart. Please continue to love Kate and Jason as you do. If you could stay in touch with Kimberly, and offer friendship, I would be eternally grateful.

Mostly, I hope you will find it within yourself to forgive me. This old broken man is tired and more than ever, hopefully, if God is merciful, waiting to be reunited with my beloved Ella.

Yours truly,

Edward Ryan

I am stunned by this letter. I do not follow instructions to destroy it. I tuck it away in my secret box I've hidden in the wine cellar. I will do as asked and get rid of it- but not today. Today, I need to sit with its contents and figure out exactly what I'm supposed to do next.

MINDY

I didn't want to come here again. If it wasn't for Big Ed and trying to be respectful and all, I would never set foot on this godforsaken property again. There are too many Kelly reminders here.

I'm attending the second Ryan memorial service in three months. Hopefully, the Ryan curse ends with them. It will be hard for me to stand around with people I know and pretend to be sad over a man who let a rapist loose in the world. I'm going to have to dig deep to pull this off.

There is a big part of me that loved Big Ed and always will. But the more damaged part of me tucked carefully down inside, hates the man who raised a rapist. General Ryan is not without blame for Kelly. We all are to blame for Kelly, but he had many more chances to stop Kelly and didn't.

This time around, Poppy stays home. The big circus funeral was too much for Poppy and the kids. As soon as the service was over, news crews were sticking phones and cameras in her face asking about Kelly's relationship with their nanny. Poppy and her burly security team handled it well. I'm fairly sure I would've told them all what they could do with those cameras and phones. What totally classless people. She couldn't even have one full day in public, to grieve her father-in-law without vultures hoping to catch her in a dramatic newsworthy moment. Celebrity is not for the fainthearted or the weak.

Kate's parents are here, they are solid midwestern *salt of the Earth* people. God love them! But that Cindy Maynard is constantly saying the wrong thing at the most inappropriate time. I guess it's a nervous reaction. If it wasn't a memorial service, it might be hysterically funny.

Kimberly skipped the private ceremony since she attended the public spectacle. I suspect she didn't want to go to either one. Once Kimberly left the cornfields, there was no looking back. I think like me, she loved Big Ed but holds him accountable for Kelly's bad life choices.

Oddly, Henry Hawthorne is also here. I never had the impression he and Ed Ryan were really friends. But who knows? They ran in a lot of the same circles. Maybe he is just here on Poppy's behalf. But he is sticking very closely to Jackson, and they are huddling in whispered conversations when they think no one is looking.

I'm proud of Jason, going to the graveside service was hard for him. He did it, with his mom and me on both sides supporting him. Jason has been very muted throughout this. I can't really tell if it's a *good* or *bad* quiet. Sometimes with him, it's like the unsettling quiet before a major storm. You don't know it's coming, until it's right on top of you and then it's too late. We keep a close eye on him, just in case.

Tessa and Jackson are the real show, though. They are incredibly awkward around each other. That's understandable. As soon as Tessa is around, he turns into a statue formerly known as Jackson. He uses as few words as possible with her and excuses himself immediately-sometimes when she is still talking. Jackson is also very weird with me. He is careful to distance himself appropriately, but I've caught him multiple times staring at me, when he didn't think I would notice. I do notice, and I do not like it. At least have the decency to end things properly with your wife before you are on the hunt for someone else. Jackson's behavior surprises and angers me. He is being very bold in his intentions with absolutely no consideration for the awful position he puts me in.

Tessa is pale, with two small pink patches on her cheeks. Those are the tell-tale signs of her taking some liquid courage. I'm not judging, and I don't blame her a bit. Coming here and facing Jackson has to be difficult. Coming here at all is hard for her. We have bad memories here. I know she still blames herself for all that happened on the fire night. It's irrational but she does. She carries a lot of guilt for not being able to convince Kate to break up with Kelly in college. Or convincing her to call off the wedding. Somehow, she thinks she could've stopped all the abuse Kate and Jason endured because of Kelly. She feels all the *feels* here, the past hurts and ones that have attached to the Ryans. No wonder, my poor girl is feeling overwhelmed. She feels everything in this world, too much. It's enough to drive her crazy.

The memorial is short, and people wander off in different directions. Tessa says her goodbyes and leaves. She has a long drive and the whole Jackson thing has her off balance. She is doing what she does when she feels overwhelmed, she retreats. And we let her.

Jason goes to town with his grandparents, to get out of the house. Jackson and Henry are down at the barn talking about who knows what? Probably the racehorses, if I'm guessing. That just leaves me and Kate rambling around in the house, not quite knowing what to do with ourselves. Kate wants to go to the gatehouse. We grab a bottle of wine, and seltzer water, some snacks and walk over. It seems like she wants some privacy, even though we were alone in the house.

I have feelings of *deja vu*. The last time we were in the gatehouse together, Kate dropped a most serious secret on us. I hope today is not a repeat! We get settled on the leather sectional and I wait for Kate to tell me whatever it is. In the past, these reveals have never been good here.

"This is probably not the right place or time. But before I lose my courage, I need to tell someone. Thankfully, you might understand because I know Tessa would judge me, not intentionally," Kate tells me while taking a big gulp of her favorite wine.

This is not going to be good. I wait, listen and brace myself for whatever is coming next. Why is this feeling like a repeat of Kelly's memorial day?

"You know when Kelly left the Reserves, rather quickly?"

"Yes," I tell her, "I vaguely remember. Kelly was always doing something impulsively, wondering where this is headed.

"He didn't voluntarily leave; he was asked to resign or face court martial charges. He had an affair with one of his subordinates, Melissa. Apparently, he forced her into a relationship and then lied about it. Anyway, I think Big Ed intervened. Kelly got off lightly and Melissa received a dishonorable discharge and had to leave the military with that on her record."

I sit for a minute, processing this. I'm not shocked or even really surprised. This is typical Kelly behavior. Get involved with someone he has no business being with and then blame it on the female. But wow, the female soldier took the brunt of this very bad decision.

"There's more," she sighs and looks down at her feet. Damn, there's always more with Kelly.

"I turned Kelly in for the affair. I knew it was going on for a while. I finally had enough and made an anonymous phone call to Kelly's unit and the Criminal Investigation Detachment. I expected Kelly to get in trouble, but I did not know they would come down so hard on her," she says, wringing her hands. That thing she does when she is nervous.

I don't quite know what to say. I don't blame her but I'm not sure what she really wants to hear right now, so I sit.

"That's when the situation with Kelly got horrible. He couldn't handle losing his commission, even though his dad had gotten him off fairly easy. He could have gone to Leavenworth for a long time. He didn't see it that way though. It was the first time he wasn't able to walk away from trouble with no consequences. That's when he beat me and hit Jason."

"Kate, you didn't know what would happen to Melissa. It's terrible but she wasn't an innocent bystander in all of this either. As bad as it was, doing that got you and Jason away from Kelly. That's the most important thing," I tell her hoping she won't continue to waste time feeling guilty over what she did.

"I ruined someone else's life, Mindy. I often wonder what happened to her. When I first found out about Kelly's death, I wondered if she was somehow involved, as crazy as that sounds. In my mind, I sent a scorned woman out into the world and caused her to kill Kelly because I could not do it myself," she begins crying hysterically.

I try my best to console her. Kelly has scarred her for life. I don't know if Kate will truly ever have peace or any real happiness. And I hate him even more for that. Kelly should have never made an entrance in this world. I did not cry one single tear when he left it, much too late, in my opinion.

Like Tessa, I am eager to leave Meadowview. Too much pain has gathered here for too long. Instead of heading home like I originally planned, I fly up to Virginia. Poppy is interested in redecorating the mansion and she wants to introduce me to a few more of her wealthy, frivolous friends with money to burn. I can't say no, after all a girl has got to support herself.

Jason

This is a freaking nightmare. Even though Grampa Ed was old, and I knew it was coming; I hate everything so much right now. Mom made me go to his memorial service here on the farm. There is no way I could've handled the official funeral service. I did watch parts of it online, it seemed like half of Washington D.C. was there. I still can't believe he's gone. Grampa Ed was the only thing that kept me and Mom going in the years AK (After Kelly). Now, what will we do?

Why the hell do we even bother anyway? Mom keeps me locked up on house arrest like a criminal most of the time, always wringing her hands and giving me the side eye. I'm not allowed to go anywhere except to therapy sessions, local errands with Neil, weekend visits with the mom grandparents and possibly to Florida for a visit with Aunt Mindy if she will ever stay her ass home long enough for me to come.

I've decided to do my own memorial for Grampa. I grabbed a bottle of his best Irish whiskey from the liquor cabinet when nobody was looking. I checked his bathroom medicine cabinet, but Mom was way ahead of me and cleared it out. I guess all of the medicine at the farm is now locked up and only warden Kate has the key.

Sitting out here at the family cemetery after dark is quiet and peaceful, in a weird way. I slipped out after supper, Mom didn't notice. She's too busy these days trying to stay on top of all of the work she's been missing. She's missed a lot of work in the last four months with all of the crazy shit that's been going on. She starts early in the morning before the sun is up and works until midnight a lot of nights. She's gonna completely burn herself out, trying to impress people that don't care about her.

Laying out under the stars, I wish I could stay out here like this forever. It's the only time I feel right with this world I'm in. The whiskey feels smooth going down, that's how you know it's a good vintage. Learned that from Grampa. This is hitting me fast. I don't know if it's the half bottle I've chugged or I haven't been lit in so long, I can't hold my booze anymore.

I brought a gun. I borrowed it off Grampa when I first got here. I found the 357 magnum in his bedside nightstand. I thought I might have to protect myself or kill Kelly if he came around. I'm surprised Mom didn't find it when she searched my room. I've kept it hidden in the secret hiding place in the floorboards underneath my bed. Grampa made it for me when I was little. He would hide letters and other stuff in there for me when he was gone. I guess Mom forgot all about it.

The gun feels heavy in my hand. Grampa took me target shooting with it one time. He says to point and shoot in the direction I wanted. The pistol is powerful enough to take down large game animals and most men, unless they are superhuman or something. It's enough to stop things in their tracks or end things.

I guess Grampa forgot about the gun. Maybe, he thought he left it somewhere else. Hopefully, there aren't any coyotes out here roaming around or any other scary things out in the woods. But hey, who am I kidding? The really scary things aren't out there in the woods. They live in houses, drive cars, go to jobs and have kids. Those animals scare the hell out of me.

My nightmares haven't gone away but they aren't at the lake cottage anymore. The fire people are gone, and they're replaced with nothing. In my newest nightmare, I'm at our house or here at the farm and they're abandoned. There's no Mom, Grampa, or anybody. It feels like I dunno, the Rapture maybe that they talk about in churches. Except there aren't any crashed cars or left behind clothes. It's just me running around freaking out, because I'm by myself. Then I sit down in the meadow by the chapel and graveyard. I hear someone calling my name, it's Chloe, she's holding out her hand. I want to go with her and get away from this creepy place. But Chloe is dead, and I can't go with her unless I'm dead too. I always wake up at this point scared as shit. I don't tell Mom or my new young therapist about my dreams. They will think I'm crazy or I'm just making it all up and give me more drugs that make me feel weird.

I'm tired, just so tired. Can I just go to sleep and wake up in an alternate reality where there was no Kelly? I'm still me, more or less, but no Kelly DNA invading my body. I could end up just like him. No matter how hard I try, or what I do. I could be just like him. That scares me a thousand times worse than the nightmares I've been having most of my life.

I lay my head on the ground. Just a little sleep and then I will sneak back into the farmhouse. Mom won't know a thing. I've got Grampa's gun to chase off wild animals and the monsters in my dreams.

— • —

TESSA

I haven't slept a good night's sleep in days now. With all that's happened in the past three months- I feel my comfortable, safe world closing in around me. I feel so alone and lost right now, not knowing who to believe or trust. I do the one thing my grandmother Esme always encouraged me to do.

Sitting here in the pews of St Anthony's in Fayetteville, it is calm. Jackson and I have attended this church on and off since we moved here four years ago. Me more *off* and Jackson more *on*, he sets aside time wherever he is to attend mass in person or virtually, if he's in a remote location. It's one of the constants about him that I admire so much.

I do what my grandmother taught me to do, I quietly begin to pray even though I am terribly out of practice.

"Father, uh Lord, God- it's me , your daughter Tessa. Contessa, your wayward daughter, I guess. First, I want to say I'm sorry for not stopping by more often. I know it's an excuse you hear a lot, but I've been busy trying to keep my life together. I bet you're shaking your head at that one. Not very original, huh? I'm also sorry for coming to mass and not paying attention. It's just this is the only place where my brain drowns out all of the noise and I can really think. God, this probably isn't the first time you've heard this either, those mass services are sometimes hard

to follow. You know when to stand, sit, sing, pray, chant- sometimes I feel a little like I'm at a football game instead of church.

I promise I'm not here to complain. I'm sure you have a lot of complaints about me. Grandmother Esme always talked to you and told me to do the same. Well, like any good Donovan female, I also don't always listen to others very well.

I'm really sorry for bringing this to you so late in the game, but what am I do? I have a husband who no longer loves me, and he might be in deep trouble. And I know someone murdered Kelly, the no-good friend that he was. I will leave him for you to deal with.

No matter what I say or do, I'm going to hurt someone. Is the truth worth risking everything?

I need a sign, I'm begging you. A vivid dream or if you're feeling particularly dramatic, a burning bush would do. Although Fr. Tom and the fire department might get upset at that one. But Lord, please reveal to me what I need to do, and I will do it.

I promise in return, to pray more and not just for green lights when I'm running late or in crisis mode. I promise to drop into your house more frequently. If necessary, I will even wear that dreadful orange, if you truly are an Auburn football fan. Even though I fully suspect you heavily favor Alabama, or at least their endless winning seasons seem to suggest that. Or maybe Lord, I'm just being silly, and you have so much on your mind, football isn't even a footnote. Please, please tell me what to do."

Not knowing what else to do, I sit quietly and then say out loud, "Amen."

"Amen," a deep male voice, softly echoes behind me. Startled, thinking I am alone, I turn around and see Fr. Tom parish priest, standing behind me, off to my left.

"I'm sorry Tessa, I didn't mean to interrupt. I wasn't eavesdropping. I needed something from our altar supply room. I thought it was you, and I wanted to wait until you were finished," he says sheepishly.

"Not at all, Fr. Tom, you have time to sit?" I ask him, gesturing to the space beside me.

"Actually, I need to get back to the school. How is Jackson? I was thinking of him just yesterday. And you and the family? I haven't seen any of the Carmichaels in a while."

I am more than a little embarrassed at this. We haven't been to church as a family in quite a long time. Jackson usually was the insistent one about church attendance. I am Methodist, he is Catholic but very set on raising the girls in his faith. Since the girls moved away, and Jackson basically quit coming home with any frequency, I quit going to church.

"All is good, just very busy, you know. Jackson is so busy; he rarely gets home much anymore. All those natural disasters, and all that," I tell him, trying to make very light conversation, so he doesn't pick up on anything else.

He furrows his brow a bit, clasps his hands together and says, "Yes, I expect so. I miss talking to him, though. We used to have weekly chats, no matter where he was. Now, it's been a long while since I last spoke to him. Is everything okay? Just work overload? I know that feeling well."

"Well, time waits for no one. I am so very happy to see you. God Bless you and your family. Please give my fondest regards to Jackson," he says quietly, patting me on the shoulder and heading up the aisle on his errand.

I climb in my Pathfinder, start the engine and sit a few minutes taking in what just happened. Then, it hits me like a load of bricks. Fr. Tom and Jackson have not spoken in a long time. This is completely out of character for Jackson. Fr. Tom, the kindly, older priest with a just a small hint of Irish lilt in his voice; is Jackson's spiritual mentor. They hit it off greatly, when we first started coming here. Jackson took to him immediately and spoke with him at least several times a week by phone. Jackson would always check in with Fr. Tom, no matter where he might be working. It was their version of "Where's Waldo". Fr. Tom enjoyed seeing the cool locations. He loved to travel but was getting up in years, and long distance travel not very likely anymore.

Jackson has not kept in contact with him. I bet if I asked Fr. Tom it would be around the same time, he started pushing to grow the business and quit coming home. Jackson has quit attending mass services. Those connections are not coincidental- not at all. They say sometimes God works in quiet and mysterious ways. That he does. I now know for sure; Jackson is up to his eyeballs in something bad.

Later in the week, my mom flies in from Florida. I need her support and unofficial legal advice. If my instincts are right, I need to know what to do about the Jackson mess. Trent is coming over today. He calls with news that he says cannot wait. Since they will both be here, I've decided to share Big Ed's letter that I've carefully hidden in a small cubby safe behind the wine cellar. It's by the door that is supposedly an underground tunnel. I need help deciding what to do about Ed's confession. This time, I can't act just on my own instincts. There is too much at stake.

Mom is happy to see Trent. She's always been a little *sweet* on him. I wonder if she ever thought he would make a better son-in-law than Jackson? That's silly and I push that thought right out of my mind. Trent has been in Huntsville, promoting a veteran's charity event. He brings a late lunch from Big Ed's pizza. It is very good! Nothing like gooey cheese and a little meat grease to blunt any bad news.

First, I share Big Ed's letter. I want to get it out of the way before I lose my nerve. I need to know what they think and if I'm way off course in believing Big Ed had anything to do with his son's death. Mom and Trent both read the letter quickly and say nothing right away. Mom has a shocked expression on her face, mirroring the one I likely had after first reading his letter. Trent breaks the silence.

"Well, that's a whopper of a deathbed confession," he says, tapping his pen furiously on the table.

"Yes, I don't quite know what to say or think," Mom says, her admiration of Big Ed seeming to diminish by the minute.

"That's a first! Claire Donovan is speechless," I sarcastically say, trying to fill up the empty space in the room.

"Okay, so am I crazy, or just reading into things, by thinking Big Ed turned his son over to Hawthorne and possibly the Mafia? That's insane," I say, shaking my head in disbelief.

"It is a definite possibility," Mom says, still in shock.

"Yep, looks like he finally hung Kelly out to dry without looking back," Trent quips.

We talk around it for a bit. We can't agree on the *why,* but we do know General Ryan told Hawthorne his precious daughter was married to a serial rapist based on the letter. The *how* of getting rid of Kelly seems messy, not like a mob hit, but it's not completely impossible.

"Let's table that for a minute and move on to what I've discovered with Jackson," he says in a serious mode that I recognize from our newspaper days. I groan a little because everything inside of me knows I will not like whatever he is about to say.

"Tessa, this took a deep dive and a wild walk on the dark web to get this. But it's legit, and I've put my best researchers and informants on it. So, listen up, this is some serious stuff. You were right, Jackson is in deep, and it's no good. My sources tell me that Martin Land has been pimping ADT and offering kickbacks for politicians willing to influence awarding big drone technology contracts to his and Jackson's company."

I look at Trent weirdly, "But isn't that..." I start.

"Illegal? Definitely," he finishes for me. "But hold onto your seat, that isn't all of it. Hawthorne, and the NY Mafia might also be in on the action. And that's where it gets very interesting," he says.

"And dangerous," Mom interjects.

"And potentially dangerous," he agrees. "Tessa, if this information is right, and I have every reason, at this point to believe it is, Jackson is going down one way or another. It involves senators, district attorneys, government contractors, Wall Street insiders, Henry Hawthorne, Anthony Marconi- New York Mafia. There are a lot of people lined up to go down with the ship if this thing breaks."

"Henry Hawthorne, Poppy's dad?" I ask incredulously.

"Yes, and you need to know my sources indicate that Jackson, Kelly, Poppy and Mindy have been running in the same social circles. They've been spotted at parties with some of these big players for the last eighteen months. It may be coincidental, and then again maybe not," he tells me knowing this will be hard for me to hear.

Hard to hear is an understatement! Jackson and Mindy have been socializing behind my back for over a year now? Jackson is possibly involved with the mafia somehow. Kelly was caught up in the middle of this too. "Whoa, Trent. Time out. I have so many questions, I don't even know where to start?"

"I know, it's too much to process and take in. Bottom line, I don't really think your friends are in this. At least not Poppy and Mindy. Kelly is anybody's guess and that might factor into his suspected murder. At this point, I don't know. What I do know is you need to prepare yourself for the possibility of an FBI visit and maybe your husband's arrest," he tells me and watches me for reaction.

"So, if I'm hearing you correctly Trent, you have reason to believe Jackson could be arrested and possibly prosecuted in this kickback scheme? And there's also a strong mafia connection to all of this as well?" Mom asks, her face going pale.

"Yes, Ms. Donovan. I believe that's correct. At least as much as I can put together. Trying to crack an ongoing FBI investigation isn't all that easy, even with the resources I have. Bottom line is Jackson is headed for trouble, big trouble. Tessa needs to protect herself, that's where you come in," he says.

"Why are y'all talking like I'm not even in the room? I'm a grown up thank you, capable of thinking and speaking for myself," it's a harsh reply but I'm so blown away by everything, lashing out is the only thing I can bring myself to do right now, even though it's wrong.

Mom takes my hand and pats it just like she's done since I was a little girl. "Sweetie, it's okay, we will figure this out. Just take a breath, breathe and know we will figure this out," she reassures me.

"Tessa, I don't mean to scare you, that's not my intention at all. But Jackson has dragged you into something huge. You need to take this very seriously and do everything your mother and I tell you to. Okay?" I've never heard this tone from Trent before in all the years I've known him, and it is scaring me.

"You need to prepare for an FBI visit. Make sure they have a warrant and identification. Do not let them bully you. If there is anything in this house or at the lake cottage that is incriminating and could tie you to Jackson's business dealings- get rid of it now," he says leaving no room for argument.

"Next, you need to go to high level security measures here. Hell, you don't even have a Ring doorbell with a camera. Get a home security system in place immediately. We will have your construction crew background checked and anybody who shows up here that you don't recognize will need to show id. No answering the door for packages, door to door preachers or girl scouts selling cookies, you got me?"

"Trent, you are scaring me. What the hell is going on?" I ask him in a shaky voice.

Mom answers for him. "Sweetie, it's not the FBI you need to worry about. It's Marconi and his thugs. If Jackson is somehow involved with them and is arrested; they will be very interested in making sure he doesn't talk," she says gently.

"If Jackson is arrested, then you need to worry. I expect the FBI won't let you leave the state, but you could stay with Finn or at the Donovan compound for a while. Construction will need to stop here for a bit. Dad and I will come back home and help you; don't you worry about that."

"Afton and Reagan, are they safe? They wouldn't go after the girls, would they?" I am so afraid right now and so very, very angry with Jackson.

"Likely not, but it may be a good idea for your daughters to take a social media break and hang a little closer to home, for a bit. Just in case Jackson does get arrested. I have some connections in Nashville and Asheville that can keep an eye on them. I also have an expert in my back pocket that can help them *disappear* on the Internet if they need to. Jonas may have to take leave of absence from his blog and sponsorship work. It might be a good time for him to start writing that book he's been interested in doing," Trent tells me with a wink.

He tries to lighten the mood, but I am terrified. My entire family may be targeted by the mafia because of Jackson's incredibly poor decision making and unbridled ambition. Not to mention, the FBI invading my privacy and home, and possible multiple interviews with them trying to prove my own innocence. Jackson, what have you gotten us into?

"So, jumping ahead here. If Jackson is arrested and has to go to trial, would I have to testify?" I ask, wondering what that would be like testifying in defense of a husband who drug me into this mess? Or testifying against my husband, the father and grandfather of our children, and sending him to prison.

"I'll take this one," Mom answers. "Maybe, I don't know. You wouldn't have to testify for the defense because of the legal separation and Jackson's long absence from home. That would hurt their case. The prosecution might call you but again, you've had such limited contact with Jackson it probably wouldn't be beneficial. Also, after the FBI goes through your phone and computer files and interviews you, it will be obvious you had no idea what was going on. Inconvenient, certainly an invasion of your personal privacy but nothing you can't survive. Jackson did you a big favor by staying far away."

Trent needs to head back to Nashville, and I am thankful for his help. I am trying to mentally prepare myself for all that lies ahead. He will check back in when he has any new developments. He cautions me not to talk to anyone about this. This new secret is ours alone to bear. It seems like when I let go of one secret there is a new one waiting to take its place. It's like somehow the void must be filled.

The night is nice, and Mom and I spend time out by the pool talking. She is doing all she can to distract me from Jackson's terrible mess. She tells me a secret that only she and Daddy know. Apparently, she's been waiting until I was old enough to know. She finally tells me why she quit being a defense attorney. I have been begging her to tell me for years and she always deferred until today. I guess today was finally the right time.

"I loved my job, and I was good at it, I didn't need the awards, high praise or compliments to tell me that," she tells me. "Using the Donovan gift didn't hurt either. I got so good at sensing people's emotions, that using it was just like breathing. I always just knew."

"My last case, you may remember. The guy accused of raping his fourteen-year-old stepdaughter. Pillar of society, good family man, people fell all over themselves defending him. Our law firm got the case, after all we were the best. This man needed the best to clear his name and walk away free. The man had sterling character witnesses including his wife, passed a lie detector test, everything. The media has already made its case that he was innocent, and it was just a case of a vengeful stepdaughter."

"Of course, I got the case, the defense attorney with the highest number of wins. I begged the senior partners to remove me from the case. I even suggested bias because of my own family situation that I couldn't fairly represent the client. Nothing I said mattered. I considered resigning and twice went into my bosses' office to do so."

"I knew after meeting with my client the first time he was guilty. No matter who or how he fooled other people, he sexually assaulted a child. I couldn't walk into the senior partners' offices and announce that I could *feel* his guilt. I would lose all credibility and maybe my job that I had worked so hard for. Besides, if I didn't take the case, someone else would. Even guilty people have the right to counsel," she says, starting to tear up.

"Oh Mom, I'm so sorry. That must've been terrible."

"It was, but I got a little revenge. I could've gone all in convincing the jury she was lying. I could have presented that she was allegedly sexually active. I could have said and done many things to get that man off. Public opinion was already in his favor. But looking at that little girl, I could not do it."

"He was sentenced to a ridiculously light sentence of 36 months in prison, with possibility of parole on good behavior and intensive counseling. He was killed in prison by a fellow inmate, never even made it to his first parole hearing. It was one of the few cases I ever lost. The next day, I walked in and resigned. No letter, no thirty-day notice, nothing other than *goodbye*. I ruined my litigation career doing that. I knew I would never be a relevant defense attorney again."

"Do you ever regret doing that?" I ask knowing her career had been important to her.

"The only regret I have, sweet daughter of mine, is not telling them to kiss my ass in the beginning when they forced me to take that case," she laughs.

"Tessa, the moral of this sad, sorry story is never let anyone or anything prevent you from doing what you know in your heart, is the right thing. You hear me? Never," she says, wiping tears with the back of her hand.

"Mom, I love you. You are one of the strongest women I know. I hope I can only be half as strong as you are," I say, hugging her.

"You, my dear one, are stronger than you will ever know."

—·—

JASON

Mom didn't think much of my private memorial for Grampa Ed. In fact, she lost her mind when she found me missing. She freaked out and sent Neil out to look for me. I'm surprised she didn't call the National Guard in to look for me. Passed out in the graveyard with an empty bottle of 18-year-old Jameson whiskey didn't go well for me. Having the gun put Mom over the edge. I didn't intend to use it but I'll never convince Mom of that.

Right now, I'm sitting in a boujee long-term mental health rehab facility in California. Aunt Kimberly lives close by, and checks on me every few days. I tried to talk my way out of going but Mom wasn't buying it. She cut me a little slack because of Bio Dad and then losing Grampa Ed. But this time, I think I've pushed her to the limit.

The main reason I haven't pitched a shit fit and refused to go is because of Grampa Ed. He left me and Mom Meadowview farm. If I meet his other requirements, then the farm will be all mine when I turn 30. He could not have left me anything better. I have always loved that old place. Some of my only good memories are there.

But the catch in getting the farm is going to long-term rehab, staying clean and continuing with my therapist. It's a hard list that he's given me to do. But he believed in me being able to do it, so I'm gonna try with everything I've got. Mom and Neil will be waiting at the farm when I get back. All of Grampa's other employees have agreed to stay on and he's left me some recommendations for hiring some more, when we need them.

Finn is interested in helping me expand the horse breeding program. Wouldn't that be awesome if one day, we bred a Kentucky Derby horse? That's Finn's dream. Grampa would be so proud.

I don't know if this *woo-woo* rehab stuff is working. But for the first time in a long time, I woke up almost happy. I don't want to get wasted; I want to stay clean. Maybe one day, there's another girl like Chloe; the sober version, waiting for me somewhere. I don't dream about fire monsters anymore. Last night, I dreamed about the farm, horses and a dark night sky filled with stars. Maybe this time, I can finally do it.

TESSA

Well it's a new year, and I very much doubt it could be too much worse than last year. Although the beginning of this year is trending that way. Trent's sources were right and on Thanksgiving day Jackson was arrested. He spent the holiday weekend with his sister and niece so at least his daughters and I were spared that humiliation.

We had Thanksgiving in Nashville with Afton. Trent stopped by during the weekend to brief all of us on safety measures we needed to take.

When Mom, Dad and I got back home to Honeywood, the house had been ransacked. Nothing taken as far as I could tell, but definitely someone was looking for something specific. All the cameras on the home security system had been disabled. It's a very unsettling feeling to have your home torn apart by criminals and then law enforcement types invading your privacy. Being fingerprinted in your own home is demoralizing.

As predicted, the FBI showed up to do preliminary *friendly* interviews. They decided after two interviews I could stay in my home or travel anywhere in the state that I felt more comfortable. They offered neither police protection nor permission to leave Sweet Home Alabama. While Mom insisted I was not a suspect, or even a person of interest; they were holding the reins pretty tight on me, for the time being.

It didn't get any better when I called my boss (and friend) Annie to update her on our current situation. I didn't want her to be blindsided. Jackson's arrest would soon be national news . I suggested taking a short leave of absence until things sorted themselves. She hesitantly told me the owners suggested an extended leave of absence until this situation settles. The owners are very conservative and in the process of seeking out investors to grow the company. I've become a liability to them with my high visibility, potential law-breaking husband. I don't blame them a bit. It's not personal- it's good business practice. Somehow, I didn't expect to also lose my career in Jackson's dumpster fire. But here we are.

Jackson spent the Christmas holidays in jail. The judge set his bail at two million dollars. He wasn't considered a flight risk, but the FBI agents assigned to my case conceded it was safer for him to stay in jail. We couldn't raise the money even if we wanted to. Anyone I might ask to help was either dead or somehow implicated in this mess.

Before his death, Big Ed sought out the services of one of the best defense lawyers in the country. Jackson would have excellent representation. He likely would not get completely out of any charges the FBI leveled against him. But he could bargain to get the best possible deal. Martin Land was also arrested and given 48 hours at home, by a lenient judge to get his affairs in order. He was escorted by deputy sheriffs and a couple of line duty cops to his mansion in Nashville. Instead of packing and saying his final farewells to his family; he went into his master bathroom and shot himself in the head. I guess he was being thoughtful by blowing out his brains there. This news made me so sad. I will always fondly remember the Martin that used to compliment my cooking like I was a five-star chef and always bring small thoughtful gifts for me and the girls. What happened to that Martin?

I haven't been allowed to see Jackson, all part of the separate and interrogated scheme, I guess. I've been called to Nashville several times for longer interviews. Staying with Afton and seeing my family is the only thing that is getting me through this terrible time. I want to talk to Mindy and Kate, but I'm not allowed to do that either. They are both on the FBI interview list and may be potentially called as prosecution witnesses if Jackson is formally charged and his case goes to trial.

The only person I am allowed to speak with about what's going on is my mother. She has been given permission to advise me in an unofficial capacity should I need legal counsel.

When Jackson is charged at his preliminary hearing, the charge sheet is long and daunting. I do not go to the hearing. Mom goes instead and brings back the news of the charges and that Jackson has been beaten up by inmates several times. They are moving him to solitary confinement for his protection. She speaks to my new FBI friends who tell her the FBI believes the beatings are warnings either from the crooked politicians or Anthony Marconi.

When the FBI no longer need me, I go to Lake James and stay with Finn in my childhood home. I want to go home to Honeywood or out to Storybook but because of the remote locations, the FBI has advised against that. It's not safe and they don't have the resources to assign enough team members to protect me at those locations. That's right, until Jackson's next hearing, I'm pretty much under house arrest. I can't visit my children, grandchildren or friends. I can't go anywhere without an FBI escort.

What they are not telling me either is that they are afraid Marconi might send out some guys to scare me. Or it might be some of the other *movers and shakers* that have been arrested in this big sting operation.

They believe someone might try to hurt me to send a message to Jackson in jail, so he won't rat any of them out. What they don't know is Jackson probably doesn't really care what happens to me. He is most interested in saving his sorry hide. If he cared about me at all, we wouldn't be in this ridiculously awful situation in the first place.

Via my mother, Trent sends word to me two days before Jackson's hearing, that he is taking a plea deal. I have no idea how he knows this. I guess it's his FBI contacts or whoever else he can get to talk off record. We arrange to meet at Storybook, he will be bringing a gun and a security team, former military types who take personal protection seriously.

Against Daddy's better judgment, Mom and I drive out to Storybook on the day of Jackson's hearing. Everyone will be distracted by that, so we should be safe at the cottage.

Trent and his security team are already there. The guys look straight out of an action movie, they have checked the house, boathouse and secured the perimeter so we can meet privately in peace. He's even put an alibi in place, if we are ever questioned by law enforcement. We are meeting to discuss a *tell all* interview featuring the scorned wife of Jackson Carmichael. Even the thought of that makes me nauseated. But we have to be prepared, just in case.

"Tessa, how are you?" Trent asks as he gives me a big hug and then hugs Mom.

"Truthfully? I don't know."

"Look I don't know how much time we have together today, so I'll get right to it. I'm sorry for not being gentle but here goes. Jackson is expected to enter a plea deal today. The FBI was hoping to take down Senator Kirby (Defense Committee), Senator Hanson (Homeland Security), New York District Attorney James Travis,

Henry Hawthorne, Anthony Marconi, and Martin Land. There may be others before it's done but these are the main principles."

"Holy hell," my mother exclaims.

"Holy hell, indeed," Trent agrees. "FBI has been leaning hard on Jackson, Martin Land and a few other low hanging fruit to get to the bigger players. Martin ain't talking obviously and Jackson remains to be seen. Others have squawked but I don't know if it will amount to anything and neither does the FBI," he says, sounding a little exasperated.

"What about Jackson, how does this all play out for him?" I ask, worried about the answer.

"Jackson, Martin Land, New York Assistant DA, some military government contractors, some Wall Street folks, all people who answer to the big players will get prison time. It sends a message to the big guys, and demonstrates the FBI is serious about prosecuting people."

"But Jackson specifically, what happens to him? I don't care about these other people," I say.

"Jackson's sentence will directly depend on whether he is willing to trade information for lighter sentencing or is holding out to protect himself and his family. People who turn evidence against the mafia and crooked politicians don't have a high survival rate in prison," he says and probably wishes he hadn't.

"Also, it's my gut feeling Jackson didn't know a whole lot and really wasn't involved in any of the deal talking. That seemed to be Martin and we know what happened to him. Jackson is smart enough to leave Marconi, Hawthorne, and the senators out of anything he might say, no matter what the Feds are offering him."

"Well, I guess we will know soon enough, what he's willing to do?" Mom says, looking at her watch. She made friendly with Jackson's attorney and got him to promise to call as soon as anything official came down from the bench.

This whole thing is making me incredibly sick. So much for the boring, lonely life I thought I had last year. If I could only rewind all of last year, I would.

"There's something else Tessa," Trent tells me. There always is, anymore.

"I can't confirm, and this stays here, never to be repeated again. Got it?" he looks at Mom and me waiting for our agreement.

"It is **very** possible that Kelly Ryan turned Jackson in to the FBI. They were heard arguing outside Kelly's mansion just a few days before Kelly died. According to the substitute night chauffeur, a youngish guy who apparently likes to make money by dishing out personal details of the rich and famous."

"Why did this driver not go to the police, or divulge when he was surely interviewed?" Mom's lawyer brain is kicking in now.

"Didn't want the attention, maybe didn't want to cut off his money stream. Who knows, why petty criminals do what they do?" Trent shrugs.

"NO, stop it! I don't want to hear anything else. Not another single word, you understand?" I say in a loud voice to Trent. It's not bad enough that I'm waiting to see if my husband who may or may not have committed a federal crime is going to prison. Or I guess how much time he is getting for taking the fall for his now dead boss and powerful people. Trent is now suggesting Jackson may have killed his own best friend. My mind cannot take anymore of this.

Trent looks pained and does not want to continue but he does. "Kate and Mindy also visited the mansion in the last month of Kelly's life. But again, I think the connection is coincidental. From all accounts, they were visiting Poppy. I don't think there's anything more going on."

I end our meeting. As much as I care about Trent and am incredibly thankful for his support; I can't deal with anything else today. We plan to get together in a few weeks after Jackson's sentencing and see where the situation stands. That is, if I still have any sanity left by then.

It's hard to believe this whole nightmare with Jackson started only a little over three months ago. It feels more like a lifetime ago. In January, he accepted a plea bargain on collusion and failure to report a federal crime charge. This is a *win* considering the long list of charges he faced.

Whether or not Jackson is guilty is beside the point. The FBI cast the net wide and arrested as many as possible involved in the case. The major players handed over subordinates and received stern reprimands or offered resignations. In a few cases, like Henry Hawthorne, they eluded authorities or left the country entirely. Hawthorne repatriated himself, Poppy and the twins back to London. No wonder Poppy didn't respond to my phone calls or text messages.

In the end, Martin Land and Kelly Ryan were named the masterminds behind the plot. This is both ridiculous and convenient. Martin was involved, Kelly was speculative, and both are dead. Neither had anyone crying out for justice to clear their names. Martin was long divorced, with a family who is deeply embarrassed by the situation. Kelly's only advocate, is recently dead. His sister Kimberly ran away years ago to be free of the long shadow of Kelly.

I'm now convinced more than ever, that with Kelly's alleged involvement in the *kickback* scheme, he was murdered. Trent and I disagree on who is the murderer. He thinks all of the evidence points to Hawthorne, or one of the crooked politicians. Kelly was always a loose cannon with impulsive judgment.

I think Kelly's death was more personal. Yes, I'm basing this theory almost entirely on gut feelings. But I know I'm right. Mindy finally told Jackson about Kelly's assault. Because of his feelings for Mindy, Jackson confronted Kelly. Jackson threatened Kelly indicating he told Poppy about the nanny affair and his sordid past. They argued loudly, got into a physical fight. Then Jackson left before things escalated to the point of no return. Next day, Kelly called the FBI seeking revenge on Jackson. Twenty-four hours later, Kelly ends up dead.

I admit, and Trent pointed out there are holes in my theory. A lot of things would have to align for this to work out. But Jackson could have easily still been in Virginia, the night of Kelly's death. How hard would it have been for him to follow Kelly, hoping for solid proof of the nanny affair? He threatened to tell Poppy, knowing this would ruin Kelly. Maybe Jackson saw an opportunity to run Kelly off the road scaring him and it all went wrong. The whole thing was quickly investigated, and Big Ed admitted discrepancies were overlooked all for saving the Hawthorne and Ryan reputations.

Trent thinks it's a stretch. Maybe it is. But Jackson's deep, long-lasting feelings might cause a man to do just about anything to avenge his love. Trent believes I'm being melodramatic and letting my own personal feelings cloud my rational judgment. He has strongly advised me to drop searching for Kelly's killer. This is unlike Trent, who travels with a security team because of the dangerous assignments he takes. He says digging too deeply into this case might be very dangerous for me, my family and even Jackson. If Kelly was really involved with these people, Trent is absolutely right. But I have to wonder if Trent isn't also trying to protect me from finding out that my husband is capable of murder. Kelly and Jackson are the only two that know for sure. One is dead and the other is obviously not talking.

Jackson is serving out his sentence at FPC Pensacola. It is a minimum-security federal prison with the reputation of being *cushy*. I suspect Big Ed somehow suspected Jackson's outcome and had a hand in this. That man knew absolutely everyone worth knowing.

The FBI and my legal advisers suggested that I not contact Jackson until things settled down. This was easy, I really had no desire to see or speak to him anyway right now. The girls keep in touch weekly but have also opted not to visit their dad. I respect their decision. Jackson's lowlife sister and niece talked to the media so much, his attorneys asked for a gag order. I guess they like the attention. Apparently, they haven't been to see Jackson or contacted him. They realize he no longer has any money to fund their lifestyles. He quickly became yesterday's news.

That's right, Jackson is pretty much penniless except for a small savings account that the FBI allowed him to keep. There's less than $7,000 in the account. Everything else, his share of ADT worth millions, his retirement account, work and personal vehicles, luxury RV, boat and nearly everything else in his name was seized by the FBI for restitution. Big Ed set aside funds for Jackson's criminal defense. Otherwise, Jackson would likely be in debt the rest of his life.

His sentence, three years with time served and opportunity for parole after 12 months is fairly light. But, with the FBI seizures and the only real mistake he made was getting involved with the wrong people, it's fairly harsh. If I am right and he killed Kelly, he is getting off very easy. Not to mention the fact that he will spend the rest of his life looking over his shoulder wondering if the corrupt politicians or mafia will make him disappear.

Mindy offers to take me to visit Jackson. I don't especially want to see my husband. Well, my former husband now, my Mom arranged a *quickie* divorce for me. It was so fast, I almost felt like a celebrity. There are so many things I would like to ask Jackson. But he is in prison, with eyes and ears everywhere, so some of these questions have to wait-maybe forever.

I do decide to visit him, just to get some closure on this crazy life chapter. Mom feels like I won't be able to move forward in my life until I see him and truly acknowledge what has happened. I have the tendency to withdraw from troubling people and situations. She is right, I do need to face this.

Mindy drops me off at the entrance of the prison. She is checking in with a local client and will be back in an hour. Plenty of time for me to see Jackson and get this over with. Prisons, like hospitals, hold a lot of residual energy. It greatly impacts me, and I fight down the urge to be violently sick all over my brand-new shoes.

I'm processed and led back to the visitation room. It's a large, bright, friendly place where you could easily forget you are behind prison walls with convicted criminals. Jackson comes into the room and sits across from me at the table. There are two guards in the room by the entrance but neither seem particularly concerned or on heightened alert. They honestly look more like library security personnel instead of prison guards.

Jackson looks good, thinner but good. I haven't seen him since Big Ed's service, and we barely spoke then. It is awkward in the space between us. We ask the normal questions, "how are you", "did the girls tell you.". This prison is so much less restrictive than other places. Other than being locked up and never allowed to leave, it's not a horrible place to be.

He tells me his attorneys believe he might be released as early as December, no later than next June. That is good news for him. I'm not sure how I really feel about that. Especially if he really did kill

Kelly, like I suspect he did. But I'm trying to follow Trent's advice and leave things alone for now. I have to believe that eventually the truth becomes public knowledge, so if he's guilty, it will come out. I know though, this is likely the very last time we will spend together. The idea of spending any more time with him after all he's done makes my skin crawl.

We run out of things to say. Or at least things we can talk about in a prison visiting room. It's almost time for Mindy to be back, so I get up ready to leave the room. Jackson asks me to sit back down a minute.

"Tessa, I'm so very sorry for everything. I know you will probably never forgive me. But I am truly sorry. All those months I didn't come home or reach out to you, it was to protect you and the girls. I had gotten myself into something I didn't know how to get out of, and I didn't want to bring it down on you. There were people involved," he stops himself. I guess realizing he shouldn't go any further. He claps both hands on the table lightly and gets ready to stand up. With his right hand, he quickly spreads his three middle fingers and raises his hand with his fingertips touching the table. It is so slight and so quick I almost missed it.

"Anyway, thank you for coming to see me, it means a lot," he says.

"You are welcome Jackson; I wish you well. Please take good care of yourself and be careful." I don't tell him I will see him again soon, because I know I won't.

He signals to the guard he is ready to leave. I watch the love of my life, the man who shared so much of my life, walk out the door forever. I wait for the second guard to signal me to follow. I collect my things, return the visitor's badge and walk through the main security check to exit the building. I am very happy to leave this place behind.

While I'm waiting for Mindy, I replay our conversation. The hand gesture, so out of place, caught my attention but why did he do that?

Was it a nervous gesture, or one of his old Sig Ep secret hand signals. I didn't know those, why would he do that. Then, it struck me. Jackson was making an "M", on the table. M for Marconi, Jackson was afraid of Marconi. That little hand signal answered a lot of questions for me. Why he didn't come home, why he was asking for money for ADT, who beat him up in jail, and why he didn't turn evidence against the big players in this case. He was terrified of Marconi and with good reason, Marconi's reputation as a ruthless mafia boss was well earned. I guess Jackson will carry that fear for a long, long time. What a terrible price to pay for unchecked ambition and getting swept away in the quest for money and power.

I'm quiet in the car on the long ride home. Mindy does her best at conversation. I am an unwilling participant. I nap a while, trying to quiet my mind and recover from the sensory overload of the prison experience. Earlier, we decided to stop in Auburn overnight. Mindy has a client in the area, and she thought it might be good to get my mind off the heaviness of the Jackson visit.

It was a great distraction visiting all our old favorite spots. We did feel incredibly old when we saw sorority girls walking across campus wearing their letters. Were we ever really that young? These days, it sure doesn't feel like it. To be so young, idealistic and with your whole life ahead of you. Would I go back and change everything, if I could?

Shortly, before we pull into Lake James, Mindy has something on her mind. She finally decides to say it.

"I know you don't want to talk about Jackson and that's okay. I want you to know, anything between Jackson and me was all in his imagination. There was **never** anyone but Theo for me."

"I believe you Mindy, we don't need to talk about this again," I tell her, really wanting to drop all talk of Jackson.

"Kelly Ryan ruined our lives in so many ways. We should've run away from him a long time ago and taken Kate with us. Men like that don't change. We are expected to put up with awful behavior and keep our mouths closed. No more, it's time for women to stand up for each other and stand up to men like Kelly and Jackson who think we are playthings, property, things to be used and discarded whenever they feel like it," she says angrily.

"Yes, Mindy. We had a lot of *should haves* in the past. I'm trying to move forward and not make the same mistakes again," I tell her and mean it.

"Tessa, it's you, me and Kate against the world. No more doing and thinking how other people think we should be and act. You understand? We are smart, capable women who don't need to be bullied by men to get ahead in life. We have each other and that may be all we need."

"Moving forward, may we never tell lies and keep secrets that harm others and threaten to destroy us," I say, offering a pretend toast. I mean this with everything in my heart.

Epilogue

The last two years have been a crazy rollercoaster ride. After my divorce and Jackson's imprisonment, I didn't see myself ever being anything close to happy or normal again. What I wouldn't have given to go back to the quiet, empty nest days of the past.

After I was quietly phased out of my position at Twisted Oak Publishing, I needed a new job. I briefly considered going to Europe and taking a reporter position with the *Stars and Stripes* news outlet. I had a great recommendation from their most famous intern, Trent James. In the end, I decided that Europe was too far away and I would miss my family very much.

Mom and Mindy convinced me to follow through with plans to renovate Honeywood and turn it into an event venue. Mom and Dad made it easier by offering up a partnership. They were homesick and wanted to move back home. They built a small cottage at Honeywood. Mom offered to manage the venue and Dad offered up his handyman services. It was a great solution that I couldn't afford to turn down.

In order to afford my share of the renovations, I sold Storybook Cottage. It made me sad, but it was no longer a place of happy memories for our family. With my mom's blessing, I sold to a newly organized non-profit organization focusing on women's issues. Storybook would be a retreat for women of domestic and intimate violence abuse.

I think Grandmother Esme would be thrilled. Mom let it slip that Mindy orchestrated a deal between Poppy and Big Ed's estate to make the financing happen.

Jason came back from California, healthy and well. He made good on his requirements to take over Meadowview farm. With Neil's guidance and Finn's grand ideas, they may just have a Kentucky Derby horse one day. Jason is thriving and I couldn't be happier.

As predicted, Jackson got released from prison shortly before the Christmas holidays. He spent time with the girls. I declined the invitation, choosing to spend time with them separately. It's too soon for us to be spending holidays together again as a divorced family. Maybe in time, but just not yet. He is planning to head out west and work on General Ryan's friend's dude ranch in Montana. Big Ed made some work connections for Jackson whenever he decides what's next for him.

Mindy is living her best life. She opened a second design store on the 30 A beach strand. She did actually find a *mini me* in Ashley Taylor-watch out world! She is also collaborating with Poppy who is bored sitting on her millions, in designing a high-end home goods line. Mindy just made the cover of *Alabama Living* as one of the state's top designers/stagers. She is on the short list to redecorate the governor's mansion. Her star is going up, up, up.

The biggest surprise of all was Kate and Finn's engagement. This caught me completely off guard and I am deliriously happy for them. Finn and Kate are buying Mom and Dad's house. Kate has decided to quit the finance business and open a small bakery in downtown Lake James.

The very last family event at Storybook cottage before she becomes a retreat is Kate and Finn's wedding. They insisted on getting married here and I couldn't turn them down. Let's close this chapter with a happy ending. The Invincible Six have become the Invincible Three and we are going to take on the world.

Kate and Finn's day is magical and everything it should be. It is the perfect ending for Before and a fabulous start for Next. It is an all-day celebration filled with love, joy and laughter. We even managed to find a DJ willing to play our 90's hits playlist. As the party is winding down, Mindy and I collapse in deck chairs on the dock. It has been a long and exhausting day. We small talk about the wedding and Ms. Cindy's wedding ideas. She will **not** be coordinating any weddings at Honeywood anytime soon. We have a great big laugh over this.

It's late and we need to go to bed. There is quite a bit of cleanup left to do tomorrow. Mindy grabs me in an uncharacteristic big hug and whispers in my ear, *"Kelly and Jackson didn't run the world. We did, I made sure of it."* It's an odd thing to say and my tired mind doesn't think anymore about it. We are happy. It was a very good day and I let it go.

A month later, at the suggestion of my former editor Annie, I'm sitting in the newly remodeled carriage house attempting to write down my experiences with Kelly and the past two years. She thinks it would be therapeutic and there might even be a book in there somewhere. I've struggled with what to say about Kelly's murder. So much has already been said and rehashed since he died. Trent begs me to leave it alone. My heart tells me to do the same because I know Jackson was involved. But there's something that just keeps nagging in the back of my mind. It's there waiting patiently for me to catch up.

Frustrated, I close out my document and stand to stretch. Going over to pour myself a diet coke, I turn up the volume on the Spotify channel I'm listening to. It's a classic 90's station, and Seal's *Kissed By A Rose* comes on. I turn up the volume, sing along and put out my best dance moves. As the song fades away, suddenly a thought projects into my mind so forcefully it almost gives me an instant migraine. A slow smile spreads across my face. I say out loud, "Mindy is Kelly's killer". And all's right with the world.

Mindy (After)

I never intentionally set out to kill Kelly. Sure, after the fire summer, I spent too many sleepless nights thinking up ways to end Kelly Ryan. Then much later on, I realized ending Kelly was too shortsighted. Totally humiliating him for the rest of his life, now that's a plan I could get behind. If there was one thing that was super important to Kelly it was his family name, and all the power that carried. Of course, the fact it was all due to his dad, was totally lost on Kelly. Never did think he was too bright.

All those years, I let Jackson talk me into keeping quiet. He was protecting Kelly, but I was protecting Theo. Knowing what Kelly did to me would've shredded Theo. The perfect couple Theo and Mindy, wouldn't have survived either.

Keeping Tessa in line proved a little more difficult though. Every so often, she would spin up about telling the *truth* to Kate and Theo. Tessa didn't even know the real truth she was protecting. Of us all, she's always been the *truth-seeker*. You could always depend on Tessa to have a strong sense of right and wrong, and no questionable gray areas for her. It is one of her adorable traits, but it's also most tiresome.

Until the year Theo died, I planned on taking that secret with me to the grave. For my own benefit- not for Kelly's sake. Then for whatever reason, I don't know if it was the brown liquor or Jackson's undying love, he had to shoot off his mouth to Theo and ruin everything. That day changed it all.

I know Theo's death certificate lists heart attack- Covid complications as the cause of death. What it should say is *death caused by best friend.* Jackson's revelation killed Theo. He would pay for that.

Getting Kelly to cheat on his wife, even the perfect female that she is, wasn't very hard. In fact, he practically did it himself, with a little help from me. I just dangled the bait. Dana Smith was a lucky find. Early Education graduate student putting herself through college by nannying for wealthy families. It took a little more digging to discover her porno blog and a very good private investigator to uncover previous extortion claims. For an envelope full of money, she was more than willing to trap Kelly. She could extort money from the Hawthorne-Ryan family and pocket the large amount I gave her. *Win-win* for her.

Getting Dana hired was easy too. Poppy and I had become friendly. We got together often discussing possibly luxury properties for sale on the 30A strand. She was also super interested in starting her own home accessories line. She had already named it *Poppy Ware.* I didn't fancy it, but that didn't matter. I casually dropped Dana's name in conversation when Poppy was looking for a new, younger nanny replacement. She hired Dana on my recommendation even though Dana was very young and very pretty. But then, when you're Poppy Hawthorne, you don't have any competition. You **are** the competition!

It would be no time at all before Kelly was sniffing around the new nanny. Days maybe a couple of weeks and he would be all in her personal space making highly inappropriate and suggestive comments.

It didn't take long- within two weeks, he was doing just that. I made sure Poppy stayed busy with our new business ventures, giving Dana plenty of time to lure him in.

The plan was to catch Kelly with Dana in a very compromising position and send the video to TMZ and other news outlets. Dana was an expert in this area. After all, she worked in porn-land. Dana didn't know my face or voice. We communicated through burner phones and couriers. After TMZ broke the sordid news, I planned to spam every major newspaper in the country with full page ads outing Kelly as a serial sleaze ball. I couldn't use the word "rape" but there were plenty other words that would get the message across.

What I didn't plan on was Jackson's involvement. After his surprising confession of love at Storybook, he decided to take matters in his own hands and avenge my honor with Kelly. I had to stop him. So, I went to Virginia and waited for him to show up.Then things went sideways.

I had plans for Jackson too. They also did not include murder. Jackson would pay by losing his company ADT, his real mistress. In the process, he would also lose Tessa. He didn't deserve her anyway. In the past year, I watched Jackson get sucked down the rabbit hole of chasing the powerful *movers and shakers* in the Beltway. If there was a D.C. party he and Martin could get an invite to, they were there. I kept running into them because of clients, and Poppy who was suddenly my new best friend.

Jackson was already on the road to Perdition. All I had to do was make a few suggestions and get him invited to the right parties. Get him introductions to the right social circles and watch it explode. I never saw his unwanted admission of love coming. And I certainly didn't expect him to go all knightley on me. Defending my honor now was just way too late.

I was in Virginia, out with Poppy when Jackson and Kelly had their big fight. I know, because I had already paid off the substitute chauffeur driver a while ago to spy on Kelly and the nanny. Apparently, words were said, blah blah blah, punches thrown and then Jackson left. I hoped that was the end of that.

The night of the accident, Dana was supposed to check in with me. Her directions were very simple. Make sure Kelly was drunk. I'd already stashed a bottle of his favorite bourbon in his massive walk-in closet. I showed up at the mansion on the day Poppy left for her trip. I had *mistakenly* gotten our meeting date wrong. Kelly was on the phone, and I was able to slip upstairs and stash the bottle, in an obvious place of course.

How hard was it to follow? Get Kelly smashed, video him in a compromising situation and get out. Pretty simple plan, right? I don't know if Dana got cold feet at the last minute or believed whatever lame garbage Kelly must've told her about being misunderstood and leaving his wife- classic cheater stuff. But she neither called, texted or delivered the video to the courier. I immediately knew something was wrong.

I parked down the street from the mansion, trying to figure out the next step. Suddenly, Kelly's red Ferrari zipped around the bend going too fast and erratically. That stupid girl was running away with him. I followed them at a close distance keeping Kelly's car in sight. He was all over the road. Why was he driving? Where was the chauffeur?

At this point, I thought I would just follow them and see what happened. I was already this invested in the process. Then, I realized if I followed Kelly and pushed too close to him: He might overcorrect and have a small accident. A 911 call on the burner phone and he would be knee deep in a very embarrassing situation.

Before I could act on this last-minute plan, a black Suburban with dark windows passed me and got immediately on Kelly's rear bumper.

Kelly accelerated; the black car accelerated. Kelly pulled in the left lane, so did the black Suburban. Kelly accelerated quickly, and the black Suburban was right on his bumper trying to force him off the road. I let off the gas slowing my car down. I didn't know what was going on now, but I didn't want any part of it. The Suburban ran Kelly off the road. Kelly overcorrected and slammed into a tree in the curve.

The black Suburban kept right on going. There were cars behind me now. I could see them pulling over. I pull over a little way in front of the accident. I am shaking so hard now, I can't stop. I'm most concerned that the black Suburban is waiting up the road to chase me too. I call 911 on the burner phone even though I know the calls have already been made. Then I get out of the car, stomp the phone to bits and hit it with a rock just to be safe. There is a small stream close to the road. I throw the phone in it and walk away. I am almost sure; Kelly Ryan is dead.

I have no idea who killed him that night and I **don't** want to find out. The next day before leaving Virginia, I call the FBI and tell them Kelly Ryan and Jackson Carmichael are possibly involved in illegal activities. They thank me for my time. I know they can trace my phone and will eventually show up at my door. I am ready.

I told Tessa at Kate and Finn's wedding that I would take care of things. And I did! Tessa is very smart; she will figure it out. But she is also very loyal and always has been. I'm so very curious to see what our little *truth seeker* will do. I guess only time will tell.

THE END

AFTERWORD

Secret Keepers deals with some heavy themes. The characters go through major struggles and dark times. Sometimes, the world can be a *hard* and *cruel* place . If you or someone you know is struggling with thoughts of suicide or have been a victim of domestic or intimate partner abuse; please reach out to someone. Let's all help one another make it through to brighter days!

National Suicide Prevention Lifeline: 1-800-273- TALK (8255)
Domestic Violence Hotline 1-800-799-7233

DISCUSSION GROUP QUESTIONS

Here are a few questions, that you are welcome to use as a guide for your Book Club discussion. HAPPY DISCUSSIONS!

1. *Secret Keepers* is told from three points of view. Which POV do you find most credible? The least? Who do you believe is giving the most accurate representation of Kelly Ryan? Tessa, Mindy or Jason? Why or why not?

2. Tessa is an empath, but she has trouble "reading" Jackson. Why is she not able to get a good sense of Jackson's emotions? Do you think she's always been unable to feel Jackson's emotions? Or is this a new thing, because of geographical and emotional distance in their marriage?

3. Tessa's marriage is slowly falling apart. Are there warning signs pointing toward this? What are they and why does Tessa not recognize what is happening? In your own past relationships, what were the signs that things weren't going well? Did you notice them or like Tessa, not realize until it was much too late?

4. Tessa's mom Claire is also an empath, stronger in her gift than Tessa. Why doesn't she tell Tessa about Jackson and

Kelly? She must sense that something is "off " with both of them. Do you know anyone who is an empath or has a strong sixth sense about things? Do people believe them or like Jackson, think it's an overactive imagination in hyperdrive?

5. *Secret Keepers* main themes are about **secrets, lies and friendship.** Tessa, Mindy and Kate's friendships are severely tested over what happened that fire summer. Have you ever had long-term friendships that ended over keeping secrets and telling lies? Would sharing secrets and telling the truth have made a difference? Why or why not?

6. Mindy and Kate suffer greatly because of Kelly's brokenness. Why do they not tell anyone until much later in the story?

7. Jackson, Big Ed, Theo and most men who know Kelly, look the other way regarding Kelly's predatory behavior, Why do they do this?

8. Why do Jackson, Theo, Mindy, Tessa and Kate put up with Kelly's awful behavior? Would you tolerate this type of behavior from a friend on a long term basis? Why or why not?

BONUS:

If you knew someone was keeping a big (and potentially harmful) secret from your family member, friend or coworker, would you tell the secret? Why or why not?

This question at my own neighborhood book club ignited the idea behind *Secret Keepers*.

—·—

FOOD FOR THOUGHT

In the South, food plays a very important role in our lives, nourishing bodies, and feeding souls. Food marks special occasions, family traditions, and even helps in times of grief when we don't quite know what to say. My husband's red beans and rice, *special* rolls, my chicken enchiladas, and Granny Florine's chicken and dumplings are highly requested dishes. They represent love, family and tradition.

Tessa serves Trent the famous Donovan family potato salad. This dish was served many times at Storybook Cottage. I'm sharing my sister-in-law Tina's recipe. It may be the best potato salad you will ever eat!

If you try this recipe or have special family recipes you would like to share with me; please do, by email lmailto:teddiepeacock@gmail.com. I promise to read all mail and would love to try out some of your favorite dishes.

DONOVAN FAMILY POTATO SALAD

Ingredients:

5 lbs potatoes washed,and cut into bite size pieces

(Do not peel potatoes)

8 hard boiled eggs, peeled and chopped into small pieces

1 jar pickle relish (drained)

1 medium onion (diced)

1 celery stalk (diced)

1 lb cooked bacon (crumbled or very small pieces)

1 to 1 1/2 cups mayonnaise (depends on consistency of potato mixture)

1 TBSP mustard

salt and pepper to taste

Instructions:

1. Wash, cut and cook potatoes until done. Should still be firm and not mushy. Rinse potatoes, let cool

2. 2. Fry or bake bacon. Crumble, or cut into small pieces, and set aside.

3. While potatoes and bacon are cooking, boil eggs. (Boil for 2-3 minutes, take off heat and let rest for 10 minutes). Peel eggs under cool running water and chop into bite-size bits.

4. Dice celery and onion.

5. Drain juice from pickle relish.

6. In a medium whisk together mayonnaise and mustard, until combined.

7. In a large serving bowl or container, combine potatoes, bacon, eggs, onion, celery and pickle relish.

8. Add the mayo mixture to the large bowl and mix together gently until ingredients are coated.

9. Add salt and pepper to taste.

10. Refrigerate for 3-4 hours prior to serving to allow flavors to meld.

(Courtesy of Tina Britton)

— · —

Acknowledgements

This is the hardest part-trying to remember everyone I should thank.

Thank you God for giving me writing ability and the courage to see this project through.

Thank you to talented graphic arts designer Drew Thompson and to Janet Kenney for finding my typos and grammar mistakes. You both made my work SO much better!

To my husband John who has always been so supportive! To my daughters, Lauren and Sara who cheer me on from the sidelines.

To the **original best friends**, Vicky Greene and Amy Rasmussen Cooper for being the very best friends.

A huge shoutout to my neighborhood Book Club; Katie, Rian, Gabby, Desiree, Jessica, Lindsey, Margaret, Katie, Anne, Kathy and Marianne. I appreciate all of you so very much!

To my friend Marie who told me to write , Jessica who helped with early edits, and my sister-in-law Tina, ever the cheerleader!

Most Importantly, Thanks to you **incredible readers** for reading, responding and sharing *Secret Keepers* . It wouldn't mean anything without YOU!

About the Author

Teddie Peacock is a former college writing instructor and author of debut novel *Secret Keepers*.

She traded in reading murder mystery books for writing her very own. Now, she (usually) knows from the very first page, who the real killer is.

Teddie and her husband live in Alabama with two rescue dogs, Molly and Josie, who definitely rule the world.

P.S. She still enjoys getting together with her book club friends, discussing good books and eating great food!

Please reach out to her : **Teddiepeacock@gmail.com. She loves hearing from her readers!**

NEXT

Did you enjoy "Secret Keepers"? I hope so, it was a project that was over 30 years in the making. It was time to bring Tessa, Mindy and Kate's story of friendship, betrayal and loyalty into being.

Please consider leaving a review on Amazon. I promise to read all reviews and carefully consider my readers' feedback in upcoming books.

Even though we tried especially hard to catch all of the grammatical errors and typos, they sometimes go in stealth mode and still slip through the cracks. If you find any, please feel free to reach out to me by email, **teddiepeacock@gmail.com**

In the meantime, I've included a small excerpt from my newest book, *Come Back Home.* ***ENJOY!***

— · —

Come Back Home (Delaney)

Sitting in the Weston County Detention Center (aka jail) in Pleasantville, Tennessee was definitely not on my *to do* list. Neither was coming back for my 15th year high school reunion. But here we are, living my very best life- Not! Okay, so I'm not really *in* jail but I **am** waiting for some very late detective to question me in connection with something bad that *might* have happened during our reunion get together. Even though no one around this place will actually tell me what is really going on.

I've been told multiple times by everyone working here at County Jail that I'm **not** in trouble, just here to answer some routine questions in a possible case. If this is true, then why have I been sitting here waiting for almost three hours? I've been drinking very stale coffee with nothing else to do except count water stained ceiling tiles and cracks in the worn linoleum floor.

But who gets a wakeup call at 6 on a Sunday morning along with a free ride to jail; if you aren't considered a possible suspect in something? Somehow I never quite saw myself back in Pleasantville, sitting in an interrogation room and wondering if I needed a lawyer?

If I get out of this place without serving 10 to 20 years for a crime I didn't commit; I'm going to fire my very expensive therapist. Then I'm driving straight out to Mom's house saying every single swear word I know, because this is ALL her fault!

When I got the reunion invitation, I should've tossed it, just like all the others. My biggest mistake was telling Mom. My second biggest mistake was telling Susan Parker, my therapist.

If only I had tossed that postcard in the trash along with all of the other junk mail I get. But no, for whatever unexplainable reason, it sat for weeks on the console table in my apartment entryway. Its bright blue color taunting me every time I left and came back home.

If only I had kept my big mouth closed in my session with my therapist when she was helping me *unpack* my childhood trauma. Things might have turned out differently.

Just as I am beginning to wonder if I'm going to spend the rest of my life here in this awful, puke colored interrogation room, the door opens. In walks a man who holds out his hand and introduces himself as Detective Chris Hunter. So, this is who I've been waiting hours to speak to. Well, at least he's young and very attractive, if that makes all of this any better.

"Delaney Quinn," I say, declining to shake his hand. My good manners left the room about two hours ago.

" So sorry about your long wait," he says,apologetically. " I was called in to work the scene of a very bad accident. I apologize for your inconvenience. Mind if I ask you a few questions about last night?"

"Actually, I do mind. However, since your department's overly enthusiastic officers showed up pounding on my hotel door at 6 a.m., well here we are, Officer," I say, spreading my hands in a shrug.

"It's Detective, ma'am," he says, not missing a beat. "Some of our newest officers get excited when there are cases other than traffic violations, and destruction of property. Or when old man Harley overdoes the bourbon and decides to lower the courthouse flag at the end of the day while naked. This case is the biggest thing we've seen in Pleasantville in a long time."

I smile just a little, old Mr. Harley hasn't changed a bit. "What case Detective Hunter? I don't know what you're talking about," I say, truly puzzled by whatever he is implying.

"Do you mind if I call you Delaney? Could you please verify your whereabouts last night?" he asks, looking intently at my face.

"Yes, actually I do, Detective. Ms. Quinn is fine. As I'm sure you already know, I was at the Alumni homecoming dance at Creekside Country Club." Something about this man is really beginning to annoy me.

He smirks a little at my sharp comeback. "Yes, do you remember what time you left the dance? Can someone verify that for us?" He asks again.

I feel a migraine coming on. I'm trying very hard to be civil here since I definitely don't have the power position. "Um, I don't know, 8:15 maybe 8:30? Honestly, I was pretty bored. I put in an appearance and drove back to the hotel. I texted my mom and my friend Lauren. I watched a little tv and fell asleep." I leave out the part that I slept like a baby because I drank almost an entire bottle of prosecco trying to erase this disastrous weekend from memory.

"Your mom and friend can confirm this, yes?" He asks me, while scribbling on a yellow note pad.

I sigh a little. "Yes Detective, now will you please tell me what this is about? I haven't gotten a phone call or been advised to call a lawyer. Is this a friendly discussion or am I in some kind of trouble here?"

He looks at me and then runs a hand over the top of his head- probably one of his quirks. " No, I hoped it would be a friendly conversation. So, you really have **no** idea what's going on? Ethan Barlowe and Olivia Harper Barlowe's son Jake, went missing last night," he tells me. His face is etched with worry.

Hearing those two names sends a shiver down my spine. When I left Pleasantville, I hoped to never hear those names or see their faces again, not in this lifetime. And I wouldn't have either. If I had just ignored my mom and *know it all* therapist and stayed home. I knew in the very core of my being that coming here was a serious mistake. I have a feeling that I'm going to find out soon just how very wrong it was coming back home.

www.ingramcontent.com/pod-product-compliance
Lightning Source LLC
Chambersburg PA
CBHW061225310726
48971CB00007B/1951